Morgan didn't kı̇~~ow~~
her phone numb~~er~~ ~~nor her address~~

All he knew was that she cleaned his office at night.

Sighing, Morgan started to stretch his long legs in front of him, but accidentally kicked something in his way. Whatever it was got caught on his toe and didn't want to be shaken off.

Curious, he peered under the table to find a pair of petite gold sandals, one long strap attached to his shoe. He reached down and freed it, then picked up both sandals and set them on his lap. Absently he examined one. The shoe was a size five and looked as if it had been barely worn.

Just as the clock on the wall struck midnight, a wide grin split his face. Brooke, his very own Cinderella, had forgotten her shoes—and it was up to him to see that she got them back.

Dear Reader,

Ever wished your life was a little bit different?
Ever wished you could look absolutely beautiful
for just one night? Ever yearned for a really great
pair of shoes?

I sure have. Brooke Anne Kressler, my heroine in
Cinderella Christmas, has, too. Luckily Brooke Anne's
daydreams lead her to an offer she can't refuse, a
glittering ball and an extremely irresistible man
named Morgan Carmichael.

Morgan's done some wishing of his own. As an
up-and-coming executive for a hotel chain, he's
pushed aside many dreams in order to focus on
his career. It takes a petite janitor wearing a pair
of gold sandals to help him reprioritize his life.

I hope you'll enjoy the adventures of Brooke Anne
and Morgan as they attempt to find each other
again after an eventful party, get ready for Christmas
and dodge the advice of a host of very opinionated
friends.

Cinderella Christmas is my first novel for Harlequin
American Romance. To see it published feels a bit
like a fairy tale to me! I hope, if you have time,
you'll visit my Web site, www.shelleygalloway.com,
and let me know what you thought. I'd love to hear
from you. Most of all, I hope you'll have a very
merry Christmas!

Best wishes,

Shelley Galloway

Cinderella Christmas

Shelley Galloway

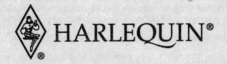

HARLEQUIN®

TORONTO • NEW YORK • LONDON
AMSTERDAM • PARIS • SYDNEY • HAMBURG
STOCKHOLM • ATHENS • TOKYO • MILAN • MADRID
PRAGUE • WARSAW • BUDAPEST • AUCKLAND

ISBN 0-373-75094-3

CINDERELLA CHRISTMAS

To Cathy Liggett, good friend and fellow author,
who one day suggested that we try writing
books about women who love shoes.

To my wonderful agent, Mary Sue Seymour,
who promised me years ago that one
day I'd be a Harlequin author.

And of course, to Tom. It takes a special man
to discuss romance writing during sales meetings.

Chapter One

Oh, the shoes were on sale now. The beautiful shoes with the three gold straps, the four-inch heel and not much else. The shoes that would showcase a flawless pedicure, the fine arch of her foot, and would set off an ivory lace gown to perfection.

Of course, to make an outfit like that work, she'd need the right kind of jewelry, Brooke Anne mused as she stared at the shoe display through the high-end shop window. Nothing too bold... Perhaps a simple diamond tennis bracelet and one-carat studs? Yes, that would lend just the right air of sophistication. Elegant, refined, classy—that was how she wanted to appear.

Hmm. She'd get her hair styled in a dramatic up-do. Something extravagant and curly, to accentuate her gray eyes and high cheekbones. Something to give herself at least the illusion of height she so desperately needed. It was hard to look statuesque when you were five foot two.

But none of that would matter when she set foot on the dance floor. Her date would hold her tightly and twirl her around and around. Balancing on the balls of her feet, she'd maneuver in sync with him. She'd finally put all those dance lessons from long ago to good use, and her date would be impressed that she could actually waltz with ease. They'd glide through the motions, spinning, dipping, stepping together. Others would stay out of their way.

No, no one would be in the way…they would have already moved aside to watch the incredible display of footwork, the vision of two bodies dancing in perfect harmony. They would stare at the woman in ivory lace, wearing the most beautiful, decadent shoes…shoes that would probably only last one evening, they were so fragile and elegant-looking.

Brooke Anne tilted her head, lost in the fantasy. At the ball, she'd hold her head high and look down upon the rest of the people, who could only waltz by counting to themselves. She'd pity the guests who'd been reduced to asking acquaintances from work or distant cousins to accompany them. They would eye her jealously as her date pressed his lean, muscular body against her, gazed at her in complete admiration, looked at her with ill-disguised longing….

And she would simply smile—not a big grin, with teeth showing, but a small one playing at the corners of her mouth. The glint in her eye would tell observers how happy she was.

She'd be like a modern-day Mona Lisa. With blond hair and gray eyes, though. And short. She'd be a short Mona Lisa. But still graceful.

And she wouldn't have a care in the world because she'd be wearing the most spectacular shoes she'd ever seen. She'd feel like…magic.

"May I help you?"

Brooke Anne stared at the slim, dignified-looking older man standing in the doorway of WJB Shoes. "Pardon?"

He pursed his lips, then spoke again. "Miss, do you need any help? I noticed that you've been looking in the window for a few minutes."

"No, thanks."

With a twinge of embarrassment, Brooke Anne turned toward the window again, catching her reflection staring back at her. She couldn't help seeing the humor in the situation. Here she was with no makeup, hair pulled back in a hurried ponytail, dressed in old jeans and a sweatshirt emblazoned with

Jovial Janitor Service. And her shoes…she was wearing old tennis shoes.

Not even designer ones in good leather, but discount-store bargain shoes. Blue-light special shoes. Ugly brown-and-orange shoes that had nothing to recommend them except a very cheap price.

Quickly, she waved goodbye to the smartly dressed salesman and walked to the next door over. After running her security card through the slot, she made her way to the sixth floor. There she used her key to open the janitor's closet, and pulled out the cart, more than ready to get to work. Today she was subbing for Tomasina, her best friend, who regularly cleaned the building.

Tomasina's baby, Vanessa, was sick, so it fell to Brooke Anne to pick up the job on such short notice. It was what you did when you owned your own company, Brooke Anne was learning.

Being a cleaning lady was not the most glamorous career in the world, but the hours were flexible and the conditions good—if you were the type who didn't mind working at night and by yourself.

Brooke Anne filled a bucket with warm water, slipped on her gloves and then checked the itemized list that she'd printed out before she left her apartment. On Thursday nights, Jovial Janitors tackled the Royal Hotels corporate headquarters, a fairly small hotel chain that was known for its customer service and careful attention to details. At least that was what it said on their framed mission statement in the lobby.

Glancing at the clock, Brooke Anne noticed that things were pretty quiet for 7:00 p.m. The Royal Hotel employees seemed to work late in cycles. Some days there were people there until ten or eleven. Others times the place was nearly empty by six. She figured this must be one of those nights.

Matter-of-factly, she began her routine, vacuuming empty offices and removing trash with practiced grace. She cleaned the east-wing bathrooms and then made her way toward the opposite side of the building, stopping at the conference room to do the scheduled dusting.

Brooke Anne hummed an old Frank Sinatra tune to herself; it'd been playing in the lobby and had stuck itself on Replay in her brain.

Retrieving a fresh rag from the cart, she was brought up short by a man in a dark suit and violet-colored silk tie glaring at the phone console, the receiver stuck to his ear. She glanced at him, unsure whether to continue dusting or leave immediately.

Different executives had different views on her presence. Some treated her much as they would a floor lamp, ignoring her completely; others felt obligated to make chitchat. Some people just smiled their hellos and then either waved her off or motioned her in. This man didn't even seem to realize she was in the room.

Since she'd already dusted two chairs, Brooke Anne decided to quietly finish her task. She looked at the man again. He was scowling, obviously unimpressed with whoever was on the other end of the phone. "I know that," he said sharply. "Tell me something I don't."

Brooke Anne wiped down the chairs as quickly as she could, eager to get out of the room before he turned his crankiness on her.

"Listen, dammit. I don't care what you think…." He paused. "Are you out of your mind? It's on Saturday night. I need someone to be there with me." He paused again, then clenched his pencil in a death grip. "Listen, Sheri, blow it off. Get someone to cover for you."

Things sounded as if they were heating up. Brooke Anne cleared her throat, waited to be acknowledged.

But the guy just went on. "I think it's a pretty easy decision. It should be." And then he looked up and caught her gaze.

Brooke Anne waited for a signal. Should she stay or should

she go? Finally, he nodded impatiently, his hand making a cleaning motion as he did so. Ah—stay there and get the job done.

"Well, I've got to tell you, I really don't appreciate you pulling this on me, and I'm going to remember it.... Fine...I know that.... Fine. Bye." He slammed down the phone and grumbled something under his breath that Brooke Anne was glad she couldn't understand.

She took a breath of her own and continued to make her way down the table. Now she was a mere two yards away from him. The Suit.

He studied her carefully, watched her work, then seemed vaguely embarrassed. "Hey," he said, "I'm sorry you had to hear that."

"No problem, sir. I'll be done in a few minutes."

His eyebrows rose in a look of surprise. Had he expected her not to be capable of stringing two sentences together? "Sure...whatever."

She lifted her head again. He was sprawled across chair number eighteen, still watching her intently with his khaki-colored eyes as if he'd never seen anyone dust a set of conference chairs before. "That was my girlfriend. Ex-girlfriend." With an impatient gesture, he corrected himself again. "Actually, we've been broken up for a while but we're trying out the 'just friends' thing. She's canceling on me for Saturday night."

Why was it that some people thought of janitors as substitute shrinks? Because he was obviously waiting for a reply, Brooke Anne said, "I'm sorry."

"Yeah, me, too. Now I don't have a date for our company Christmas party."

She moved to chair number fourteen. Dusted the armrests, then ran her cloth along the back. "What are you going to do?" she asked, since he seemed to be looking for conversation.

He raked his hands through his short hair. Unable to help it, she stared at him, analyzing each feature. His hair was a true mix of colors—not quite blond, not quite brown— making Brooke Anne wish it was daylight, so she could see what it would do in the sun. He had a ruddy complexion and a firm jaw. A tender mouth. He looked like someone she would want to know.

Better.

Brooke Anne's eyes fell to his silk tie again and she firmly reminded herself that she was wearing dollar-store shoes and a sweatshirt with a big mop on it. They had absolutely nothing in common. But…what if they did?

He answered her then. "I don't know. I wouldn't care except that it's kind of expected, you know?"

She stared at him blankly.

"I mean, everyone's going to be there, showing off their trophy wives and perfect marriages," Mr. Executive explained. "Dinner's always a sit-down affair, assigned seats. Now I'm going to have an empty chair beside me. It's going to be obvious I don't have a date."

His problems seemed so trite, so simple. He was worried about a vacant seat next to him? Didn't those types of worries disappear sometime around junior high?

She shrugged. "Couldn't you just say your girlfriend—uh, ex-girlfriend—couldn't make it?"

"Not with this crowd. Nobody *can't* make it. Everybody who gets an invitation comes. Heck, I know a guy who missed his mother's seventy-fifth birthday extravaganza to come to this thing. Guys skip their daughters' dance recitals. Damn."

Sounded to her as though everyone had their priorities confused. Brooke Anne started on chair fifteen. "Don't you have a sister or someone you could take?"

His eyes brightened for a moment, then dimmed. "Nope. My sister, Caroline, flew to south Florida for the weekend, to get a break from the cold. She left this morning."

Brooke Anne almost slapped her palm against her head. Of course. Caroline was vacationing for the weekend. To escape the weather. Why hadn't Brooke Anne thought of that? Instead she tried for a small, tight smile. "That's too bad."

The man rapped his fingers on the table, watching her wipe down the legs of a chair. He had the grace to look embarrassed. "Sorry. I guess I sound like an idiot. It's just that these darn dinners are almost like a grown-up show-and-tell. It'll be my first opportunity to spend some time with the new CEO the board hired, and I didn't want anything to go wrong."

Understanding dawned. She felt the same way about family get-togethers—especially since the Russell fiasco. "You don't sound like an idiot," she murmured. And surprised herself when she realized she was telling the truth.

He smiled at that, and it completely transformed his face. The worry lines around his eyes vanished, and the most appealing dimple appeared in his left cheek. Not a big one, just a little mark that she hadn't expected. He really was striking.

"Maybe you could go with your secretary or something," she suggested.

"Nah…my secretary's married, and almost old enough to be my mother."

"Hmm."

"What I need is someone to look good, not make a scene and be able to dance."

"Dance?"

"Yeah. The president has a real thing for ballroom dancing. He and his wife are actually in one of those dancing clubs— they meet every Friday night and practice."

She thought of her own Friday nights, usually spent nursing a cold soda and soaking a sore pair of feet. Who knew people in this world had time for such stuff?

Mr. Too-Handsome-in-a-Gray-Suit smiled again. "You'd be surprised to hear about the number of our employees who've been attending the Jim Langley Dance Studio on the sly. I swear, you'd think that the president was getting a kickback."

"What kind of dancing?"

"Mr. Brownlee favors waltzing, the fox-trot and swing."

"Do you know all those?"

"Enough not to embarrass myself too badly on the dance floor. Sheri and I went to eight lessons back in October. We do all right. Besides, no one wants to look *too* good when the Brownlees get on the floor, anyway." He gazed at her for a minute, then bent over and laid his head in his hands. "So, Miss, uh…Jovial Janitor, who can I find—who'll look good in a ball gown and knows how to dance—by tomorrow night?"

"I'm sure you'll find someone."

He scowled again, though that dimple spoiled the effect. "Come on, nobody knows how to rhumba except people in this office."

"Um…I can dance," she stated, then glanced at him, horrified that she'd actually said the words aloud. Why had she done that?

His head popped up. "What?"

"Um, I know how to do all that stuff…you know, waltz and everything." When he continued to stare at her as if she'd grown horns, she expanded. "Just to let you know that maybe more people can rhumba than you might think."

He tilted his head. Narrowed his eyes. All at once he seemed to be seeing someone behind the Jovial Janitor sweatshirt. "You may be right about that."

Chapter Two

That had been fun, Brooke Anne thought mockingly as she left the conference room and made her way down the hall. Deftly, she guided her cart around the corner and began to clean the break room. Although it technically wasn't on the list, Tomasina had written a note that said she usually wiped down the counters and washed any coffee cups left in the sink.

Sure enough, the executives had a healthy habit of caffeine consumption. Brooke Anne filled the sink with soapy water and set to work, happy to have something to do besides recall the expression on the man's face when she'd dared to mention that she could dance.

It had been priceless.

Well, maybe that wasn't the right description. Embarrassing was more apt. He'd looked at her the way an eight-year-old might look at a bug under a magnifying glass. With bemused interest. Or the way her mother and father looked at her over supper when she went home to Nebraska and never made any mention of having another boyfriend.

Or the way the shoe guy had looked at her when she'd been practically drooling over those shoes.

Pitiful.

Nobody seemed to see that there was a real woman under all the custodial garb. That the entire sum of Brooke Anne

Kressler's interests did not consist of cleaning bathrooms and constructing thousand-piece puzzles.

There was a completely feminine part of her that liked pretty dresses and fancy dinners.

She'd actually read an Emily Post book just to know how to reply to a formal invitation to tea, in case she ever received one.

She liked dancing and putting on makeup.

It wasn't her fault that she never did any of those things. Life just got in the way of her dreams, that was all. It wasn't possible to spend money on silk dresses when your company needed to hire another employee. It was hard to date when you were cleaning office buildings at night. And impossible to vacuum in gold sandals, even if they would make her feel ten feet tall.

After setting the sparkling-clean cups on the counter to dry, Brooke Anne pushed in the chairs and was just about to turn off the light when Mr. Suit appeared in the doorway.

"Um, may I talk to you for a moment?"

She glanced at him again. Noticed that he was taller than she'd thought, and built almost like a swimmer, with broad shoulders and narrow hips. Then firmly tapped down any more observations that were about to spring up. She had nothing in common with him—absolutely nothing.

"Miss?"

She met his gaze. Realized she was keeping him standing there, waiting. "Yes? Did you need something cleaned in your office?"

"No," he said, shaking his head. "I just wanted to make sure I didn't offend you or anything when you said you could rhumba."

"Not at all," she answered, wondering why he'd even care.

He looked relieved. "Listen, um, I'm…my name is Morgan Carmichael."

She nodded. "Nice to meet you."

"Do you have a moment to sit down?"

They sat at the table she'd just wiped. Mr. Morgan Carmichael rested his elbows on the surface, then pulled them away when he found it was still damp. Brooke Anne kept her hands in her lap.

"I know this party must sound pretty dumb to someone like you…."

Her eyes widened. *Someone like her?* Lord.

He continued. "But, hey, I've got to go to this thing. You don't know me from the average guy on the street, but I'm trustworthy and usually pretty easy to be around."

What was he getting at? Brooke Anne nodded at him, waiting for him to go on.

"So, would you consider going to this party with me?"

"As your date?"

"Well, more like a paid escort." He nodded, as if he liked that description. "Look—I'd pay you for your time," he replied hurriedly. "Christmas will be here soon. Maybe the extra cash would come in handy."

The "someone like her" comment still stung; she couldn't deny it. And the "extra-cash" aside wasn't flattering, either. She might be in need of extra cash, but she wasn't in danger of visiting a bread line.

Did she really want to be in this guy's company ever again? No. "Sorry, but I don't think so."

He looked wounded. "I'd pay you well."

"It's not the money, believe it or not."

He stared hard at her, as if he was trying to read her mind. "Is it me? Yeah, I bet it is," he said, with a wry expression. "You don't know a thing about me, do you?"

Brooke Anne held up her hand to stop him. He might be attractive, but there was nothing about him that she was interested in knowing.

But he didn't even glance in her direction. "I've been working for Royal Hotels for three years now. I'm the product purchasing manager. My team and I are in charge of a majority of the purchases that are made for the hotel chain."

He seemed so proud of his job. Proud enough to make her grimace. "I wasn't aware there were jobs like that."

But her cool tone didn't seem to bother him in the slightest. "Wait, there's more about me that you need to know." He paused for a breath. "I graduated from the University of Texas with my bachelor's and then got my MBA here in Cincinnati. I have one sister, who also happens to live here. My parents live in Dallas, now."

This was way more about Mr. Carmichael than she wanted to know. And none of it inspired her to get to know him better. Brooke Anne leaned forward. "Listen, it's not—"

He cut her off again, and began speaking quickly. "Most people think of me as a decent kind of guy. I work hard, play racquetball three times a week and even make it to church most Sundays."

Oh, that church comment. She was softening; she could feel it. She had to talk fast. "Mr. Carmichael, I'm sure you're very nice, but I don't think we'd suit each other."

He met her eyes. "It's Morgan. And we don't need to suit each other. It would only be for one night. I can get along with anyone for five hours." He reddened, no doubt realizing how his words must have sounded out loud. "Scratch that. What I'm saying is that I'm desperate, you can dance and the evening wouldn't be a total waste of your time—oh, I forgot to mention I had a beagle growing up and I'm addicted to puzzles."

Maybe it was his remarkable looks that piqued her interest, or the sincerity of his grayish-green eyes. Maybe it was the dog, or his admitting that he liked puzzles, too. She felt herself waffling.

"I'm sorry, sir, but—"

"It's Morgan. And I *am* a nice guy. Even though I didn't sound that way with Sheri. She just frustrates the heck out of me." He cocked his head and stared at Brooke Anne. "Have you ever felt like that with someone? Attracted to them, but really frustrated?"

Russell came to mind. Russell, who'd managed to make her the laughingstock of Nebraska in two swift moves. "Oh, yeah. I've felt that way before. It's a pretty awful feeling."

The man's expression softened with her understanding. "Then maybe you know what I mean? About being in a bind?"

Brooke Anne wasn't sure what led her to nod, but she did. She knew all about obligations and wishes. And lost dreams. Against her better judgment, she found herself saying, "All right, Morgan, I'll be your date."

A look of complete relief swept across his face. "Thanks a lot. I promise you won't regret this."

She already did, though she couldn't say why. "So this is a formal affair?"

The dimple appeared again. "Yeah, it is." He shifted and pulled out a thin, dark-brown wallet, then grabbed three one-hundred-dollar bills from its folds. "Here. This is for you to get a dress for the dance."

"No, I couldn't accept."

"You've got to. After all, you're doing this as a favor to me. You'll need it to buy a gown." He paused for a moment, glanced at her feet and pulled out another pair of hundreds. "Here. You'll need shoes, too."

Shoes? She took the money without hesitation. The bills felt crisp and unfamiliar in her hand. She gripped the money a little harder. "Thanks."

"And does five hundred dollars sound fair to pay you for the night?"

She just about choked. "Another five hundred?"

"You know, as your fee for putting up with me for the evening?"

Five hundred for a dress and shoes? Five hundred to put up with him for a night? She cleared her throat. "I think I can work with this arrangement."

"Great. I'll pay you Saturday night."

"That will be fine."

He eyed her hair, then, and Brooke Anne instinctively knew he was wondering if she could style it any differently. "I'll do my hair and makeup, too, Morgan." When he looked doubtful, she added, "I had practice doing it when I took dance lessons in high school."

"Oh, great. That's great."

She nodded. "What time?"

"How about seven? There are cocktails from seven until eight, then the dinner starts. Dancing is later. Where shall I pick you up?"

"Don't. I'll just meet you there."

He looked worried. "It would probably be easier if I picked you up," he protested.

"I'd feel better meeting you there. And if for some reason I don't show, at least *you'll* be there."

He looked startled by her lame attempt at humor. "Yeah, but…"

"I promise I'll show. Where is this dance?"

"The Willowbrook Room of the Excelsior Royal Hotel."

Well, well. The Willowbrook Room was an especially swanky club on the penthouse level of the hotel. It was a place she'd only seen pictures of in the society pages. She tried hard to act blasé. "Excellent. I'll see you then."

They stood up, Morgan eyeing her carefully. "You sure you can dance?"

She did a little pirouette and smiled. "I can."

"All right, see you then."

"Saturday. Seven p.m. Willowbrook Room."

Morgan stepped out the door, then popped back in, a horrified expression on his face. "I don't even know your name."

"It's Brooke Anne."

"That's a pretty name. Bye, Brooke. Thanks again."

Brooke Anne chuckled to herself. People always mistook Anne to be her last name. Oh, well, no harm done. She'd answered to just plain Brooke plenty of times…and it wasn't like he'd ever need to know her last name, anyway.

With that, she turned off the kitchen light and sauntered down the hall. The Royal Hotels' corporate offices were clean, the hour was late and she had her very own ball to get ready for.

Chapter Three

Okay. What did a girl do with five hundred dollars in cash, a dress and shoes to buy, a heavy mass of hair to fix and a ball to attend in just over twenty-four hours?

Eat toast and pray, Brooke Anne thought wryly, as she scanned the latest issue of *Town & Country Magazine* one more time. She'd bought it on impulse when she was going home last night, thinking it might give her some insight into the latest fashions for society ladies.

If *Town & Country* was to be her guide, it looked as though cool blondes, statuesque redheads and old money were in style. Not to mention designer handbags and trinkets from Fifth Avenue shops. At the moment, she only owned mop-adorned sweatshirts, fashion jewelry and an assortment of T-shirts from restaurants in town. None of that was going to cut it.

Since she'd be living the *Town & Country* life, at least for a few hours, Brooke Anne knew there was only one thing to do: seek professional help. And that source would be in the form of a rather austere-looking man in a well-fitted suit at the shoe store. No matter what, she was going to buy those shoes, even if they cost the whole amount that Morgan had given her. Those shoes were special. And maybe the salesman could help get the rest of her that way, too. He looked as if he had enough style and class for both of them.

But when she walked into the shoe boutique two hours later, Brooke Anne began to seriously reconsider her decision. The store reeked of good taste and luxury. The smell of new leather and expensive cologne teased her nostrils. The temperature of the room was perfect—not too cool, and not too warm—which wasn't an easy achievement, since it seemed that in late November most Cincinnati stores blasted each customer with a burst of hot air.

The wine-colored carpet was deep and plush, the kind that showed every single stray thread or speck. Yet it was immaculate and still carried the marks of fresh vacuuming. Brooke Anne briefly wondered how they managed to keep it looking like that.

She ventured in farther, all too aware of how her own sneakers stood out among the beautiful sandals and designer pumps.

But those feelings were quickly forgotten when she saw the gold sandals.

"May I help you?" The same salesman who'd approached her the day before appeared by her side. His voice was curiously comforting, as if the question that he probably asked a hundred times a day was actually sincere.

"Yes, please. I'm interested in this pair of sandals."

His eyes flicked to her outfit of faded Levi's, black turtleneck sweater and worn tennis shoes. "In size…"

"Sorry. Size five, please. Narrow, if you have them."

"Narrow, too?" As if he favored small feet, the corners of his lips turned up, stretching his thin face. "Very well, ma'am. If you'll have a seat?"

His immediate acquiescence was refreshing. Brooke Anne didn't know what she'd expected from the well-dressed gentleman, but she had a feeling that it had involved a surly look and a begrudging temperament. Taking his advice, she sank into a tapestry-covered high-backed chair, removed her sneakers and waited.

He returned within a minute, bearing two boxes of shoes and a packet of knee-high panty hose. "Here we are. I brought out two pairs, the size five and five and a half. Let's see how these fit." He sat down across from her on a little leather stool, looking strangely prim and proper, for such a tall man positioned on such a small stool. He patted the slanted front of the bench. "If you would place your foot here, please, my dear."

So this was what *real* shoe stores were like, Brooke Anne thought wryly as she removed her sock and placed her foot on the indicated spot. Buying shoes here was equivalent to the difference between traveling first class and economy on an airplane. In spite of herself, she was prepared to enjoy every minute of the experience.

"If I'm not mistaken, you were visiting our store last night."

His words, so clipped and formal, played against a faint Southern accent nicely. Brooke Anne wondered where he was originally from. Virginia? Tennessee? London? It was hard to tell.

She glanced at the man's discreet name tag, a slim gold bar with *Warren* written in script across it. "Yes, although yesterday I was just looking through the window."

"I'm glad you came back," he replied, in such a way that her presence sounded like a favor. He passed her a smoothly folded knee-high sock, and carefully, she pulled it on.

"Me, too," she said.

He opened the shoe box with no small amount of flair and eyed her carefully, his light blue eyes taking in each wrinkle of her sweater. "You must be going somewhere very special."

Brooke Anne couldn't even answer at first, she was so spellbound by the pair of shoes waiting in their box, ready to be tried on. "Yes, yes I am," she stammered. "I'm going to a ball."

"A ball? How interesting."

He picked up a sandal, lowered it to her foot and gently slipped it on. The leather felt cool and firm. Her foot arched automatically to conform to the high slope. Brooke Anne bit her lip to hold back a sigh.

After he buckled the strap around her ankle, he helped her move her foot to the floor. "Stand up, please. Let's take a look, shall we?"

She did as he asked and found she couldn't hold the sigh in any longer. "It fits."

"Yes, indeed it does," he said with a nod. "I thought it would. You definitely are a size five, narrow. One doesn't see too many of those." He glanced at her again, as if he was about to say something but decided against it. "Well now, let's put the other one on."

Wearing both sandals now, Brooke Anne stepped lightly across the room, loving the feel of the thin straps holding on the delicate shoes. Enjoying the sensation of being four inches taller. Unable to stop herself, she spontaneously did a little twirl.

Warren stood to the side, a pleased expression playing across his features, as if he truly delighted in someone appreciating his wares. "What are you wearing tonight, if you don't mind my asking?"

Reality came crashing back. "I'm not sure."

"Pardon me?"

"I've got to go find a dress."

Thin, precisely-groomed eyebrows clicked together. "Most people do things in the reverse order, if I may say so."

"Not this girl. I've been in love with these shoes ever since I spotted them in the window three weeks ago."

He nodded understandingly. "I know exactly what you mean. They are *perfect* party shoes. They will make any outfit." He paused. "You're leaving it a little late. You've delayed your shopping trip a tad too long, don't you think?"

For some reason, it was easy to talk to Warren. "Not really. I was just invited last night. I'm the guy's replacement date."

"I've never heard of such a thing." Warren's mouth pursed. "Doesn't say much for your gentleman friend."

"Oh, he's no friend, it's business."

"Business?"

She had to smile; Warren looked completely taken aback. "It's for a company Christmas party. The guy who asked me—

Morgan? He needed someone who knew how to waltz. I, his cleaning lady, fit the bill."

"How fortunate for him," Warren said dryly.

Brooke Anne laughed. "It's not as bad as it sounds."

"Well, it doesn't sound particularly good."

Warren was right, she supposed, but there was no time for regrets. "I've got a bit of a dilemma. I only have a day to get myself ready for a ball." She glanced discreetly at the price of the shoes. One hundred and fifty dollars. Way more than she'd ever spent on a pair of shoes, but not as much as she'd feared. "And…I'm kind of on a budget."

Warren's eyes shifted to the price tag. "Is that so, miss?"

Now was not the time to cling to her pride. Lord knew she clung to that enough in all the other areas of her life. "Any idea what I should do next? I still need to buy a dress and some accessories."

Warren ran a finger over the crease in his slacks, then fiddled with the neatly knotted paisley tie under his chin. "Exactly how much time do you have for your transformation?"

"I need to be at the Willowbrook Room by seven on Saturday night."

Warren sat down while she remained standing in front of him. "Hmm," he murmured.

Perhaps more explanation was needed? "I have to go from jeans, flyaway hair and chipped nails to a high-class society lady in one day." She laughed at her description. "Just call me a modern-day Cinderella!"

Once again Warren studied her with those light, clear, speculative eyes. "That type of girl, my dear, is truly my favorite kind."

Chapter Four

"What you need is a plan. A plan of good taste," Warren stated cryptically.

"What I need is an ivory-colored dress that doesn't cost too much."

"Precisely how much are you planning to spend, my dear?"

She did a quick mental calculation. "After the shoes, about $350."

Warren eyed her again. "You need to go to Time Worn Treasures."

"Time what?"

"Time Worn Treasures. It's a resale shop."

Going through someone else's old clothes didn't have much appeal. "I don't know…I was kind of thinking I'd go to the mall, see what was on sale."

Warren actually winced. "Surely not. There aren't any gowns there that would fit your personality, in my opinion."

"My personality?"

He waved a hand at her. "Yes. You positively sparkle. Yet there is a certain cautiousness to you, as if you've been hurt by someone in the past."

Once again, Brooke Anne thought of her ex-boyfriend, Russell, and how his rejection of her had, indeed, hurt her badly. But Warren's "sparkling" reference made her smile. "The sale racks at the mall may not meld too well with my personality, but I have a feeling they'll be the perfect match for my wallet."

Warren clasped his hands behind his back and rolled forward on his heels. "I think not. You'll find a lovely dress, full of flair, at Time Worn Treasures, for much less than two hundred dollars," he said. "You might even have money left over to, uh, do something with those hands of yours."

Brooke Anne stared down at her fingers in wonder. Never in her life would she have expected the state of her hands to draw a comment from a shoe salesman. Of course, never in her life had she ever encountered someone like Warren. He was in a shoe-salesman class all his own. "My hands?"

He sighed. "Your nails are chipped and cracked. You've got cuticles that look as if they're in a race to climb up your nails. And your skin—" He looked away, as if he couldn't even bear to continue.

Brooke Anne knew better, but she went ahead and asked. "My skin?"

"Red."

"Red?"

"Red and scaly. You need to get dipped."

"Dipped?" This conversation was the strangest one she'd ever had. "In what?"

"Paraffin wax, dear." At her complete look of bewilderment, Warren held up a hand. "Wait here."

Then, in a flash he returned, carrying a fine leather notebook and a Montblanc fountain pen. "Here. Call this lady. Tell Patricia that Warren sent you and that you need the works."

"The works? But I thought I only needed a manicure…and maybe some help with my hair?" Images of her hard-earned money floating toward a phantom Patricia filled her mind.

"You're going to need more than that. Your hair needs to be colored, your eyebrows waxed, and your feet—" He sniffed again. "Let me just say that they are in dire need of a pedicure!"

"But they're just feet!"

"Feet that are going to be ensconced in these exquisite shoes! You don't want to ruin the effect with unkempt-looking toes, do you?"

Warren made it sound as if her feet were radioactive. What could she say? She shook her head slightly, overwhelmed.

Warren nodded. "Actually, with everything we need to do, there's no time to spare." He glanced at his gold Rolex. "I'll call Patricia right this minute. She'll take care of you, I promise. And she always has one or two beauty-school students she privately trains—they do all the work for half the price. Your money should more than cover the dress and the treatments." Like a fairy godmother…uh, godfather, he waved a hand. "Go on, now. You've got a hundred things to do."

Brooke Anne did as she was told. Warren knew fashion, and he knew the right places to shop. It was obviously in her best interests if she just nodded her head and followed his directions.

THAT FRIDAY FOUND Morgan sitting in front of his laptop, trying to sort through the fifty-three e-mails he'd received in the last twenty-four hours, when Breva, his assistant of two years, wandered in, her arms laden with files.

"M.C., we've got a whole stack of paperwork to go through if you want to be ready for that conference call on Monday morning."

Since her voice brooked no room for argument, he clicked off his e-mail and turned to her. "I'm ready."

Breva was old enough to be his aunt, though she was completely different than any female currently in the Carmichael clan. Where the women in his family worried about their homes, tennis games and appearances, Breva worried about world peace, her three children and keeping Morgan on task.

In her usual no-nonsense manner, she pulled up a chair and sorted through the files until she found the latest draft of his presentation. She also slid a thick leather folder full of letters that needed signatures across his desk. Morgan looked at the packet with distaste.

"Things never seem to ease up, do they?"

Breva glanced at him over a pair of very stylish angular frames. "Do you want them to?"

The question caught him off guard. "I don't know...but just for once I'd like to have my desk cleared off."

"When you figure out how to do that, call me," Breva responded dryly. "My stack of papers is as high as yours. Of course, with my luck, you'll just push all your papers off your desk and onto mine."

He had to laugh at that. "Who, me?"

Breva grinned. "The sad part is that I really wouldn't even mind...as long as you keep all these boxes full of hotel stuff out of my space."

Morgan gestured to a long line of cardboard boxes with towels and hand soaps peeking out. "Some people actually think that we have a glamorous job."

"They're wrong. There's nothing glamorous about choosing products for a chain of hotels."

"We must've done some glamorous stuff in the past..."

Breva groaned. "Remember when we got stuck delivering Easter baskets to the kids? That was fun."

It had been anything but. The Easter-candy vendor had had a chip on his shoulder and cat fur stuck to his jacket.

Morgan played along. "No, I'm sure we actually got to order cool stuff one time. Fountain pens, maybe? That guy was decent."

"The pen guy was okay." She crossed her legs smartly, her long black skirt flaring out as she did so. "Hey, remember the night when we called in everyone to test toilet paper?" she asked with a smirk. "I'll never forget seeing everyone caress their cheeks with various brands of toilet paper. People using words like 'powder-soft' and 'velvety.' It was so funny."

"Yeah, it was." Morgan leaned back in his chair. "It was a

heck of a lot better than sorting through all these account files. I'm glad you're here."

She gave a long-suffering sigh. "Once again, I feel compelled to tell you—"

"I know, I know. I wouldn't be anywhere without you," Morgan quipped. "It's true. I can hardly function when you're out of the office. Before long we'll be permanently attached at the hip."

She eyed him over her frames.

Immediately, he amended that thought. "Well, I've gotten used to you ordering me around. You're better than my mom."

The faintest smile formed on her lips. Morgan grinned, as well. Breva was very much a June Cleaver type of mother. She was highly involved in her children's lives, and couldn't say enough great things about them. To call her the exact opposite of his own mother was an understatement.

"So, is Aaron looking forward to tomorrow night?"

Breva rolled her eyes. "Oh, yes. All the best construction workers enjoy tangoing on their nights off."

"I seem to remember the two of you holding your own last year."

Breva smiled complacently. "We did. Aaron may look one hundred percent beefy male, but he's got a tender side, too." Her dark eyes flickered mischievously. "But don't tell him I said that. Is Sheri looking forward to the dance?"

Morgan couldn't help noticing the remarkably cool tone in which his assistant spoke of Sheri. "No, she's not. She called me last night and canceled."

Breva dropped her pencil. "What? She can't do that to you."

"I guess no one told her that."

"Let me just state for the record that I never did care for her very much."

"I got that impression."

"You have to go…. What are you going to do?"

Morgan was grateful to be speaking to a person who completely understood the gravity of the situation. Looking good and schmoozing at the Christmas party was a job responsibility, not an optional activity. People who didn't work there just didn't get that. "I got a substitute."

"And she is?"

"Someone I just met." He couldn't bring himself to tell Breva that he was taking the building's janitor. Not that she would think less of Brooke, or less of him for finding such an ill-fitting replacement, but he simply wasn't ready to respond to the speculative gleam in Breva's eye or to her questions. "You don't know her," he said truthfully. Hell, *he* didn't know her. He hoped he'd even be able to recognize her.

But Breva wasn't about to let it go. "I might. Who is she?"

"I'm not telling."

She drummed her fingers on the table. "I bet I can guess."

"You won't."

"Come on. Susan E. down in marketing?"

"Negative."

"Danielle in accounting? She's always had the hots for you."

He bit his lip to keep from smiling at her jargon—then was brought up short as her words finally registered. "Danielle does? Nobody ever told me that. How come?"

"You didn't need to know." Breva had picked up her pencil again, and rapidly tapped it on his desk. "Jayne in promotions?"

"Nope. Breva, I'm not going to tell you." Morgan held the manila file folder she'd brought in front of her, hoping she'd take the hint.

She didn't. "Does she work here?"

"Kind of."

"Aha! She's an outside vendor, like Sheri."

"Nope."

"Hmm. That Crystal girl."

"Which Crystal is that?" he asked, hoping he sounded as if he really didn't know.

Breva crossed her arms over her chest. "You know. 'Oh, Mr.

Carmichael, I just love that tie you have on,'" she purred in a breathless whisper.

He laughed. "Not Crystal, Breva."

"Give me a hint."

"Not on your life. You can be surprised when you see her Saturday night."

Breva quirked an eyebrow and asked the inevitable. "Can she dance?"

"She says so. We'll see."

Finally Breva's pencil-tapping stopped. "Gosh, I hope so."

And with that, they got back to business, sorting through his correspondence, making changes to his PowerPoint presentation, completing tasks that were on Breva's to-do list.

But Morgan had a hard time concentrating. Visions of the tiny cleaning lady kept floating through his mind. That little pirouette. Dusting the chairs, staring at him. He wondered what she'd think of the office politics that seemed to permeate every aspect of his business. For once he'd like to get away from all of that—just do his work without feeling he had to vie for power at the same time.

Somehow he didn't think Brooke would put up with the game they all played—feigning phony interest in each other's lives, not laughing until the president did, purposely coming in five strokes behind the VP of sales during golf games.

Pretending to enjoy ballroom dancing.

Pretending to look forward to a holiday get-together that had Grinch undertones.

Brooke would probably shrug her shoulders at everyone's petty problems.

Wouldn't she?

Shouldn't he?

He should. He knew that. But for the moment, he was so caught up in all of it, he wasn't sure if he could get out, or would even know how to function in a world where other people weren't after his job, or the next promotion, or the next big account.

Maybe it was because he'd been raised that way. Expectations were paramount. Appearance was everything. People didn't hug friends or long-lost relatives. Everything was in its place. Contained.

Something told him that Brooke probably *hadn't* been raised like that. She was probably a touchy-feely girl. The kind who hugged her parents when she saw them. She probably believed in frank, deep conversations and late-night laughter.

He couldn't remember the last time he'd engaged in either.

Frowning, Morgan realized he was lacking in attributes. No wonder Sheri'd had no problem canceling on him the minute something else came up.

The phone rang. Breva answered and put it on hold before letting him know it was Jerry, their paper goods supplier.

Before he picked it up, Morgan gave one last thought to why he did so well at Royal.

The formality of the company suited him. He didn't know how to hug spontaneously or give warm fuzzies. He wasn't comfortable having meaningful conversations and forming attachments.

The corporate life, with its many idiosyncrasies, was where he fit in.

Chapter Five

Brooke Anne twirled in front of the mirror one more time. The ivory crepe de chine billowed out, then fell, cascading in a puddle around her ankles. The fabric was soft and airy. Heavenly. She felt like an angel and looked like one too—or as close to an angel as she was ever going to get, she reflected wryly.

And her shoes… They sparkled like bright beacons, summoning people to take a closer look at her toes, painted a pretty coral.

Her hair was pinned up, and her lips looked pouty and lush in the berry-colored lipstick. She felt attractive and sexy, alluring and mysterious.

In short, she felt perfect.

She could already imagine the look on Morgan Carmichael's face when he saw her. *Oh, Brooke Anne,* he'd say, unable to tear his eyes from her figure, her intricate up-do…her newly waxed eyebrows. *You're beautiful.*

She'd smile gently, telling him without words that she knew she looked terrific. Morgan would pull her into his arms, she'd smell his warm, woodsy aftershave and feel giddy. And then they'd skillfully step across the dance floor, to the beat of an intimate samba.

No, Brooke Anne amended, they'd spin. They'd spin to life, with laughter in their movements. He'd rub his thumb against her hand, and she'd shiver at his touch, and then he'd say, *Brooke Anne, your hands are so soft and creamy-feeling. Nothing like the red, scaly hands you sported only forty-eight hours ago.*

They've been dipped, she would respond. He'd hold her close, and the pounding of his heart would be so strong, so bold that she'd swear she could hear it reverberate through the room…that it sounded like her own heart knocking in excitement.

Knocking that was loud and forceful.

Brooke Anne's vision cleared. She stared at the reflection in the mirror, as she realized the knocking was real—not her heart at all.

Someone was at her door.

Brooke Anne hurried across the room, taking shorter steps than usual in the narrow skirt. With a deep breath, she pulled open the door, then wished she could close it right back again. Tomasina stood in the hallway, looking fired up and completely put-upon.

Brooke Anne stepped back. Her guest wandered in. "Thought I'd stop on by for a minute, give you an update," she said as she strolled past Brooke Anne, her relaxed gait seeming to take double the time of anyone else's. As usual, her gaze scanned the room for anything new, then finally settled on her friend. Two perfectly shaped eyebrows jumped up in surprise. "Hey, honey," she drawled, "don't you look fine."

If Tomasina said she looked fine, Brooke Anne knew she must. Tomasina wasn't one to be free with her compliments. "Thanks. How's your baby doing?"

"Better. Vanessa just had a cold, but with those things, you never know." She stared at Brooke Anne, her expression more telling than a hundred words. Brooke Anne bit back a smile. Tomasina was an eternal pessimist, as well as one of the most cantankerous people she knew. Kind of like Schleprock in the old Flintstone cartoons. Things were never great with her.

Rarely were they good. Tomasina also happened to be the best friend she could ever hope to have.

"I'm glad Vanessa's better," Brooke Anne replied. Suddenly feeling a little overdressed, she waved her hands across her front. "Guess what? I have a date."

Tomasina's dark eyes raked up and down her. "To where, a ball?"

"Yes, as a matter of fact," Brooke chirped, "complete with champagne and hors d'oeuvres and ballroom dancing."

Tomi did not look impressed. She seated herself on Brooke Anne's brown velour couch and stated, "You'd have a lot more fun at the bar down the street. The beer's cheap, there's all-you-can-eat pretzels and they don't make you wear ball gowns."

"I'll keep that in mind for next time."

Her friend nodded. "So, who you going with?"

"No one you'd know. It's kind of a blind date."

Her eyes narrowed, distrust evident. "How blind?"

"Well, I've met the guy, I just don't know him very well. His first date canceled on him at the last minute."

"Nothing too special about that," Tomasina harrumphed as she crossed one muscular leg on top of the other. Tomi favored cleaning office buildings with ankle weights on. "How'd you get the dress and those fine-looking shoes?"

Brooke Anne didn't want to lie. "He paid me some money to go with him."

"Oh, Brooke Anne."

"I know what you're thinking, but don't. This won't be so bad. I need the money...and I've been wanting these shoes."

Tomi pursed her lips and stared at her for a good long minute. Finally, she started talking again. "Are you worried about tonight?"

Was she? "No. Well, a little. It's at the Willowbrook Room."

"Wow."

"Yeah. Obviously, I don't hang out there regularly."

Tomasina grinned. "I've been there before."

"Really?"

"Oh, yeah. It's beautiful."

Brooke Anne was impressed and a bit surprised, though she knew she shouldn't have been. Tomi was beautiful and vivacious, with more friends than she could count. "When did you go there?"

"Couple of months ago. Ronnie had a delivery, and I went up with him. They gave us a Coke, right at the bar."

It took Brooke a moment to digest her words. Then she burst out laughing.

Tomi started laughing, too. "Girl, you should've seen your face. Can you really see me dancing it up at the Willowbrook Room?"

Brooke Anne almost told Tomi about the paycheck she'd be receiving from Morgan, but didn't have the heart to go into it. She needed that money to pay Tomi her bonus, and didn't want Tomi feeling the least bit guilty about accepting it.

"I'd better get going," she said. "I can't be late."

"All right. How're you going to get there?"

"In my van."

"Your *van?* Come on, girl. You've got to do better than that. I'll give you a lift."

Tomasina drove a turquoise Pinto just because she wanted to. It had fuzzy, electric-blue seat covers and a permanent collection of head-bobbing animals on the back dashboard. People literally stopped in their tracks when the Pinto came roaring into view. If anything could be worse than arriving in a Jovial Janitor van, that would be it.

Not that she had any intention of sharing *that* thought with Tomi. "Thanks, but I want to take my van so I'll have a ride home."

Tomi glanced at her rhinestone-adorned, magenta acrylic nails, then fired a question. "Why isn't this guy picking you up?"

"It seemed better if he didn't."

Tomasina folded her arms over an ample bosom. "But you're okay about dancing with him?"

Brooke Anne shrugged.

Tomasina looked her up and down again. "Humph."

Sensing that Tomi was gearing up to spout out a long, drawn-out soliloquy, Brooke Anne started speaking fast. "I'll see you on Monday," she said as she opened the door, giving Tomi no choice but to get up and leave. "Thanks for coming by. I'm glad Vanessa's doing better."

"Me, too."

"Good night!"

"Good night," Tomasina replied with much less enthusiasm. "Hey, Brooke Anne?"

"Yes?"

"Have fun tonight, but be careful. You know what I mean?"

Brooke Anne nodded. "I do, and I will," she said as she gave Tomi a quick hug. "I've got to go."

As soon as she'd closed the door, Brooke Anne pulled on a wrap, grabbed her beaded evening bag and set out. Her stomach was in knots, but she felt warm and flushed and eager. She was ready for an adventure.

Ready to feel beautiful and statuesque…even for one night. If only for one night.

Chapter Six

She was late. How could she be late? Morgan checked his
watch again, then scanned the crowd milling about in the lobby
of the Excelsior Royal Hotel. Familiar faces returned his
glance. Inwardly, Morgan groaned. Already it was starting.

People had their best social smiles pasted on, and were attempting to look interested and bored at the same time. Women
were eyeing other women as potential rivals, measuring each
other's jewels, gowns and hair styles.

Later on, things would only get worse. Casual conversations
would morph into rumors about lifestyles and weight-man-
agement problems, followed by unsubstantiated gossip. And he
sure as hell knew that he didn't want to be the subject of any
snide remarks. He needed his date and he needed to mingle,
fast.

There was no way he wanted to stand by himself much longer
without an excuse. He needed a reason as to why he was at the
party by himself. Maybe he'd say Sheri had gotten pneumonia
and her doctor wouldn't release her from the hospital. Would
that be an acceptable reason to blow off the party? Car accident?
Amputation? They had possibilities, but still sounded weak.

Maybe her mother could have died. Yeah, no one would
blame him for showing up alone if there was a death....

"Mr. Carmichael?"

He turned toward the voice and stood in awe. A gorgeous blonde stared up at him, gray eyes wide and unsure.

"I'm sorry I'm late. I had a little trouble getting here and, well, I've been wandering around for ten minutes. It seems there are two entrances to this party, and a whole lot of people mingling together…and all the men are in black tuxedos…." Her voice drifted off. He could tell she was wondering why he was standing there like a fool, a blank look on his face.

Did he have a reason for standing in front of her, mute?

Not really, unless you counted the fact that he was staring at the loveliest little janitor he'd ever seen in his life.

His date.

"Don't worry about it. You're not too late—I was kind of early," he lied.

She was clearly relieved at his words. "I'm glad. You look very handsome, Mr. Carmichael."

"Morgan, remember? We're on a date."

She chuckled. "All right. *Morgan.* I'll remember."

He continued to stare at her, and wondered how a woman who normally wore old tennis shoes and mops on her sweatshirts could have transformed herself into such a knockout.

The ivory dress she wore accentuated her every curve. Its wispy, sheer fabric reminded him of a nightgown. That made him want to run his hands over it, check what it felt like. The dress flowed to the ground, and for a moment, when the door opened behind them, the gown molded to her legs. Legs that were long and firm and beautifully shaped, in those gold sandals.

"Let's go upstairs." He held out his arm for her to take. "I'm glad you're here."

"Morgan," she murmured when they entered the elevator. Her voice sounded a full octave lower than he recalled. "What do you want me to do when we get there? Say to people?"

"Try not to say too much," he replied without thinking, then amended his words. "But when you do talk about yourself, gloss over the part about being the building's janitor…. Maybe just say you own your own business?"

"I think I can handle that," she murmured in obvious amusement.

Feeling like a heel for having said such a thing to her, he added, "Don't worry about anything else…you look very pretty. And if you can dance, we'll have it made."

"I can dance."

She squeezed his arm in reassurance, and he realized he was actually proud that she was by his side. This woman was lovely, had a ready smile and seemed eager to fit in. Already, she was a vast improvement over Sheri. "You ready, Brooke?" he asked as they approached the center ballroom, the doors held open by two men in hotel uniforms. A live orchestra version of "Silent Night." Its familiar melody floated out of the room, along with a thread of laughter.

"Ready as I'll ever be," she said.

He patted her hand. "Don't worry, this'll be fun. Something to laugh about years from now."

Morgan pasted a relaxed smile on his face and entered the room, knowing he looked exactly as he intended to look: successful, self-assured and attractive, with a cool blonde on his arm. Things were going to be just fine.

It was hard for Brooke Anne to keep her cool; she was so tempted to stare around her in wonder. The grand ballroom was magical. Gold and ivory balloons decorated the center of each table, gold-foil-wrapped gifts lay on silver chargers at each place setting and wooden reindeer and Christmas trees decorated the borders of the room. Tiny gold and white lights twinkled everywhere.

And the people. There had to be at least three hundred people in the room, all dressed to the nines. Gems sparkled and richly colored gowns clung to beautiful figures. The scents of freshly applied cologne mixed with freshly cut pine and roses.

People stood in groups of four or six, talking avidly. The whole atmosphere gave Brooke Anne a strange feeling, like being on the set of *Dynasty*.

Who knew that people in Cincinnati entertained like this? Apparently a lot did!

Brooke Anne glanced over at Morgan. He definitely looked as if he belonged in this crowd. Handsome and polished, rich and carefree. She caught her reflection in a mirror and was surprised to find that, at the moment, she appeared to fit in, too. She looked happy, almost tall, and radiant.

Resolutely, Brooke decided she was going to have the best time at this office party that she possibly could. Who knew when she'd get another chance to attend such a chichi gathering? She'd put on her best smile, dance as much as she could and enjoy her pretty dress and flat-out sexy shoes.

"Ah, here's Gary," Morgan said at her side. "Let's go over and talk to him." He guided her to a tanned, slim man with salt-and-pepper hair who sported a rich burgundy brocade vest. Gary looked pleased to see them.

"Morgan, where've you been? We've been solving all the world's problems and were just about to tackle the Bengals."

Morgan laughed. "I came just in time." He tilted his head in the direction of the elevators. "We've been downstairs for a little while, watching everyone come in. I'd like to introduce you to Brooke. Brooke, please meet Gary and his wife, Kathy."

"Nice to meet you," Gary said with a smile.

"Hello," Brooke Anne responded politely.

"I love your dress," Kathy gushed as she switched places with Gary. "Where did you get it?"

"At Time Worn Treasures."

"The resale shop?" Kathy sounded surprised.

Brooke Anne cringed inwardly. Oh, no. Was she not supposed to mention resale shops, either? Well, too late now. "Yes, they had a lot of formal gowns to choose from."

Kathy examined her dress appreciatively. "Oh, I'm going to

have to go there. We have another party to attend next weekend." She shrugged. "You know how that goes, I'm sure."

"It's a busy time of year," Brooke Anne said noncommittally.

"Do you have children?"

"No, I don't. Do you and Gary?"

Kathy beamed and opened up her evening bag. "Four. We just got their photos taken. Come see."

The next thing Brooke Anne knew, she was looking at Kathy's pictures and complimenting her on her beautiful children. A few other women noticed the photographs, and soon Brooke Anne was being introduced to them and listening to stories about kids and babies and Christmas toys.

As they moved to a more brightly lit area to get a better look at the photos, Brooke Anne reflected that this group of women was not too different from most of the others she knew. They all had the same universal stories to share about labor pains, spills on the carpet and trips to the mall to visit Santa. Brooke Anne even found herself telling a story about her sister's two girls and how they had decided to wash the dog in the ornamental fish pond outside their house.

Waiters approached and brought them flutes of champagne. Brooke Anne sipped her drink with care and began to slowly relax. She could do this. She could fit in with these women. She'd just be herself. And if her nerves threatened to get the best of her, well, she'd just think of the money. True, she was really just a spruced-up janitor, but Morgan Carmichael had known exactly what he was getting when he asked her to accompany him to this ball. Hadn't he?

The man himself suddenly appeared by her side. He was wearing a bemused expression, as if intrigued by her immediate acceptance into the circle of women.

"Ladies, I'm going to claim my date again," he said, with enough of a flirty tone to cause the ladies to look at each other knowingly. "The dancing is about to start."

Brooke Anne let him take her hand and lead her away. His

fingers felt firm and warm clasped around hers. She felt a connection to him that she couldn't deny, and wondered why that was. Was she so attuned to Morgan's every move because she was simply trying to get a good read on him? Or was she completely smitten?

She glanced at him. He met her gaze, and a wealth of emotions they were too afraid to verbalize seemed to pass between them.

Morgan gently removed the champagne glass from her grasp and set it on a waiter's tray. Then, as the orchestra played the opening bars of "A Christmas Waltz," Morgan pulled her into his arms.

Although he was easily eight inches taller than she was, they fit well together. His left hand on the small of her back felt possessive and warm. She had no problem tilting her head to gaze into his eyes. It was as if she'd been in his arms before—it truly felt like the most natural place in the world to be.

Morgan Carmichael was a man who could waltz with the best of them. Obviously, he'd taken those dance lessons a little more seriously than he'd let on. There was no counting involved, or clumsy footwork, or any of the faulty movements that two people usually made the first time they partnered together. He was an expert leader; she was being twirled by someone who could have given lessons himself.

"You were right," he murmured after a few minutes.

"About what?"

"You can dance." The dimple appeared in his cheek again. "At the risk of sounding like Fred Astaire, I'll even say that you dance divinely."

"Thank you," she said, feeling somewhat like Ginger Rogers. "You dance well, too."

He rolled his eyes. "I need to work on turns some more. That's what my teacher said."

"Take it from me, you're doing great."

Morgan grinned at the compliment. They moved toward the

edge of the dance floor and then glided to the center again. "So, you hanging in there? I know these parties can be tough."

"Absolutely. Those ladies are very nice."

"Yeah, I guess they are. You fit right in."

"All women can talk about kids and chores," she said, realizing that perhaps she had more in common with them than she'd previously thought.

The comment seemed to take him by surprise. "Do you have children?"

"I don't. Do you?"

"No."

"Gosh, I guess we really don't know anything about each other."

The reality of their relationship veered front and center once again. Her stomach tensed. They didn't even *have* a relationship...did they?

"Is there anything I should know about you before I make a fool of myself?" Morgan asked quietly.

"Such as?"

"I don't know—life-changing situations, schooling?"

It was as if he was asking her to condense her whole life into one sentence. The request was both amusing and bizarre. How did one do that? "No, I don't believe so. The biggest life thing was when I was in fifth grade and got my hair stuck in the electric mixer."

"Stuck? In the motor?"

"No. In the meringue I was beating in the bowl!" She laughed at the memory. "Nothing compares to the angst and embarrassment of having most of your hair cut off because it was practically glued to a pair of beaters. Your turn."

"My turn?"

"Tell me something about you—something I need to know."

"Well, at work—"

She squeezed his hand hard to stop his words. "Not about work. About *you*. Something personal."

He pursed his lips. He couldn't remember the last time he'd been asked to do that, the last time he'd wanted to share anything personal about himself with anyone else. "I'm not quite sure how to do this."

"Please, Morgan. I'm trying to get to *know* you…not judge you."

"Um…" He hesitated. It had been a long time since he'd spoken without worrying about the impression he would make. "My two front teeth aren't real. Does that count?"

She gave him a pretty smile. "Definitely. What happened?"

"Well, I really wanted a go-cart when I was twelve, but my parents said no way."

"Uh-oh. I know what's coming!"

Morgan laughed. "I decided to make my own. I got hold of an old lawn mower engine."

"And…"

"I made myself a go-cart, all right. But I forgot one important thing."

"What?"

"A brake. I was forced to use the garage door as a convenient crash site."

She shook her head. "Oh, Morgan."

He spun her again. "I'll have to tell you about my mom's reaction one day." He glanced around them, a thoughtful expression on his face. "Boy, I hadn't thought of that in years."

Something about the manner in which he said it made her heart pound. He sounded wistful, tender—almost like a normal person. One hundred and eighty degrees different from the man she'd met on Thursday night, so concerned with appearances that he seemed to have forgotten what real problems were. With that in mind, she spoke. "Maybe it's time you did some thinking about that—you know, what's really important in life."

His eyebrows rose in surprise. "If bad experiences like electric mixers and go-carts matter…"

"It all matters," she said with feeling. "Everything always matters."

His eyes warmed at her words. "Maybe I should give it some thought, then."

The music ended with a flourish of notes from the pianist. For a fleeting instant, Morgan pressed her close to him, so her body was flush against his. Her gown felt as insignificant as tissue paper against his tuxedo. A hot curl of desire formed within her, despite the fact that her mind was saying a romance between them would be hopeless.

But what if it wasn't? She had a connection with him, a bond she couldn't deny.

What if his date's canceling on him was fate? What if they were meant to be together?

Those thoughts were hard to abandon as a colleague of Morgan's approached them and asked if she could fox-trot.

"Of course," she said with a smile and was promptly whisked off by his co-worker, hoping Morgan would be just a teensy bit jealous to see her in someone else's arms.

She glanced in his direction and caught his eye for a brief moment. Once again, time seemed to stand still as their eyes connected from all the way across the room.

Chapter Seven

Morgan wasn't sure if he wanted to think about how he felt seeing Brooke dancing in Stan's arms, her head turned up to him like a fresh daisy in the sun. A mixture of emotions coursed through him. But one thing was for sure: he was attracted to her. He wanted to spend more time with her and investigate these feelings.

There was something about her that made him forget all the inconsequential stuff in his life. When they'd danced, he hadn't given a single thought to his place in the company or the business goals he wanted to achieve.

He'd managed to forget about the lectures from his father, who always reminded him to put his personal feelings last. And the judging eyes of his mother, who'd skipped his football games because she hadn't been sure he'd play every quarter.

He could only think about the woman who'd accompanied him to the party, her shining gray eyes and the way she'd fit so nicely next to him.

And that was a good thing.

Restlessly, he wandered from one group of people to the next, engaging in meaningless small talk while keeping an eye out for Brooke and Stan. But the music seemed to last forever, and Brooke's attention was solely on Stan. Morgan tapped his foot impatiently when he caught Stan leaning just a little too close to speak to Brooke. Shouldn't that bother her? Wasn't Stan invading her space or something?

Morgan hoped Brooke had noticed Stan's wedding ring. The guy was married. He had no business whispering to her. Or letting his hand linger so comfortably on her waist....

"Hey, M.C., how are you this evening?" a familiar voice asked, snapping his attention away from the dance floor. It was Breva, her eyes scanning the crowd for his date.

"I'm fine, Breva. You look very pretty in red, if I might say. It's nice to see you, too, Aaron," he added as he held out a hand to her husband.

"Thank you," Breva replied, while Aaron nodded in response. "So, where's this date of yours? I've been trying to get a peek at her."

"She's over there, dancing with Stan Ashworth."

"Ah."

"*Ah?* What is that supposed to mean?"

A hint of mischief tinged Breva's tone. "Well, they seem to be having a very good time together, don't you think?"

Why was it that his fifty-year-old assistant talked as if she were perpetually fifteen? "Stan's married," Morgan said.

"Since when has that stopped Stan?"

Alarm spread through Morgan's stomach. "What do you know that I don't?" Brooke was, after all, his responsibility for the evening. At least that was what he told himself to explain his sudden uneasiness.

Aaron shook his head. "I wouldn't worry about it, Morgan. Breva's just giving you grief."

But Breva didn't seem ready to end her teasing. "By the way, I was talking to Michelle down in human resources yesterday, and boy, did I hear an earful!"

"About who?" Morgan inquired. Heck, he could gossip with the best of them.

"Well, she did mention a certain product purchasing manager—"

"Brev," Aaron warned.

That must have been the tone she listened to, because she stopped right then. Morgan was tempted to pursue it, but saw Brooke approaching them. "Be nice," he hissed to his secretary.

"I'm sorry I didn't see your dance end—I would've come to get you," he said, stepping forward to take Brooke's hand. After a small pause, she placed it in his.

"Hello," she said to Aaron and Breva.

"Hi, there," Breva answered. "I'm Breva Henry, and this is my husband, Aaron. M.C. was just telling us all about you."

Brooke looked taken aback. "M.C.?"

"Breva's my assistant," Morgan said, trying to imagine how confusing the plethora of names and titles must be for Brooke. "I can't get anything done without her, and she reminds me of that constantly. Back when we first met, I wanted her to call me Morgan, she wanted Mr. Carmichael, so we settled on my initials. Most of the time, anyway."

"How're you surviving your first Royal Hotels ball?" Aaron asked. "This is my fourth one."

"Oh, you're practically a veteran!"

"They're not so bad once you learn to pay no attention to most of the people."

"Aaron!" Breva chided.

Brooke smiled at Aaron. "I'm enjoying myself, actually. I love to dance, so it's a nice opportunity for me."

"I know what you mean," Aaron replied kindly. "I'm in construction, and this isn't something the guys go out and do on a regular basis. Or ever."

"How much convincing did Breva have to do to get you here the first time?"

"I had to promise a lot of things that are better left unsaid," Breva said with a laugh.

Aaron rolled his eyes. "Let me just say that the dance lessons were worth every bit of what I got in return," he said with an impish smile.

The force between them was hard to ignore, although Morgan would've liked to. He eyed the two of them with resentment, something he'd never felt before. He envied their security with each other and their playful banter. Feeling he had to diffuse the electricity in the air, he muttered inanely, "Well, at least we all know how to dance now."

"I saw you doing the fox-trot with Stan," Breva said to Brooke. "When did you learn ballroom dancing?"

She laughed. "I started taking lessons in junior high. It's kind of funny, but I've always liked to dance, especially the old-fashioned kinds of dances. One day when I was little, I watched a ballroom dancing competition on TV. The women were wearing gorgeous flowing gowns, and the men had on tuxedos with tails…and I was immediately hooked. I wanted to be one of those beautiful ladies, with their perfect makeup and serene expressions. I wanted to be twirled and dipped—" She stopped suddenly and pressed a hand to her mouth. "Oh, I'm sorry. I didn't mean to go on and on about something so silly."

Morgan shook his head when she met his eyes. She hadn't sounded silly at all, just honest. Adorable.

Aaron seemed enchanted. "The music's starting again. May I have this dance, Brooke?"

And before Morgan could even utter a word or try to cut in, Aaron was escorting Brooke onto the floor as the music flowed through the room.

Breva gazed at them with amusement. "Well, there you have it—the only two people in the entire room who are having a completely wonderful time. Everybody else looks like they're on the prowl for brownie points from the president."

Morgan had to laugh at her description. It was true. Last year, when he'd taken Sheri, both had been so intent on saying the right things and pandering to senior management that they'd actually seen very little of each other. Their conversation had centered entirely on work, and they'd spent the whole night dancing with other partners.

No wonder they had broken up just months afterward. It had been evident—at least to him—that any sparks between them had more to do with business than romance.

Only now did he realize the irony of that night. He'd been with a gorgeous woman, had wined and dined her all evening, yet the only thing they'd talked about had been rumors of who in the company was getting the largest Christmas bonus.

"Why are we here, Brev?" Morgan asked, in spite of the knowledge that he should probably just keep his mouth shut.

She looked at him in concern. "Because it's the thing to do. Because we have to be here if we want to keep our jobs. And we like our jobs."

"Do we?"

"I like the money. The power. So do you."

That he couldn't deny. "It's true."

She gestured toward several of their associates, who were also observing the dancing from the sidelines. Some wore obvious fake smiles, others had worry lines on their foreheads. "We're not the only ones who feel this way."

"I know," Morgan sighed as he watched one of the directors take his wife on a stumbling turn around the dance floor. Since that particular director was known for being especially fond of NASCAR racing and bowling, his presence on the dance floor could only be described as a command performance. Morgan threw Breva an amused look when the other man twirled his date with a little too much gusto. "I think Chris is actually getting better."

Breva arched an eyebrow. "I don't think so." Gesturing to her husband and Brooke, she said, "The thing of it is, you need your own Aaron."

"Is that right?"

"Yep. You need someone as down to earth as Aaron, who'll flatly tell you that work is over when you try to bring it up at night. I've told my children to do that, as well."

"Do you listen when he tells you to stop thinking about work?"

"Not always…but he finds ways to distract me," Breva said with a secret smile. "The fact is, Morgan, we all need to be reminded sometimes of what's really important in life. There's got to be more than office gossip and paychecks to keep us going."

They watched the parade of couples on the dance floor in silence for a few moments. Breva chuckled when Aaron and Brooke accidentally ran into the vice president of service, and then began visiting with him and his wife as if they were out on the golf course. "I like Brooke, Morgan. I hope you keep her around for a while."

"I like her, too," he stated, surprising even himself.

"You going to take her out again?"

"I don't know," he replied slowly, then revealed something he was hesitant to admit even to himself. "For some reason it feels like this is a one-night thing…that this is my only opportunity to get in good with her, and if I blow it, I might never see her again."

"I'd give you more credit than that, M.C. You need to think that way, too."

"I'll try. It's just that tonight, I seem to be thinking almost like a real human being. Tomorrow I'll probably go back to being an idiot."

"Not if you hold on to her."

Morgan saw Aaron and Brooke laughing while they waltzed, and couldn't help himself any longer. He wanted to be near her, to get a taste of that laugh, of her vibrancy. If he was only going to have her for one night, he didn't want to waste a minute of it.

Chapter Eight

Brooke Anne's evening was like a dream come true. Actually, it was better. It was real. She was being whisked away by a handsome executive who appeared content to stay glued to her side. He stared at her as if she was beautiful. No daydream that she'd ever had could come close to this.

Morgan Carmichael looked dashing and powerful. He had a ready smile for everyone—and a secret, sensual one for her alone. He acted like her personal Prince Charming, her own knight in shining armor. He seemed prepared to defend her honor, slay her dragons and fight off marauding knights just to make her happy.

Luckily for him, she was content simply to dance.

And dance they did. They tangoed and cha-cha'd and waltzed throughout the evening. And when they waltzed, he held her tightly against him, and she could feel the muscles in his arms and chest. She reveled in his self-assured steps and allowed her gaze to linger on the planes of his face, the shape of his lips.

He wasn't the sullen, quiet dance partner she'd imagined he would be. He talked to her. After further prodding, Morgan told her about growing up with his older sister, about his adventures in the woods when he was a boy and about his seemingly idyllic childhood.

In turn, she told him about her family vacations, complete with their run-down station wagon and a carsick dog. The conversation was light and revealing and gave Brooke Anne a true insight into the man she'd become enormously attracted to.

After waiting patiently while she took two brief turns on the floor with Stan and Aaron and introducing her to a variety of people he knew, Morgan seemed to let his possessive side come out.

His hand lingered on the small of her back, and his breath was warm against her neck as he whispered silly comments about different people in the room. He smelled spicy and masculine, and when their eyes met in the middle of a conversation, the look he gave her was decidedly warm.

She was lulled into being tempted by his interest. Tempted to believe they could have a future together. Tempted to forget she was getting paid to be there, and that she could've never afforded her dress or shoes without his financial assistance.

It was tempting to pretend she always painted her nails that shade of coral, that she truly did regularly schedule pedicures and manicures. That she hadn't arrived in a Jovial Janitor van.

Which was why, when he asked her to accompany him to the enclosed balcony, she didn't hesitate.

"Thanks," he said, as soon as he closed the sliding door behind them. "I couldn't wait to take a breather. It was getting hot in there."

"It's cold out here."

Concern crept into his eyes. "Are you chilled? I forgot that you're only wearing that lacy dress."

"I'm all right."

"Here, take my jacket," he offered, sliding it over her shoulders before she could refuse. Brooke Anne couldn't resist pulling it around her and losing herself in its warmth.

The lining of his jacket felt comforting and slick against her skin. Immediately, she caught the scent of his cologne. Feeling his coat around her was almost as good as his arms.

"In spite of our circumstances, I'm having a good time, Morgan."

"I am, too. Actually, I'm having the best time I ever had at one of these affairs. You're a wonderful dancer and a great date."

"Thanks."

He paused. "I was just telling Breva how much I've enjoyed getting to know you. You're so different from most of the girls I've dated."

"How so?"

"You're more real, if that makes any sense."

"Real?"

"I feel like I can be myself with you…. That's good."

"Tonight is a lot different than I thought it would be, too," Brooke Anne admitted.

"How so?"

She smiled at the echo of her own words. "I guess because my first impression of you wasn't all that great. You seemed a bit…shallow, the way you were so worried about having the right date and everything."

He stepped closer. "And now?"

His proximity made her breath catch. "Now I realize we're not really so different."

A new understanding infused the air between them. No longer did she feel like his employee. No longer did she feel unsure of what to say to him. She was hoping for more. More of the type of thing that wasn't scripted or in their plans for the evening.

Brooke Anne's awareness of the flecks in his eyes, the faint scar on his jaw, the pleasure she felt just being next to him suddenly increased, and a shiver ran through her.

Morgan noticed and wrapped his hands around her shoulders. Their warmth transfixed her, and she closed her eyes briefly, reveling in his touch.

"You're cold, Brooke…. I'm sorry." But instead of offering to take her inside, he enveloped her in a hug, his arms sliding under his jacket to circle her waist.

It was only natural to lift her arms to his neck and nuzzle her face against his chest.

"Better?" he whispered.

"Almost," she said, then cringed in mortification. How could she have said that aloud?

"You still cold?" he murmured huskily. "What do you need, Brooke?"

She knew what he was asking. Any sane person intent on regaining body heat would be heading toward the glass doors as quickly as possible.

She wanted a kiss, and she wanted it from Morgan. She wanted to feel his lips against hers, to melt into his embrace. So she did the only thing any bright, forward-thinking girl would do: she tilted her head up to him in an unspoken request.

With a slight smile tugging at the corners of his lips, he muttered, "I was hoping you'd say that." And then, finally, his mouth touched hers. He was gentle and slow, tenderly giving her a taste of what she wanted so badly. She sighed as his lips brushed against hers—once, twice. Moaned when he trailed his lips over her cheek to her jaw.

But it wasn't enough.

Thankful for her heels, she stood on tiptoe and buried her fingers in his hair, then strained to deepen her exploration.

And once again it seemed he'd only been waiting for her consent.

His hands pressed her upper back toward him, then one hand snaked up to trace the tendons of her neck. All the while, he savored her mouth, teasing her, delighting her with his patience and expertise. He was a passionate and thoughtful kisser, and she appreciated every second of it. She never wanted this to end, and—truth be told—she was already anticipating their next embrace. Looking forward to future dates and moonlit walks and furtive kisses on dark balconies. She wanted to hold on to him and never let go.

When his hands circled her rib cage, then slid down to her waist, she leaned into him. When his lips grazed her shoulder, then the tender slope of her breasts, she braced herself for the onslaught of sensation she knew would come.

She wasn't disappointed.

No longer were they relative strangers on a first date. They were Morgan and Brooke Anne, two almost lovers. Two people lost in the sensation of each others' body, intent on finding satisfaction in each others' arms.

She curved her hips to meet his. Moaned softly when his thumb swept her breast. Drew closer to his warmth. His desire. She arched her back, heard his breath hitch unevenly—then gasped when he broke the contact. Cautiously, she glanced up at him.

He stepped back, his face mirroring her own emotions. He looked mesmerized and a little stunned by what had just happened. His lips were swollen, his eyes dark and cloudy.

A chime rang in the distance, followed by the muffled call of someone announcing that dinner was about to be served.

A new awareness permeated the air.

She felt his ragged sigh on her cheek when he cleared his throat.

"Wow," he said, then chuckled. His dimple appeared. "You're probably not going to believe this, but I don't think I've ever been as affected by one kiss in my entire life."

"I believe it," she answered, seeing no reason to point out that they'd just shared far more than one innocent kiss.

Morgan combed his fingers through his hair. "I guess we should go on in. The people at our table will be looking for us."

"All right."

"And, uh…Brooke?"

"Yes?"

"I'm really glad you came," he said quietly.

"I am, too." She exchanged a knowing smile with him, then realized she was still wearing his coat. "I think you're going to need this," she said jokingly, and pulled it off. Immediately, the chilly air seeped through the thin fabric of her gown.

Morgan slipped his suit jacket on and straightened his bow tie. "You're still beautiful. Do I look okay, or am I all rumpled?"

"You're still beautiful, too," she teased.

His answering grin was a gift in itself as he opened the door, then guided her to their waiting chairs at table number seventeen.

Chapter Nine

Each table seated ten people, and Brooke Anne was disappointed that neither Breva and her husband, nor any of the women she'd met earlier, were seated with them. If Morgan was disappointed by their table partners, too, he didn't let on.

He'd managed to transform himself once again. In the space of a split second, it seemed, he'd adopted his professional demeanor, joking with some people and brusquely introducing Brooke to the others. His manner was cool and distant, as though he was completely aware of his colleagues' scrutiny.

Almost as soon as they'd been seated, uniformed waiters in navy jackets, black trousers and white gloves served a shrimp appetizer. Brooke Anne took her cue from the others about which fork to use.

And she took care to be just a silent observer during the dinner conversation. There was talk of a recent takeover by a competitor's company—something that made a man named Bruce very uncomfortable. Morgan seemed to be doing his best to calm Bruce's nerves, but it didn't look as if he was having much success.

After a time, the shrimp plates were removed and small Caesar salads were served, three large croutons decorating the center of each. Morgan's attention was drawn to another co-worker, so Brooke Anne turned to the dark-haired woman on her left.

She introduced herself shyly. "My name is Brooke Anne."

"I'm Cassie Edwards."

Brooke Anne nodded politely. "This is a wonderful salad," she said inanely when Cassie evidently had nothing else to offer. "I bet this is quite an undertaking for the staff—serving a party this large."

"Does it seem large to you?" the brunette asked archly. "Anthony and I went to a party last week at least two times the size of this gathering." She took a minuscule bite of salad. "I don't remember seeing you before. Are you a new friend of Morgan's?"

"Yes, I am. This is our first date, actually."

"How nice for you. Our Morgan is considered quite a catch, you know."

Brooke Anne caught every veiled hint thrown her way— Cassie was making it clear that she deemed Morgan to be out of her league. But recalling the sweetness of Morgan's kiss, she decided to volley a few shots of her own. "I'm very lucky, then. Have you known him long?"

"As long as he's been with the company. Three years now."

"You must know a lot of the people here."

"Oh, yes, but not very well," Cassie said, taking another small bite of salad. "At these parties, it's next to impossible to speak with everyone. You have to pick and choose who you spend time with. It's a wife's duty to make sure she speaks to everyone who counts."

"My goodness."

Cassie nodded sagely. "We spent a whole fifteen minutes speaking with the new CEO. That was quite a coup. Have you had a chance to meet him yet?"

"No."

"Or his wife? She's very fond of gardening."

"I'll keep that in mind."

"What about Mr. Brownlee, the president? I actually *danced* with him this evening. Anthony was so excited to see me in his arms! Who have you danced with?"

Brooke Anne had never been part of a conversation as strange as this one. The woman was treating networking like a full-fledged job. "I've been dancing with Morgan. And with Aaron...Morgan's assistant's husband."

The other woman's lips pursed. "Who else?"

"Um, Stan someone. I don't remember his last name."

"Was it Stan Ashworth? One of the vice presidents?"

"Gosh, I think so. Is he the man who has thinning blond hair and twin girls and likes to ski?"

Cassie looked taken aback. "Listen, I hate to be the one to tell you this, but you've been doing Morgan a disservice," she said quietly.

A feeling of dread settled in the pit of Brooke Anne's stomach. "What do you mean?"

"I mean that the purpose of these parties is for Morgan to have opportunities to mingle with people who matter. If you can't help him do that, then you're really of no use to him."

Her shock at Cassie's words must have been written all over her face. Brooke Anne glanced at Morgan. He'd moved his salad away, untouched, and was still deep in conversation with the man next to him.

"I'm sorry?" she asked. "I don't think I heard you correctly."

Cassie narrowed her eyes, as if she was weighing how much energy she should expend on Brooke Anne. "I'm just saying that if you expected romance from this party, you came to the wrong place. Morgan needs someone here to help him further his career. His job is what's most important to him, anyway." She let out an artificial laugh. "But I'm sure you've realized that."

"No, I hadn't," Brooke Anne answered honestly. Memories of Morgan shrugging out of his coat on their private balcony flashed through her mind. And the kiss. That wonderful, heart-stopping, luxurious kiss. That had to mean something, didn't it?

Minutes went by. The waiters came again to carry away the

salad plates and fill their stemmed glasses with a sparkling wine. Brooke Anne took a fortifying sip and waited for things to go back to the way they'd been between Morgan and her. She waited for him to turn with a sexy smile and whisper that he wished they were alone.

Except that Morgan's interest was now focused on the fate of two specific stocks, and he seemed to have the undivided attention of half the table. The others were either talking quietly among themselves or scanning the crowd.

Then the sound of tinkling glasses, the signal for a speech, rang through the air. All conversation stopped, and an elderly man whom Brooke Anne recognized as the CEO from a photograph in the building began to speak.

She shifted in her chair. Due to Morgan's lack of attention, Cassie's daggerlike words and the imposed boredom of the meal, she noticed that her feet had begun to hurt.

As inconspicuously as possible, she leaned down and inspected one of her heels. She was more than a little dismayed to find that her beautiful shoes had rubbed a raw blister there. A stinging sensation burned deep.

Realizing that her other foot was probably in equally bad shape, and that they were destined to sit through several more courses, Brooke Anne slipped her sandals off and curled her toes in the soft pile of the carpet.

The relief was immediate.

She forced herself to sit quietly and listen to the year's progress in the stock market, as well as the CEO's perspective on the state of the economy and the country in general. No one besides her appeared to be bored or uncomfortable.

She was glad when, after thirty minutes, the man finally stopped speaking. More wine was poured and dinner was served. Rare prime rib and baked potatoes were distributed quickly, as if the waiters had had the plates ready for quite some time.

Although the meal wasn't piping hot, and the meat was

rarer than she liked it, Brooke Anne dived in with gusto. She was hungry and restless and feeling very confused by her date's abrupt change in attitude. So far, the only thing Morgan had said to her during dinner was "Looks good, doesn't it?"

But the wine must've given Cassie a much-needed conversational boost. She chattered away to Brooke Anne about Morgan's stellar career and his former girlfriend, Sheri, who worked as a representative for one of the product lines Royal Hotels employed.

Brooke Anne couldn't help being interested in the woman from his past. "What's she like?"

"Oh, she's terrific," Cassie said with glee. "I've known her forever. We were in the same sorority."

"You went to college together?"

"We went to the same college," Cassie hedged, making Brooke Anne wonder if perhaps the two of them had attended at different times.

"How did Morgan and Sheri meet?"

"They knew each other through work…but I have to admit I'm the one who formally introduced them," Cassie stated proudly. "They're two of a kind, you know."

"How is that?"

"They both like the same things—power, money and really expensive cars."

Brooke Anne began to laugh, then realized Cassie was serious. "You sound like you know them well."

Cassie glanced at her husband, and Brooke Anne spied a brief flash of remorse in her eyes. "I know what it's like to want those things," Cassie admitted. "Growing up, that's all I dreamed about."

Ah. So Cassie had a vulnerable spot. "I know a thing or two about dreams," Brooke Anne volunteered. "Growing up, I couldn't wait to be independent. It was a great day in my life when I started my own business."

Cassie smiled, though a hint of bitterness clouded her features. "I can only imagine."

Well, that took care of that conversational thread. Returning to Morgan, she asked, "So, what happened between them? Morgan told me they broke up a while ago, that they were just friends."

"That was the rumor, but I think that Sheri was just waiting for Morgan to come to his senses." She shrugged. "But then again, you're here and she isn't, so who knows what is really going on between the two of them?" Thankfully, Cassie's husband asked her a question, and Brooke Anne was saved from further investigating the inner workings of Morgan's relationship with his ex-girlfriend.

She laid her fork carefully on her plate and peeked at Morgan again. He was sipping wine and appeared to be in thought. Brooke Anne wondered what he was thinking about. Doubts surfaced. Had their kiss, in fact, meant nothing to him? Had his hints of furthering their relationship been just talk?

He met her gaze and she felt a quick stab of guilt. Probably, rule number one in being a date for hire was not to gossip about the man with the paycheck.

Rule number two was probably to stay peppy and pleasant. "How's your dinner? Was your prime rib good?" she asked with false brightness.

Morgan tilted his head. "I could ask you the same question. We had the same meal," he teased gently.

She felt heat creep up her neck. Time to move on to another topic. "I was just thinking about Christmas. Have you started your shopping yet?"

His lips twitched. "Not yet. What about you?"

"I just have a couple more presents to go. I'm not sure I told you, but I dress up as an elf at Children's Hospital. I need to get a couple of games for the kids. And Barbies. There's an angel Barbie that's on every little girl's Christmas list."

"That sounds like fun. I can just see you shopping for those dolls. You know, I'd love to get involved with something like—" He stopped abruptly as his attention was drawn to the door. "Excuse me. There's someone I need to speak to."

With that, he got up and strode over to the front entrance, leaving Brooke Anne alone, feeling completely confused. The waiter came by again, picked up her half-eaten dinner and asked if she'd like dessert.

After nodding, she turned in her seat to see who had just appeared.

Someone tall, tanned and elegant. And she had a possessive hand on Morgan's biceps.

Inwardly, Brooke Anne groaned.

Chapter Ten

"What are you doing here, Sheri?" Morgan demanded. He clenched his hands and did his best to keep his expression neutral and composed—so he wouldn't look as if he was about to strangle her.

She beamed at him in triumph. "My plans changed suddenly, so I was able to come over and give you a little surprise!" She scanned the room as she dramatically slid off her fur coat, revealing a scarlet beaded gown underneath. The dress was form-fitting, its neckline low. A diamond-encrusted heart peeked out from her generous cleavage, beckoning others to get a closer look.

Sheri was the kind of woman who could scream for attention without uttering a word, and Morgan had usually been happy to answer her cries.

But at the moment, all he could do was wonder how to get rid of her without causing a scene.

It wasn't going to be easy; Sheri didn't take rejection lightly. He glanced over at Brooke Anne, who, to his relief, appeared oblivious to his absence. Again, Morgan was thankful for the many differences between the two women.

"Let's step over here and talk for a minute," he murmured.

But Sheri was already checking out the crowd. "Oh, I see Louise and Dan are here, and there's Bill. Have you talked to him about his contract yet?"

"No."

"What about Mr. Lancaster?" She fired off the question. "Any word about his deal with Emerson Paper? If he gets that account, things are going to be great for you. What do you think? How's he doing tonight? Is he in a good mood?"

Her questions came fast and furious, a sure sign that she was on "party alert." Last year it had amused him, and he'd shared her belief that every minute at the ball should be used to make connections. He'd been impressed when she'd discussed her intentions to circulate at the party with all the strategy of a field commander. Now, however, he was desperately planning her retreat. "Listen, Sheri. I'm here with somebody else."

She stared at him blankly. "What?"

"I came with someone else. There's no place for you here. You need to go home."

She studied him, incredulous. "But I was your date. You wanted me to be here with you."

"You're remembering it wrong. We agreed to go together because I needed a date and you didn't have any other plans for tonight. Then, you canceled on me."

She didn't deny his words. "So I was replaced in forty-eight hours?"

Maybe it was because her voice had grown louder. Perhaps he just felt like being a jerk. Whatever the case, he couldn't stop himself from speaking frankly. "No. It only took an hour."

She raised her hand, and for a second he was sure she was going to slap him. "I don't know why you're telling me this right now," she snapped, her eyes instantly watering. "Today's been terrible, especially with everything going on with my dog and with work. And then I went to all the trouble of getting dressed up to be here with you and…and…"

There'd been a time in his life when her act would have worked. He would've felt terrible for being so rude, and his heart would have gone out to her when he saw the tears begin to trickle down her face.

But not anymore. Now he knew her crying had as much to do with her genuine feelings as a soap star's tears did on TV. "Sheri, I've got to get back to my date, and you need to go home. Before you embarrass yourself."

"That sounds just like you, Morgan. So cold. So calculating. Always concerned with how things look. What people will think."

Her words hit close to home. Too close. She was right. His inability to relax his guard made him worry he was as cold and aloof as his parents.

It chilled him to hear it from Sheri, of all people.

Her manner became businesslike again. "So, who is she?" she asked, her shoulders stiffening.

"It doesn't matter."

Sheri's gaze panned the tables, looking for vacant chairs. "Is that her, in the black dress?"

"Sheri…"

"What? I don't even get to see who replaced me within an hour?" Turning toward their right, she motioned in Brooke Anne's direction. "What about that blonde? Is that her? She looks familiar. Where does she work?"

"For God's sake, Sheri!" he hissed.

But the tears were on again and her voice was carrying. Already she'd grabbed the waiters' attention. Morgan knew that if they stayed there another minute people would begin talking about the two of them—and about how he'd left his date at the table alone. With a shake of his head, he took Sheri's elbow and guided her out of the room.

He didn't even notice her triumphant glance at the crowd as they retreated to the hall.

BROOKE ANNE COULDN'T believe her eyes. Not only had Morgan practically ignored her during dinner, but now he'd *left the room* with another woman. This had to be an all-time dating low, even for hired dates.

What was she going to do if he didn't return? Get up and leave? Wait for him at the table until he decided to remember she was there? Mill around the room and try to look happy, even though she'd been jilted? Her head started to pound. She ate an extra big bite of her chocolate cheesecake for comfort.

"That was Sheri Vincent," Cassie said.

Like she needed this right now. Swallowing quickly, Brooke Anne turned to Cassie. "Oh, really?"

"They must've decided to give their relationship another go. Didn't she look stunning in that red gown?" Cassie gushed. "It takes a special person to pull off a dress like that."

Brooke Anne was wondering why a dress so skimpy didn't *fall* off. "It was very red, that's for sure."

"You should've seen them together last year. Morgan wore a dark bronze vest and Sheri had on a gold sequined gown. They looked like two people at the Oscars! What a striking couple they make."

"She is pretty."

"Did you notice the way Morgan took her arm when he pulled her out the door?" Cassie continued. "I bet he can't wait to get her alone. They must be getting back together right now."

The idea made Brooke Anne's stomach flutter with agitation. Cassie was probably right. And it was what she deserved, wasn't it? What had she been thinking, anyway? That she and Morgan were actually going to be a couple?

That all their differences were going to disappear? That it suddenly wasn't going to matter that tonight was like a fairy tale to her, but gala evenings were a part of Morgan's life?

"I wonder what I should do," Brooke Anne muttered to herself.

Cassie must've heard her. Once again, her expression was cold and haughty. "There's no doubt in my mind that it would be best for everyone if you'd just leave," she said archly. "I mean, you wouldn't want to spoil Morgan's career by staying where you aren't wanted, would you?"

The way she spoke, combined with her icy gaze, gave Brooke Anne a sick feeling of hopelessness.

"They'll be back any second," Cassie was saying. "If you're here, where is Sheri going to sit?"

Brooke Anne opened her mouth to protest but was cut off before she could utter a word.

"And the president's about to give his speech, too. You won't be able to get up while he's talking. If you stay, you'll cause a scene."

So many thoughts ran through her mind. Morgan, her promise to be his date for the whole evening, his words…her paycheck. "But—"

Cassie leaned in close and lowered her voice. "I don't know how to be any clearer, Brooke. You don't belong here. You need to leave."

"I can't just take off while Morgan's gone. What will he think?"

"He won't even notice you've left. You got a free dinner out of this—what more do you want?" The woman grabbed Brooke Anne's arm. "Oh, here comes Mr. Brownlee. If you're going to leave, you'd better go now. There—" Cassie pointed one crimson nail in the direction of a marked exit "—right out the back door. Hurry!"

Without further hesitation, Brooke Anne did just that. She scooped up her handbag and made her way as quickly as possible to the exit. Without looking back, she opened the door and pulled it shut behind her.

After asking a member of the waitstaff for the closest route to the parking garage, she turned the corner, then walked swiftly down two flights of stairs.

It was only when her feet touched the cold concrete floor of the parking garage that she realized she'd forgotten to put her shoes back on.

What could she do? It was twenty degrees out and those sandals were the reason she was even there. She had to at least try to retrieve them.

Stealthily, she sneaked back into the dining room, then noticed two things. First, the president was speaking and the huge room was as silent as an empty office building.

Second, Morgan's chair was still empty. Had he gone ahead and left with Sheri? Thank goodness she wasn't still sitting there by herself, waiting for him. That would have been extremely embarrassing.

She stepped a little farther into the room, attempting to peer under the table to find her shoes. But as she leaned forward, her hip collided with a foodcart, its shrill squeaking causing more than one head to turn her way. Two men nearby visibly winced, apparently at the thought of someone interrupting Mr. Brownlee.

Great. Now she not only had no shoes, but she'd practically caused a scene. With a sigh, Brooke Anne walked out of the room. Nothing was worth this embarrassment. Not even a pair of really beautiful high heels. Not even a really magical night.

IT HAD TAKEN SOME DOING, but Sheri was now out of his life. Morgan hurried back to the table, ignoring the dark look he got from the president for walking through the room during his speech.

When he reached the table, he sat down wearily and glanced toward Brooke's chair. When he didn't find her next to him, he looked in the direction of the ladies' room. He knew he needed to explain things to her, tell her he hadn't meant to abandon her during their meal, that his only intention had been to get Sheri out of the room, fast.

The president droned on.

He bent toward John. "Have you seen Brooke, my date?"

"Not for about ten minutes. She left right after they served dessert."

"Really? You think she's okay?"

John gave him a bemused smile. "I have no idea. Ask Cassie. They seemed to be having a pretty good conversation."

He leaned across the empty seat beside him. "Cassie, where's Brooke?"

Cassie's eyes widened. "Where's Sheri?"

"Sheri left—she couldn't stay," he said impatiently. "Any idea where Brooke is?"

"She left."

"What do you mean, *left?*"

Cassie shrugged. "I thought you were back together with Sheri, judging by the way you couldn't keep your hands off her."

He looked at her in alarm. "What are you saying?"

"I'm saying I told her you'd probably prefer her to leave," Cassie said, her expression becoming wary.

"You *what?*"

"Morgan, I thought you and Sheri were getting back together."

Morgan could only stare at her.

Cassie glanced over at her husband, saw his look of surprise and squirmed. "I was trying to help."

"Cassie—"

She interrupted him. "I didn't know that she *meant* anything to you."

Although two executives from his department glared at him for talking, Morgan knew he had to get to the bottom of what had happened. Surely Cassie hadn't actually told his date to leave without him—that was low even for this crowd. "Listen, I was standing in front of the main exit. Which way did she go?"

"I couldn't tell you, Morgan."

He gritted his teeth. Couldn't…or wouldn't? He knew very well the type of spiteful person Cassie was.

And here he'd left Brooke alone at the table—hell, alone at the party—while he'd gone off to take care of Sheri, and he hadn't even given her a word of explanation or warning about Cassie.

He closed his eyes in frustration.

Finally Mr. Brownlee finished his speech, they all dutifully applauded, the orchestra resumed playing and his co-workers began to stand up and mingle again.

Cassie seemed to know she'd made a major faux pas, and took off right away. Morgan remained at the table long after everyone else had departed, and cursed himself.

He'd acted like an ass to the first girl who'd really mattered to him in years, and now he was going to have to find a way to make it up to her.

And, he realized with a shock, pay her. Christmas was a month away and she had probably been counting on that money.

Abruptly, it occurred to him that he didn't know Brooke's full name, her phone number or her address. All he knew was that she cleaned his office at night.

And that she dressed as an elf at Children's Hospital during the Christmas season.

And that she'd gotten her hair caught in an electric mixer when she was a little girl.

That she enjoyed dancing and had a beautiful smile.

That she looked pretty in ivory, had flyaway blond hair and sparkling gray eyes.

That her lips were soft and full and that she tasted like a dream. And her body had felt right in his arms.

He knew then that he'd move a lot of mountains to make sure he saw her again.

Sighing, Morgan started to stretch his long legs in front of him, but accidentally kicked something in his way. Whatever it was got caught on his toe and didn't want to be shaken off.

Curious, he peered under the table to find a pair of petite gold sandals, one long strap attached to the toe of his shoe. He reached down and freed it, then picked up both sandals and set them on his lap. Absently, he examined one. The shoe was a size five and looked as if it had been barely worn. The straps were unbuckled and the soles were brand-new.

Just as the clock on the wall struck midnight, a wide grin split Morgan's face. Brooke, his very own Cinderella, had forgotten her shoes—and it was up to him to see that she got them back.

Chapter Eleven

Brooke Anne flexed her toes into her soft, cushy slippers and tried to pretend that there was nothing she'd rather be doing on a Sunday morning than working on her newest jigsaw puzzle. After all, Sundays were usually her favorite day—a day when she sometimes made it to church and to her favorite doughnut shop for two doughnuts, one glazed and one chocolate-covered. Or, if she slept in, as she had today, she'd just stay home. Lounge about in a soft nightgown, extra-large terry robe and cozy slippers. For someone who was so cheap with shoes, Brooke Anne always made sure that her slippers were new and fluffy.

She'd make a good pot of coffee, flavored with hazelnut or French vanilla, and she'd turn the television on low while she worked on a puzzle.

She loved the puzzles from the Hallmark store, and she took care to pick one that corresponded with the season. Currently, she was working on a Thomas Kinkade winter scene.

Putting together a fifteen hundred piece puzzle depicting a horse-drawn carriage making its way through the snow was fun.

Well, it was relaxing, she amended. Relaxing for a girl who couldn't afford to splurge on luxuries like massages and spa treatments.

Unable to stop herself, she took stock of her present situation. She was an independent entrepreneur with a lack of funds and a good disposition. Christmas was coming and the four women who worked for her would each expect a bonus.

Her parents would ask why she wasn't coming home for the holidays.

Brooke Anne moved two yellow-tinged pieces around the table, aimlessly trying to find a home for them. But her heart wasn't in it. And at the moment, she wasn't even concerned about her family or her finances.

She was concentrating on one thing, and one thing only.

A man.

A man named Morgan Carmichael.

A man named Morgan Carmichael who'd blown her off when his ex-girlfriend came back. She should hate him. She should be mad as hell at him.

But all she could think about was the feeling of being in his arms. The way the corners of his eyes had crinkled when he'd laughed. How his whole body had attuned to hers when they'd danced…and kissed.

A tremor coursed through her at the memory. Drat her body. It seemed she just had to think of him and it would react. Not good, when she didn't want to ever see the man again—even if he did owe her money. Money that would've come in very handy about now, with Christmas coming.

Finally, giving up all pretense of putting together the puzzle, Brooke Anne walked to the window, framed with twinkling multicolored lights. She looked out at the cold, gray morning. It was a perfect day to stay inside.

She should make some lists and figure out how to turn the two hundred dollars she had squirreled away into acceptable presents for ten people.

A knock at her door disturbed her musings.

Tomasina had come to pay her a call again. Brooke Anne was hesitant about seeing her. Tomasina had a clear, no-nonsense outlook on life that Brooke Anne didn't feel up to embracing.

"What's up?" Tomi asked, looking very festive in a red sweat suit and green socks.

Brooke Anne smiled wanly at the question. "Not a lot, obviously. I was just about to get another cup of coffee. Would you like one?"

Tomi glanced at her friend with concern. "I would," she answered as she followed her into the kitchen.

Brooke Anne refilled her own cup, then poured a generous mug for Tomi and set out a carton of cream and a container of sugar. Tomasina liked her coffee rich and sweet.

"Well, I'm waiting," Tomi said as soon as she'd planted herself at Brooke Anne's card table in the living room. "How was your evening?"

How could she tell her without dissolving into tears? "Interesting."

"As in how?"

"As in I danced a lot, basically fell in love, had a great kiss out on a moonlit balcony, got ignored during dinner, and then was told to leave by a witchy wife when my date's ex-girlfriend showed up." Brooke Anne paused and took a small sip of coffee. She was kind of proud of herself for having summarized her evening so succinctly.

Tomi winced while stirring her coffee. "Anything else?"

"Hmm. What else can I add? Oh, yeah. I forgot my shoes, which just happened to be the whole reason I said okay to this date, and I didn't even get paid, which would have made all the heartache at least bearable."

Tomasina's eyebrows pulled together as she digested the outpouring of information. "How was the food?" she asked then, a teasing smile tugging at the corners of her mouth.

Brooke Anne chuckled. Leave it to Tomi to get to the heart of things. That's why she appreciated her friendship so much.

"You know what? The prime rib was almost raw...but the cheesecake was excellent."

"What kind of cheesecake?"

"Chocolate, with a dark cookie crust and fresh whipped cream."

Tomi nodded her head in appreciation. "That alone must have been worth some heartache."

"Some," Brooke Anne agreed. They sat quietly for a moment, Tomi automatically moving the puzzle pieces in front of her.

"Real shame about how it all turned out," Tomi said after a time.

"Yeah."

"How're you going to get your shoes back?"

"I'm not."

"Why not? Girl, they're yours, bought and paid for!"

"I never want to see Morgan Carmichael again."

Tomasina pushed her coffee cup aside and stared at Brooke Anne, incredulous. "Not even to get your shoes? Your money?"

Recalling his too-handsome features and his soft hair, which had felt so good under her fingers, made her shudder. No way did she want to get near him again. "Not ever again. It's just not worth it."

"I don't know what to say about that."

Brooke Anne figured with enough time, Tomasina would have plenty to say. "I shouldn't have seen him in the first place," she explained. "I shouldn't have danced with him, enjoyed myself so much. We're too different."

Tomasina sighed. "Brooke Anne."

"Tomi, he's too rich for me."

Her friend laughed. "Too rich? Is that possible?"

Brooke Anne couldn't help but smile at that. "All right. How about...too different. We have nothing in common. Morgan belongs in that glittering, superficial world. Not me."

"So you're going to lose him?"

Had she ever truly had him? "I'm going to lose all of my pride if I try and pretend to be somebody I'm not."

"Oh, honey," Tomi said with a grimace. "You've got it bad."

Maybe it was her friend's calm assessment of the way things really were. Maybe it was forcing herself to admit that her feelings had been hurt. Regardless, it was enough to finally make her cry.

"I can't believe I ran off last night," Brooke Anne said shakily, tears falling down her face. "I can't believe things started out so good and ended so bad."

Tomi, like the good mother that she was, scooted her chair closer and patted Brooke Anne's back. "That no-good two-timing loser," she murmured.

"And I was having so much fun, too." Brooke sniffed. "I danced with a few different people, and for a while, I really did seem to fit right in."

"I bet you did," Tomi said soothingly.

"Morgan kept telling me that I looked beautiful."

"I saw you with my own eyes. He was right."

"I felt like a princess." She hiccupped. "And when we waltzed—you should've seen us—we were two bodies moving in perfect harmony."

"I've never waltzed."

"Oh, Tomi, it was wonderful. We were *gliding* across the dance floor. Morgan spun me so fast, all I could do was hold on tight."

"I'm more interested in how you got that kiss."

"It wasn't just one kiss—there were a bunch of them."

Tomi leaned back. "A whole make-out session, huh?"

"No, it wasn't like that. It was sweet. And passionate. Exactly how I always imagined it would be with the right person. I didn't want it to end."

"Well, why did it?"

"We were on the balcony, in the cold, and they rang for dinner."

"So, you went inside, and things went to hell?"

"Pretty much," Brooke Anne admitted miserably. "I sat next to this strange woman who only talked about Morgan's ex-girlfriend." And, Brooke Anne realized, Cassie had made it clear that she hadn't really fit in at all. That one kiss couldn't change the fact that they were from separate worlds. That she'd never belong.

An image of Russell, her ex-boyfriend, popped into her mind. Russell had told her he loved her, then discovered Suzanne, a pretty, young checkout girl at Wal-Mart. Brooke Anne hadn't stood a chance after that. Especially since she'd thought she'd been days away from receiving the very nice diamond that she heard Suzanne now sported on her finger.

The ring that everyone in her family had assumed would be hers.

Tomi pursed her lips in disapproval. "And what was the man of the hour doing at the time?"

"Talking business with everyone else."

"And then he took off and left you?"

"Yep, more or less."

"Girl, you ought to say good riddance and goodbye. Guys like him are a dime a dozen."

"Not guys who can dance and look great in a tux."

"It's not what's on the outside that counts," Tomi said primly.

"You sound just like my mother."

"Good. You need some old-fashioned advice. Turn this page of your life and move on. If it's a guy in a fancy suit you're interested in, there's one of those on every corner."

"Those are the Salvation Army Santas, Tomi."

"Well, the way you described this guy, I'd say those pretend Santas and this Morgan Carmichael have a lot in common. They're all trying to be something they're not."

Brooke Anne slumped back in her chair. Tomasina did have a point there. "But what should I do next time I see him? Part of me is going to want to apologize for running out on him, and the other part is just going to want my money and my shoes back."

"Do you want to see him again?"

No. Well, not really. "I don't think so."

Tomasina smiled. "Then don't. We both know you've had your share of bad men in your life."

"Just Russell."

"Just Russell? Don't 'Just Russell' me! That boy in Nebraska broke your heart, and you're still trying to mend it now—three years later!"

"I've got a good job—"

"Jobs have nothing to do with love, and you know that. Look. When Russell be-bopped over to that bimbo Suzanne and left you high and dry, you were supposed to use that as a learning experience. You know, to stay away from men who were going to cause you heartache."

"I've learned."

"Have you? It seems all you've done is put off dating completely. All I ever hear about is how you stay at home in slippers and do puzzles. You never go out and get social."

Tomi's idea of socializing would put Brooke Anne in the hospital. "So…even though I liked kissing Morgan I should stay away from him because he's trouble?"

"T-r-o-u-b-l-e." Tomi sighed. "Hey, don't worry about seeing him. Royal Hotels is my account, anyway."

"But—"

"If I see this Morgan, I won't say a word about you. I'll just let him cool his, uh, heels for a little bit."

Brooke Anne winced at Tomi's play on words. "Then what?"

Tomasina shrugged. "If he wants to find you, he will. Otherwise, in a week or so I'll ask him for your money and your shoes." She snapped her fingers. "Piece of cake."

"You wouldn't mind doing that?"

"Not at all," Tomasina said with a smile. "Now, let me tell you about my evening. It was better than good."

Brooke Anne wrapped her hands around her mug and leaned forward. "Tell me every little bit," she commanded.

Tomi laughed. "No problem. It started when Ronnie got us a babysitter for Vanessa."

"I didn't know he knew how to do that," Brooke Anne teased. Tomi was always complaining that her husband never organized their dates—he just showed up.

"Ronnie surprised me. And then, things got really good at the movies," Tomi added with a wink.

Brooke Anne settled in more comfortably. Suddenly the dreary day seemed a little brighter. "Then what happened, Tomi? Don't skimp on the details."

"Oh, honey. I don't know if you're anywhere near ready to hear the rest," Tomi teased. "But if you think you can handle it…"

She went on. Brooke Anne got them both another cup of coffee and brought out a box of Chips Ahoy cookies that she'd been saving for a special day. Somehow all her problems seemed manageable again.

Just before she left, Tomi pulled out a sheet of paper. "I almost forgot to give this to you."

Brooke Anne scanned the sheet with concern. "What is it?"

"A cleaning request. Someone left a message on the answering machine. I called the lady back. She lives in one of those mansions in Indian Hill and is desperate for a rush job." Tomasina raised her voice two octaves. "Her regular maid service is all booked up."

Brooke Anne laughed—both at Tomi's voice and the irony of it all. Clients always thought that they were the only ones who got busy over the holidays. "And we aren't?"

Tomi shrugged. "Normally, I figure you'd tell that gal to go jump in a lake or something, but with the date gone bad and everything…"

Tomasina's voice drifted off, and Brooke Anne smiled grimly. She knew exactly what Tomi was getting at. Tomi wanted her bonus and it was Brooke's responsibility to make sure she got it.

Carefully, she folded the note and set it next to her date book. "I'll call this lady first thing in the morning, Tomi. Maybe you and I can knock it out at the end of the week?"

Her friend winked at her, visibly relieved. "Check with my boss. If she says I'm free, I'll be there."

As Brooke Anne watched the blue Pinto drive off, she had an uneasy feeling that maybe she'd never really been meant to be with Morgan Carmichael. Money to him could be forgotten and misplaced. She'd always worked like a dog and all she had to show for it was bills.

Bills and dishpan hands.

Chapter Twelve

It was seven o'clock on Thursday night, and Morgan plucked the pair of gold sandals out of his bag and displayed them in clear view on his desktop.

He'd decided to stay late and catch Brooke Anne when she came to clean.

He couldn't wait to see her pretty face and tell her he was sorry. And then he needed to try and make amends.

Of course, Breva hadn't hesitated to let him know every day of the past week that he'd deserved every single thing that had happened. On the hour, she'd chimed in with little tidbits about how she'd never liked Sheri in the first place, how he'd run off the only nice girl he'd ever met, and how he'd managed to completely embarrass himself in front of every person at the company Christmas party.

Good assistants like her were hard to find.

Morgan had considered waiting for Brooke Anne on Monday night, but that had seemed too eager. On Tuesday he'd had a dinner meeting. Wednesday he just hadn't felt like subjecting himself to her hurt glances and accusations. But today he couldn't help it.

He wanted to see her. He wanted to hear about her day and talk about mundane things. His week had been filled with meetings that went on for too long, arguments over expenditures and a surprise visit from the CEO of the company. Morgan felt frazzled and more tired than he cared to admit.

But things would be better once Brooke showed up. He was sure of it. He'd give her the shoes and the money he owed her, ask her if she wanted to go out for a late dinner, and then find out more about her stint as an elf at Children's Hospital. He could be himself again—

—or someone he wanted to be. Someone who was good at relationships and had no problem connecting with other people on a personal level. He could give her a hug hello and practice the art of meaningful conversation.

At least for a little while.

He was starting to believe that all the things he'd held so dear before—power, money, social status—really meant very little. It had hit him the hardest Sunday afternoon, when he'd realized he didn't have a single person to call to talk about Brooke, Sheri or to ask what to do with a pair of gold shoes.

Maybe he'd convince Brooke Anne to come over to his house this weekend and help him put up a tree. They could go shopping for ornaments and lights and celebrate their handiwork with a cup of eggnog in front of a crackling fire…which would lead to a couple of kisses.

Scratch that. It would lead to a very passionate make-out session on the floor next to the tree. Just imagining how Brooke would look wearing little more than splashes of color from the twinkling lights made his mouth go dry. He'd bet that her legs were just as silky as they'd appeared peeking out from under that dress, that her stomach was flat and velvety soft….

"'That's the way, uh-huh, uh-huh…'"

Morgan let go of the shoe he was holding as a beautiful, rich voice continued to sing down the hall.

"'Uh-huh, uh-huh…'"

Whoever it was didn't seem to know the lyrics to the KC and the Sunshine Band song any better than he did. The voice was stuck on that same line like a broken record. He went to investigate, and in the kitchen found a tall, lanky woman with cappuccino-colored skin and black silky hair, singing her heart out while washing dishes. She was wearing a white Jovial Janitors sweatshirt.

"Excuse me…."

The woman was really belting it out. "'Do a little dance… make a little…"

He tried again, louder. "Excuse me."

She let out a shriek and spun in his direction. "What are you doing, sneaking up on people in the middle of the night?"

"I've been trying to get your attention, and it's hardly the middle of the night. It's seven-thirty."

The woman gave him a withering glance and looked as if she was considering the pros and cons of launching her washrag at him. "Do you need something, sir?" There was condescension in her tone.

"Yes, as a matter of fact. I'm looking for the girl who usually cleans this office."

"That *girl* would be me."

"No, someone else. I'm looking for Brooke. Do you know her? She's petite with blond hair. She was here cleaning a week ago."

The woman's eyes turned appraising. "You met her last Thursday?"

Morgan nodded. "Yeah. Brooke. Is she in one of the offices down the hall?"

The woman's eyes narrowed. "What do you want her for?"

Because he needed information, he bit back a sharp retort. Something told him that, for some reason, this woman was practically itching for a fight. "I have something to give her. Could you tell me where I could find her?"

"There's no Brooke here," she replied, setting down her dishcloth and stepping forward.

"Is she sick?" he asked.

"Look, I don't know why you want Brooke, but this company is my account."

"So why was she here last week?"

No answer.

"Listen, it's important. Can't you give me some information?"

One minute passed. "No."

The woman was turning surly, and he didn't know why. Again he strove for patience. "Could you give me her phone number?"

"Are you crazy?"

Frustrated now beyond words, Morgan sat on the edge of a circular table. "Look, I need to see Brooke, and if she's not here, I need to get ahold of her. Cut me a break and help me out."

The woman didn't look at all cowed by his tone. She merely leaned against the opposite table, folded her arms across her chest and glared at him.

"Do you even know Brooke?" he asked, exasperated.

Her eyes narrowed. "Brooke who?"

"Brooke…Anne?"

One eyebrow raised. "Anne? Is Anne her last name?"

Her contemptuous stare made him uncomfortable. "I believe so."

"So, you're not even sure."

Honestly, this woman could've given Perry Mason a run for his money. Morgan shrugged. "I don't know her all that well."

"Well, I don't know *you* too well. What's your name?"

"Morgan Carmichael. And you are…"

"Tomasina Edwards."

"Pretty name."

She treated him to a superior look. "It is."

"Do you know the Brooke I'm talking about?"

"I do."

Lord, it was as if they were going in circles. "Will you please let me know how I can get in touch with her?"

Tomasina gave him another hard stare, then shook her head. "I don't think so."

Maybe a little subtle bullying would help. "Look, I'm going to find Brooke's whereabouts one way or another. In fact, I could just call Jovial Janitors right now and ask to speak with her."

Tomasina's lips twitched. "First of all, no one is ever there to answer the phone. It's switched to be picked up by a machine."

"Why is that?"

"Do you think we just hang out in the office all day?" She shook her head. "Why don't you tell me why you want to talk to her. What did she do, touch your desk by accident?" she asked sarcastically. "Erase something on the whiteboard in your room?"

"This has nothing to do with cleaning. It's personal."

The woman eyed him for a long moment, as if making a monumental decision about his right to speak to her friend. In spite of himself, Morgan stood at attention, waiting for her approval.

Apparently, it wasn't his to be had. "No, I don't think so."

They were obviously at a standstill—and Tomasina was matching him word for word in obstinateness. "Why the hell not?" he demanded.

"Because I don't think I like you, that's why. Brooke's nice and doesn't appreciate people swearing. She's got delicate sensibilities."

"Ah, so you do know her well."

"Never said I didn't." Tomasina narrowed her eyes at him again, glanced at the clock and frowned. "I've got to finish up here. My baby's at home with her daddy, and they've no doubt got my dinner ready. How about you just give me a note to pass on to Brooke? She can deal with you if she feels like it."

"That's all you'll do for me?"

"Uh-huh. Take it or leave it."

Great. He was now at this Tomasina's mercy. There was something about her militant stance that made Morgan positive she wasn't about to change her mind. But as Brooke's pretty smile popped into his mind, he realized he was willing to do just about anything to see her again.

"All right," he said slowly. "I need to go fetch some paper from my office. Promise you won't leave before I get back?"

She looked amused. "Scout's honor."

Feeling as if he was in junior high, Morgan hurried to his office, pulled out a sheet of monogrammed paper and tried to think of something to say that would bring Brooke back into his life. His pen hovered over the paper.

Brooke,
   I have your shoes and the money I owe you. Please stop by on Monday to get them.
Morgan.

There. Though there was nothing the least bit romantic about his note, it was straightforward and to the point. That had to count for something, right? Hastily, he folded it up just as Tomasina came walking down the hall.

"Here. Will you please give it to her?"

"Maybe." Without a flicker of guilt, the woman opened up the letter and scanned it quickly. "Now, this is just the type of note to make my heart go pitter-pat."

Tomasina was right. As far as love notes went, this one sucked. Still, he held his ground. "I'm not trying to make anyone's heart, uh, do that. I'm just trying to get in touch with Brooke."

She met his gaze. "And here I was thinking that she meant something special to you," she said softly.

"She might." Biting the bullet, he said, "What's she like?"

That same eyebrow rose again. "Don't you know?"

"Not well enough," he said, though privately he recalled that she had tiny feet and an elegant neck, and she'd smelled like vanilla and…almond?

But he wanted to know more. "Tell me one thing about her."

"Brooke Anne is the dreamiest little thing you'll ever meet," Tomasina said after a moment's reflection. "And she can really scrub a floor."

With that, she stuffed the note in her jeans pocket and sauntered away.

Morgan went back to his office and carefully slipped the shoes back in a drawer. He'd need them on Monday.

Chapter Thirteen

"Gosh, Mom…I don't know," Brooke Anne hedged as she contemplated throwing the phone out the window.

"But dear, what else will you do over the holidays?"

"I've got a million parties to go to, Mom." *Well, to clean for.*

"But your sisters and brothers will be here, and all the kids. They'd love to see their favorite aunt."

That was a direct hit. Her mother knew her nieces and nephews were her weakness. Of course, she'd be sure to run into Russell, her ex-boyfriend, as well. With Suzanne and their new baby. Did she really want to see him again? Remember that she'd been jilted by him in front of all of her friends?

No way. Looking at the blank calendar, she tried to sound regretful. "Gosh, Mom, I'm sorry, but I just can't get away this year."

"Tell me one good reason why."

There was no way she could tell her mother the whole truth, that she just didn't have the funds for a trip to Nebraska. That she couldn't bear to see Russell again. That she didn't want to see all her siblings married and happy and be reminded that she was alone. Still.

If she admitted any of those things her mother would turn chatty. Start in on her speech about how Brooke Anne should move closer to home. How they could *help* her, *be there* for her. Introduce her to some *good* men. How Mrs. Vance two streets over had a divorced son just about her age. How she needed to stop daydreaming so much and *live*.

Oh, it would be awful.

Thinking quickly, Brooke improvised. "I…I met a man."

"Brooke Anne! Really?" The way her mother said it was the way other people reacted to scientific discoveries.

"Uh-huh."

"What's his name?"

"Morgan. He's an executive with a hotel chain. He's the product purchasing manager." There. That sounded impressive. And it wasn't even a lie. Mentally she gave herself a pat on the back.

"What kind of job is that?"

"I don't know, Mom. A good one, I guess."

"And you're going to spend the holidays together?"

That sounded good. "Yep. He practically begged me to stay here," Brooke Anne said, as she fingered his note for about the hundredth time. "I'm sorry, but I promised him I'd try." She glanced at her reflection in the living-room mirror, for fear her nose had grown from all of these tall tales she was spouting.

"Maybe you could bring him home with you. Has he ever been to Nebraska before?"

To her mom, Nebraska was one of the great, untapped places of the world, just like in the *National Geographic* magazine.

Somehow, Brooke Anne didn't think Morgan Carmichael was the Nebraska type. "I don't know if he's been there or not."

"If he came home with you, we could all meet him."

Like that would be fun. She could introduce Morgan to her overprotective mother and let him hear about how Russell had broken up with her in front of her friends and family. "That would've been nice, Mom, but—" she racked her brain "—he's asked me to go to his parents' house Christmas Eve. We're going to have a turkey there and then go to midnight Mass." Brooke Anne rolled her eyes. Sure, why not add church in there, too? Why not just keep those lies coming?

"Well, goodness. It sounds serious."

"I wouldn't go that far," Brooke Anne said with only the barest sense of remorse. She was seeking self-preservation, after all.

"Do you think he's *the one?*"

Oh, there was so much her mother left unsaid. Brooke Anne knew she meant *is he the one, finally?* The way Russell had almost been. Fighting an onslaught of nerves, Brooke Anne wandered over to her puzzle and furiously tried to pop one of the pieces into place. "I don't know."

"Well, if he wants you there for Christmas, I'd say there's a good chance he might be, Brooke Anne. Maybe your father and I could pay you a visit in January. Get to know this Morgan a little better."

"January in Cincinnati isn't all that great, Mom. Maybe you should come in the spring instead." Yeah, surely by spring she'd have her life figured out.

"But we might have some serious planning to do. You'd need my help."

"Serious Planning" meant wedding plans. Brooke Anne tried again to press a puzzle piece into the wrong spot. Tension started to build in her shoulders. She jammed the piece in harder.

It was time to get off the phone, fast. "Gosh, will you look at the time? I've got to go."

"Where?"

She thought quickly. "Work. And then a dinner date. Bye, Mom."

Brooke Anne hung up, then grabbed her coat. She really did need to leave. She and Tomi were going to go clean the shrill-voiced society lady's home. The one who was desperate to have a clean house for her *soiree.*

She and Tomi had had a good laugh at that. What exactly was a soiree, anyway? How many people did that involve? What kind of food did they serve? It was a great mystery.

Before the soiree cleaning, Brooke Anne had something far

more important to do. She'd promised the volunteer coordinator at the hospital that she'd pick up a few more Barbie dolls on her way there. One of her jobs as a Christmas elf was to help wrap the hundreds of donated items. Then they'd match the toys they received with the children's wishes.

Minutes later she was striding toward the neighborhood toy store when Warren, the shoe salesman, caught her eye from his shop window. Seeing as she at least owed him a thank-you for his help with her makeover, she crossed the street. His face lit up when she approached.

"Well, if it isn't Cincinnati's very own Cinderella. How did things go?"

"I looked the best I ever have," she said, sidestepping his question. "Thanks to your assistance."

He nodded in response. "Glad to help. How were your shoes?"

"My shoes were lovely," she said, and hoped he didn't hear the tinge of regret in her voice. Warren didn't need to know that they'd given her blisters and were now lost forever.

"And your young man? How was he?"

"Fine…at least in the beginning."

"But not in the end?"

"No, my prince kind of turned out to be a frog."

"Oh?"

"I left early."

Warren studied her, his eyes traveling downward to her brown-and-orange sneakers. "Are you coming in to get more shoes?" he asked hopefully. "Perhaps some leather tasseled loafers?"

"No, I'm sorry, I've got to go buy some Barbie dolls for the hospital, then get to work."

"All right. Take care, Brooke Anne. Come by soon for some hot tea, even if you're not in the market for shoes."

He sounded so sincere that Brooke Anne immediately took him up on the offer. "Thank you. I will, soon."

She ran into the toy store and bought a dozen angel Barbies

with the credit card the volunteer had given her for the purchase, before setting out on her way again.

The weather was cool and crisp, with no sign of rain or snow in the air, rare for Cincinnati in the winter. She'd decided to take advantage of the day and walk to the drop-off point for the toys. Then she'd quickly pick up her Jovial Janitor van and drive to Tomasina's.

It gave her a lot of time to think about the note that Tomi had delivered yesterday afternoon.

Tomi had handed her Morgan's letter with scarcely a word, something that was surprising in itself. And when she'd read the missive—she could hardly call it anything but that—Brooke Anne had felt chilled to the bone.

His two meager sentences didn't exude any of the warmth she'd felt from him at the beginning of their date. Had she just imagined the connection between them?

Maybe whatever connection they'd had didn't matter anymore, now that he was back with his ex-girlfriend. Maybe now that their date was over, he had no thoughts of Brooke Anne except bad ones. Perhaps she was but a bitter reminder of a date gone wrong, and all that remained was an incomplete business transaction between them.

All she knew was that she sure as heck wasn't in any rush to see him, especially since he'd summoned her in a note. Who did he think he was, anyway?

Of course, she *had* asked Tomi to help her keep *her* distance….

As she walked along the sidewalk, Brooke Anne watched the people of Cincinnati go about their business, and reflected on her situation. She didn't need a man in her life—well, not a man who made her sad. She'd cried more than enough tears over Russell.

There were a lot of good things to concentrate on. Jovial Janitors was her very own business, and she had really great friends she knew she could always rely on. Like Tomasina. And Tomasina's little family was practically her own.

If Morgan wasn't romantically interested in her, she could handle it. One day she'd be able to forget just how handsome he'd looked in that tuxedo.

Yep. She didn't *need* Morgan. She'd just fallen for him, in a silly, teenaged kind of way.

And no matter what, she had to put him out of her mind—fast. After all, she had a mansion to clean.

Chapter Fourteen

"By my way of thinking, it's only going to take us a solid twelve hours to clean this place top to bottom," Tomasina muttered as they pulled up to the side of the soiree house in the prestigious community of Indian Hill, later that day.

With a groan, Brooke Anne had to agree. The place was gargantuan. "Are you sure this is the right address?" she asked, hoping against hope that maybe they were at the wrong home.

"I'm positive," Tomi said, scanning the note again. "I took care to double-check her address and directions. Well, on the bright side, we'll get to charge an arm and a leg, right?"

"As well as a few other body parts," Brooke Anne replied. With a sigh, she stepped out of the van into the cool winter air. "Let's get this over with."

"Roger that."

Carrying a pailful of cleaning supplies, Brooke Anne made her way to the front of the home and rang the doorbell.

Tomi followed a good two steps behind, lugging her own bucket. "Do you think we were supposed to go around back?"

"What, like the help in old movies? Come on, Tomi, it's just a house. Besides, we did park off to the side."

The beautiful etched-glass door was opened by a petite woman in high heels, designer jeans and a sweater that Brooke

Anne had seen in the window of a very exclusive boutique. "Are you the cleaning girls?"

"That's us," Tomi said dryly. Tomi really hated being called a cleaning girl.

"I'm Brooke Anne Kressler, owner of Jovial Janitors," Brooke Anne interjected.

"Nice to meet you. I'm Caroline Hart," the auburn-haired woman said with a smile. "I'm desperate. People will be here in four hours!"

Brooke Anne tried not to wince at Ms. Hart's high-pitched squeal. The woman was obviously feeling a little stressed about her upcoming event. "Well, if you'll just show us which rooms you'd like cleaned, we'll get right to work."

Ms. Hart stepped back and motioned them inside a marble foyer decorated with gilt cherubs holding handfuls of Christmas garlands. They were kind of cute, if a little ostentatious, Brooke Anne decided.

The woman then led the way through several rooms, each with a fancy name. Brooke Anne couldn't help raising her eyebrows at her friend after they'd peered into the library, the parlor and the conservatory, each one more elaborate than the last. They were all decorated to the hilt and then adorned with an extra layer of Christmas glitz.

"Would you like us to dust everything, ma'am?" Brooke Anne asked. If Caroline Hart was hoping to have every expensive knickknack removed and wiped down with polish, each room could take four hours!

"Just do what you can," she said with a chuckle. "I know it's an enormous task."

Ms. Hart quickly clip-clopped down the hall, pointing out three bathrooms and yet another cozy sitting area.

"You won't need to worry about the bedrooms, private baths or the kitchen. But if you have time, please vacuum the billiard room in the basement."

"Will do," Tomi said. "You have a very pretty house, Ms. Hart."

Their client looked genuinely pleased. "Thanks. At first I was worried that my husband and I wouldn't feel comfortable in such a big old place, but we've grown to love it."

After they'd discussed payment, cleaning supplies and other details, Ms. Hart headed toward the back of the house. "Some guests might be arriving before you leave. If you see them before I do, can you let them know I'll be in the sunroom?"

"Sure thing," Brooke Anne replied. As soon as they were alone, she shared an incredulous smile with Tomi. "Can you believe this place? It's bigger than some office buildings we clean!"

"It's bigger and fancier than the Union Center Museum," Tomi added with a grin. "And all those names. Conservatory? Sunroom?" She rolled her eyes. "Why not just call them 'More Rooms to Clean'? Who in the world needs five sitting rooms?"

"Obviously Caroline Hart does." Brooke Anne glanced at her watch. It was time to get down to business. Four hours was going to fly by with so much to do. "How do you want to tackle this? Work together or separately?"

"Separately, of course. I'll take the bathrooms, you start dusting the statues in the conservatory!"

"That was the library."

Tomi pursed her lips. "Let's just call it the ugly gnome room."

"I think those 'gnomes' are probably pretty valuable."

"You take them, girl!"

After giving Tomi a high five, Brooke Anne left her partner and went off to dust and vacuum. As she made her way through each area, she decided that she really couldn't find fault with either Caroline or her house.

After all, it wasn't any of her business how the woman spent her time or money. And she did seem rather nice. Lord knew Brooke Anne and Tomasina had met their share of difficult people, most with a lot less class and money.

She couldn't help wondering what it would be like to live this way. She tried to imagine spending hundreds of dollars to get seven rooms cleaned professionally for a bunch of snooty friends.

And the rooms looked as if an interior decorator had designed every one of them. They were right out of one of the pages of *Town & Country* magazine. She'd have a hard time sipping tea and doing her puzzles in this house. Why, she'd probably have a heart attack if she spilled anything on the antique Oriental rugs!

Ms. Hart came down after three hours to see how they were doing. "My, everything looks wonderful," she said to Brooke Anne as she walked into the study off the front hall. "You two did a great job."

"Thank you," she replied, trying not to stare at the woman's new outfit. She'd changed into a silky red-and-black pantsuit. It clung to every inch of her perfectly proportioned figure and set off her striking head of auburn hair. A chunky gold necklace completed her outfit. "You look very nice."

Caroline's face lit up as though Brooke Anne had just announced she'd won the lottery. "Thanks. It's new! But the best part of the whole outfit is the shoes. Look!"

There, on her feet were a pair of black high-heeled sandals. *Yes, she knew exactly how nice those shoes were.* They were her exact shoes, only in black instead of gold. "Those are beautiful."

"I got them at WJB Shoes."

What could Brooke Anne say? That she'd bought the same pair last week? That she went to that store all the time in her ugly tennis shoes? "They're very pretty."

Caroline flashed her bright smile again. "Thanks! So, are you and your partner just about finished?"

Brooke Anne consulted her watch. "I'd say we'll be out of here within thirty minutes."

"Great. Here's your payment," she said, handing her a thick envelope. "I put a little extra in there since you two have been so nice."

Brooke couldn't help grinning as she slid the envelope into her jacket pocket. "Call us if you're ever in a bind again, ma'am."

"I will," Ms. Hart said, just as the doorbell rang. "I'd better go get that."

Brooke Anne had turned around to finish dusting a set of candlesticks when she heard an eerily familiar voice. Cautiously, she peeked out from behind the desk to see who'd entered.

Standing right there in the foyer, in a smartly tailored navy-blue suit, was Morgan Carmichael, with a gorgeous brunette by his side. As if frozen to the spot, Brooke Anne watched him hug Caroline, present her with a bottle of champagne, then guide his companion toward one of the back rooms.

In seconds, they were out of sight.

Her heart sank. Although the brunette wasn't the Sheri woman who Cassie had told her about at the gala, she was just as attractive and elegant-looking as Caroline was. And Morgan and she looked to be pretty close.

With a deep sigh, Brooke Anne sat down on the carpet behind the desk and tried to pull herself together. But it was hard.

Even though she knew it was ridiculous, she'd been hoping that when she and Morgan finally saw each other again, all of their differences would've magically fallen away and there would still be that stellar, vibrant spark between them.

But seeing him in these surroundings made everything all too clear. Morgan belonged here. He knew women like Caroline. He hung out at mansions like this one all the time.

He knew what a soiree was.

She just knew how to clean the rooms for one.

"Brooke Anne?" Tomi called from the doorway. "You ready?"

"Yeah. Hold on."

Tomi stepped inside, then bent down to catch Brooke Anne's eye. "Why are you sitting on the carpet?"

"No reason. I...dropped a rag. But I've got it now."

"There's already a crowd in the kitchen, and I do believe they're headed toward the front parlor as we speak," Tomi said.

Lifting her nose in the air, she said loftily, "Let's depart, shall we?"

With a half-hearted chuckle, Brooke Anne picked up her pail and followed Tomasina out the door to the van.

As they were pulling out of the driveway, Tomi turned to her. "Did she pay you?"

"Oh, yeah. We'll have to count it when we get back to the shop. She said she gave us a little something extra."

"Good."

"You know what?" Tomi said. "I was so prepared to hate that rich woman. I was so ready to put down her house and her decorations and her whole life. But…she was nice."

It felt worse, hearing her private thoughts spoken out loud. "Yeah," Brooke Anne said. She still couldn't believe that she'd actually seen Morgan at Caroline Hart's house.

Tomi kept talking. "I mean, that Ms. Hart didn't have to be so sociable. And her house, though too fancy for me, was kind of cool, huh?"

It was. It was cool and sophisticated. "There were a lot of neat things," she admitted, knowing that her words sounded weak.

But Tomi didn't seem to notice. "Did you see that mink fur throw? Or those beaded fruit? Or the leopard-spotted china set?"

"I did."

"They were nice. Real nice. And Ms. Hart and I chatted all about animal prints when she asked if I wanted a glass of iced tea." Tomi paused a moment, then continued. "You know, Brooke Anne, today showed me that I could handle being rich, no problem." She just kept chatting along. "If I ever get rich, I'm going to be cool, too. Cool and *nice*."

"I hope so!"

"You know what? I'll even invite you to my soiree. That is, if I ever figure out exactly what happens at one."

Brooke Anne burst out laughing, unable to stay in her funk

with Tomi babbling so excitedly. "If you ever have a soiree, I'll be there with bells on," she said.

And then giggled with her best friend all the way home.

Chapter Fifteen

As soon as she got home that evening, Brooke Anne wrote Morgan back. She needed to get her shoes and the money and move on with her life. What happened at Caroline Hart's house had made that crystal clear.

> Morgan,
> Please give my check and my shoes to Tomasina. She'll make sure they get to me.
> Brooke Anne

After reading it twice, she couldn't resist adding a little more.

> I hope you are doing well. I'll remember our dances fondly.

There. Let that be a lesson to Morgan Carmichael. It *was* possible to write a businesslike note and still be friendly.

"IF I'M GOING TO START being a letter carrier, I'm going to need a raise," Tomi declared from across her breakfast bar.

Brooke Anne had stopped off at Tomi's before running to the office. She liked hanging out at her house. Tomi favored a bold decorating style that was anything but staid. Currently, she was into the nautical look. The kitchen was painted in shades of turquoise and blue. Brightly colored fish made out of wood and stone graced the counters. Vanessa, Tomi's two-year-old, loved the fun atmosphere, and so did Brooke Anne.

But Tomi's décor did nothing to quell Brooke Anne's disappointment at her friend's reaction. "A raise? Is that all you have to say? I'm in the middle of a major crisis here!"

Tomi made a few googly-eyed faces at Vanessa before turning back to Brooke Anne. "You're right. I can say more. How about… This is the worst letter I've ever read in my life. No, make that the second worst. The worst was from your Romeo."

"*Romeo?* He's not *my* anything," Brooke Anne hissed, looking up as Tomi's husband, Ronnie, entered the room.

"Don't mind me," he said, stopping to brush a kiss on Tomasina's brow. "I'll be getting out of your hair in a minute."

"You don't have to hurry. I'll be leaving soon," Brooke Anne told him.

Ronnie tilted his head, studying her. "You okay?"

"I've been better. How come all men can't be like you?"

"Like me?"

Tomi nodded. "You're special."

That earned her another kiss.

"You ought to take a seat and give us some perspective, Ron. Our girl's really in a bad way."

Brooke Anne squirmed. "It's not that bad…I've just got some issues with a man I kind of dated."

"Kind of?" Ronnie echoed.

"It's complicated."

"You've got man trouble?" he asked.

"Does she ever. By the basketful," Tomi added.

"Then I'm outta here. Bye, babe," he said to Tomi, after he kissed Vanessa's cheek about ten times. "See you."

"See you," Tomi called out, then stared at Brooke Anne.

"Your man, your Morgan… He could be *your* Romeo if you'd just stop being so stubborn and give the guy a chance."

Something was up. "My *man?* Tomi, what's going on?"

When Tomi just sat there, looking obstinate, she asked, "Have you switched sides?"

"No. Not really. I'm just trying to stay out of the middle. And do my job, and take care of my family." Tomi narrowed her eyes. "Seems to me that I'm a lot busier than you. You ought to be delivering your own mail."

"I thought we agreed I should avoid Morgan."

"That was before I noticed how under your skin he was. I think it's time you talked to him."

"Tomi!"

"Well, at least go deliver your letter."

"Oh, yeah, like I'm going to sneak into the Royal Hotel offices and put it on his desk myself," Brooke Anne said.

"Yes, you are. I'm so glad you're going to take care of this so I can head straight home after work."

Brooke Anne's stomach roiled in panic. Now she wished she had told Tomi that she'd spied Morgan at Caroline's house. Maybe if she knew her friend would be a little more forgiving.

For now, though, she was willing to sound desperate. "Tomasina, you can't do this to me."

"Christmas is coming. Did you know that play cabins are a lot harder to put together than you'd think? I've got a lot to do, Brooke Anne."

"But—"

"Next Friday is our bonus day," Tomi interjected with a raised hand. "It's circled on my calendar. You won't want to forget that."

No, she didn't. Even with the extra money from last night, both women knew that Brooke Anne was in no position to walk away from Morgan's cash. "I won't forget," she muttered.

Tomi's lips curved upward as she handed Vanessa two saltines.

Glancing at her friend, Brooke Anne spoke quietly. "Hey, Tomi…what did you think of him?"

"I don't know."

"Come on. Does he seem all bad?" she asked. "Do you think I've completely misunderstood him? I mean, maybe he had a perfectly legitimate reason for leaving the dinner."

Tomi fussed with Vanessa. "Brooke, I only saw him for a few moments."

"Am I going crazy, imagining the two of us together? I mean…he's rich."

"Money isn't everything."

"It's a lot," she protested. Just thinking about seeing Morgan again—even if only to pick up her check—made Brooke Anne's stomach hurt. Perhaps it would be best to simply dip into her savings and forget about retrieving that money. "Maybe I should just forget about him and the shoes," she said.

Tomi's expression became soft as she turned toward her. "Brooke Anne, you have to give people a shot. Everyone has their good and bad sides. And good and bad days. Give things time."

Even though she knew what Tomi meant, a part of Brooke Anne didn't want to keep waiting and investing time to find out if the man she liked was Mr. Right. Hesitantly, she tried to explain herself. "Remember how I told you about Russell?"

"Uh-huh."

"I really liked him, Tomi. I thought we were going to get married. *Everyone* thought we were going to get married. But then one day Russell showed up with a photo of Suzanne instead of a ring. It was at a barbecue and all my friends were there. It was all I could do to stand there and not burst into tears."

"I remember you telling me about Suzanne, the bimbo replacement."

Brooke Anne smiled at the description. "Yes. But now that I think about it…maybe Suzanne wasn't a bimbo at all. Maybe she was nice. Maybe she was the right girl for Russell, and I didn't want to believe that. They have a baby now."

"It hurts, huh?"

"Yeah. It hurts a lot." She gazed at Tomi, who was cuddling Vanessa close.

"Tomi, I think I've been hiding. I think I've been telling myself that I'm fine with Jovial Janitors and living on my own. But maybe I haven't been. Maybe I do need someone to love."

Tomi looked at Vanessa, then at the door where Ronnie had exited. "Everyone does."

"And all that mess with Russell… Maybe even though he wasn't the right guy for me…maybe someone else is."

Tomi reached out and clasped Brooke Anne's hand. "Of course you need love," she said. "Of course Russell wasn't for you. Who knows if this Morgan guy is. But maybe it's time to think about giving him a chance."

To acknowledge that scared Brooke Anne half to death. "I don't know…"

Tomi rolled her eyes, a sure sign that she knew her friend wasn't being completely honest about her feelings.

"I think I like him," Brooke Anne finally said. "I can't stop thinking about him, even though I know I should. But we're so different. I mean, what would we talk about?"

"Beats me," Tomi said with a sad shake of her head. "But if you can't stop thinking about him…maybe you need to see him again. Right?"

"Right. Thanks."

Tomi squeezed Brooke Anne's hand, then let go of it and walked to the door. "Go on, now, girl. You've got things to do, and I've got to figure out how to build a cabin without Vanessa seeing it. Wish me luck."

"Good luck," Brooke Anne said as she stepped onto the porch, pocketing the note Tomi had given back to her. Yep, it had to be done. She had to go deliver the note herself. And if he was there…well, so much the better.

Maybe.

Chapter Sixteen

"What did you do on the weekend, Morgan?"

Morgan looked up as Breva entered his office, carrying a batch of folders and a shopping bag that appeared to be filled to the brim with toilet paper. "I went to my sister's house for a party."

Breva sat down in the chair across from him. "Caroline?" she asked with a smile. "How is that rich sister of yours?"

Morgan grinned. "Just as loony as ever. She decided to host a soiree."

"Isn't that just a fancy name for a party?"

"Damned if I know. My cousin Barbara and I kept giving Caroline grief about it. Twice Barbara offered to perform her third grade recital piece on Caroline's grand piano."

Breva winced. "What did Caroline say about that?"

"To shut up and act refined," Morgan said, laughing at the memory. "Then her husband came in and got things going."

"Oh, yeah?"

"Bob can make a mean martini."

"I've met him before, right?"

"Yep, he came in once last year when Caroline took him out shopping."

"When I saw him, he hadn't shaved in two days and was wearing jeans and boots. You'd never know he was a gazillionaire."

"Nope," Morgan agreed. "The way he tells it, it's not his

fault he inherited a boatload of money. Someone had to." He shook his head. "Bob does good things with it, though. Anyway, during the soiree slash party, he took us downstairs to play pool. It was fun."

"Well, your evening kind of makes my time with the grandkids sound pretty boring."

"I doubt it," Morgan said. He knew Breva loved being with her grandchildren. "I bet it was like a three-ring circus there at your house this weekend."

"It was, but it was fun."

Morgan nodded his head. "It kind of felt like a circus at my sister's house, too. I'm glad I have Caroline. My parents are so much work, but Caroline makes me smile…inside, if you know what I mean."

"I know exactly what you mean. That's what family is for, M.C." She shook the large shopping bag she was holding. "Well. Speaking of circuses, ready to get back to the real world, boss?"

"That depends. What's in the sack?"

"Toilet paper."

He couldn't help scowling. "Haven't we looked at enough?"

"This is for the ladies' restrooms at the A-list hotels in the East. Someone somewhere decided that the toilet paper needed to coordinate with the hand towels."

That sounded like a complete pain. "Can't you take care of it?"

"What? And let you miss out on all the fun? I don't think so. Besides, you're the one who has to sign off on it."

"If my mother had had any idea she was raising me to rate toilet paper—"

"If your mother had any sense—which she doesn't, by the way—she would be proud of you."

Morgan ducked his head for a moment, too aware of the truth behind Breva's words. She was completely right about his mom. His mother was a cold woman who had never really attempted to form a bond with him. Again, he was grateful to have Breva in his life.

She was the mother figure he'd always wanted. And a damn good assistant.

He raised his head as she ceremoniously dumped all the rolls and packages of hand towels on his desk. "Hop to it, M.C. They're waiting for a reply."

He squeezed a roll, just to make her smile. "This one— Number J7594—feels nice."

"But is it A-list-ladies'-room nice?"

Morgan picked up another and tossed it to her. "You're a lady. What do you think?"

She rubbed the roll against her cheek. "It feels good to me."

Unable to help themselves, they started laughing. "I guess my bosses won't care that I attended a bona fide soiree just the other day."

Breva shook her head in mock sympathy. "Nope. Every day can't be a party, M.C. Some days are only fit for TP."

"That says it all," he replied, then pulled out a sheet of paper and prepared to check costs, stock availability and softness.

MORGAN YAWNED AGAIN and fought to keep his eyes open. It may have only been seven o'clock, but his body was telling him it was time to sleep. Although he and Breva had gotten a kick out of rating the toilet paper, the rest of his day had been taken up by an endless supply of paperwork and conference calls.

It had been a bear of a Monday.

He grimaced as he eyed the mountain of papers that never seemed to shrink. He'd almost snarled at Breva when she'd brought in the last stack before she'd left for the day.

Invoices needed to be checked. Commissions verified. It was part of his job, and as much as it drove him crazy, he didn't complain. At least, not that often.

He glanced at the clock again: 7:10 p.m.

Slowly, his problems at work were replaced by thoughts of

Brooke. He had no idea if she was going to stop by tonight…
but he really hoped she would.

Of course, there remained the question of what he was going
to say to her if they actually did meet. Should he tell her he was
sorry? Mention that they ought to go out again, but this time on
a real date? He sighed and ran his fingers through his hair, trying to think of something to say to a woman he'd practically
abandoned during a dance—a woman who had then deserted
him.

He closed his eyes and silently tried out some lines. *"Hi,
Brooke. Long time, no see."* Ouch. *"As long as you're here, why
don't we go get a bite to eat?"* Cheesy. *"I really like your
shoes."* Morgan groaned. Yawned. He could just imagine what
she'd say to that comment. She'd probably think he was a
creep with a shoe fetish.

Morgan sank lower in his chair, pushed his feet out in front
of him. Maybe he should just be straightforward? *"Brooke, I've
been thinking about you for days, and I'd love to take you out
again. Will you give me another chance?"*

He thought that sounded pretty good as he drifted off to
sleep.

IT TOOK ALL OF Brooke Anne's strength to enter the Royal Hotels headquarters with her key and walk down the long hallway to Morgan Carmichael's office. But since Tomasina—the
traitor—had abandoned her, she had little choice.

As she stood outside his door, clutching her note, she had
to admit she couldn't wait to see him again. Her pulse had
quickened in anticipation. She felt excited and nervous and embarrassed that one person could cause such a stir within her.

But then again, maybe it was only natural. Morgan's kisses
had been so tender, so promising. And when he touched her, it
had made her feel all jittery and hot inside.

Russell had never made her feel like that.

Brooke Anne steadied herself against the wall. She had to

calm down, or she'd just sound like a flighty teenager, and he'd hand her the check and her shoes and get rid of her as fast as was humanly possible.

With that in mind, she turned toward his door, straightened her shoulders in an effort to look a full inch taller, and knocked.

No answer.

She tried the handle. His door wasn't locked. "Mr. Carmichael? Morgan?" she said before peeking in.

There he was, sitting at his chair. Most likely too busy to even look up from his desk. Brooke Anne stepped inside the office and cleared her throat to get his attention, but he didn't budge. Then she noticed that his eyes were closed and he was breathing softly.

He was sound asleep.

Surrounding him were more stacks of papers than anyone should rightfully have to deal with. There were open files and brochures lying in heaps. A pair of wooden dice and a few executive-looking toys were scattered around.

It was a real mess.

Brooke Anne was tempted to straighten things up a bit, but then Morgan shifted in his seat and turned his head to the left. She sat down in the chair across from him and just stared. He looked so cute asleep!

Every line in his face had been smoothed away, and appeared calm and serene. Momentarily, she imagined sleeping next to him every night. Would he want to cuddle her close when they turned off the lights? Slip an arm around her middle, so her back would stay warm against his stomach?

In her fantasy, she'd wear a pretty silk nightgown and Morgan would wear boxer shorts with animals printed on them. He'd kiss her and tell her he loved her, and after they'd passionately made love exactly as they do in the movies, they'd gently drift off to sleep.

But just before she'd sink into slumber, he'd whisper in her ear, "You're so wonderful, Brooke. So amazing. I love you so much."

Her keys clanked to the floor.

With a start, Brooke Anne shook herself. She needed to stop these daydreams and focus on reality. This man didn't want a future with her—he wanted to give her a paycheck for going out with him! He hadn't asked her to come by because he liked her—he wanted to get her out of his life and fulfill a commitment.

He didn't need her. He had modelesque brunettes and Caroline Hart and soirees in Indian Hill!

She placed the carefully folded note on his desk. She'd turned away and taken two steps toward the door when she stopped and studied him again.

What if he did need her?

What if he did like her…more than just a little bit?

Did he look cold? Spying an overcoat thrown over a pile of boxes, she picked it up and carefully covered him with it. She couldn't resist smoothing it over his shoulders and straightening it across his legs.

"Oh, Morgan," she whispered, tracing a finger along his cheek, "if things were different, we'd be perfect together." Unable to help herself, Brooke Anne brushed a kiss across his forehead.

Morgan's body twitched but his eyes remained closed.

She kissed his temple, pressed her hand to his chest. Smelled the remnants of the same cologne he'd worn on their date. Felt the heat radiating from underneath his blue button-down. She slid her palm over his firm muscles and imagined touching his bare skin. The smooth planes of his chest. A bare thigh.

Morgan breathed deeply.

Brooke Anne stared at him in shock. What was she doing, fondling a sleeping executive?

She moved away, ready to hurry out of the room, then was struck by the sight of the whiteboard next to the door.

Recalling her rather unimaginative note, she stared at the board. It was practically beckoning her to write something else. Anything to let Morgan know that he was more to her than just the purveyor of a paycheck, and a distant memory.

Brooke Anne picked up the red marker sitting in the bottom tray and glanced back at Morgan.

Still sleeping soundly.

She pulled off the cap. Held the marker over the board. Did she dare open herself up to him? Make herself vulnerable?

She thought about the way Russell had described his feelings for Suzanne and how ardently devoted Tomasina was to her family. And she heard her mother's endless questions about her own nonexistent love life echoing in her ears. Brooke Anne knew she had to do this. She could either give this relationship a try, or always wonder what might have been.

She touched the marker to the board and wrote:

Morgan,
    Things are fine with me.
    I've been busy buying angel Barbies for the hospital. And cleaning houses. I started a new puzzle. And I put up Christmas lights on the balcony of my apartment. They twinkle at night and make me think of stars.

Morgan shifted again in his sleep. Quickly, she put the cap back on the marker, then hurried out of the room, stopping only long enough to close the door tightly behind her.

She walked briskly down the hallway, chastising herself for covering him up with the coat. Berating herself for writing on his whiteboard. But she'd had to cover him…. He'd looked so cold and lonely. *And warm and irresistible, and she'd wanted an excuse to touch him.*

And the note…had been a risk worth taking…right?

Scowling, she pushed the elevator button firmly and tapped her foot. All right. The truth was that she was mesmerized by the guy, and she hardly even knew him! And what she did know wasn't all that good. He was self-centered and career-driven. Rich.

They had nothing in common. If they ever did go out on an actual date, it would be uncomfortable. What would they talk about, anyway? How she'd spied him in Caroline Hart's foyer while she'd been spot-cleaning his friend's carpet?

Just the idea of that conversation made her squirm.

But, they had gotten along very well when they were on the balcony, and they'd had a thousand things to say when they were dancing. Hadn't they?

Or was she just so used to living in her little fantasy world that she'd imagined there was more between them than there ever was? After all, he'd ignored her throughout the entire meal. What did that say?

Brooke Anne shook her head in confusion. She needed to get home and stop thinking about what amounted to one measly night in her life. She needed to listen to her mother. She needed to think about somebody other than a certain irresistible product purchasing manager.

With that firm resolve, she stepped into the elevator and smiled to herself, imagining Morgan's reaction when he woke up and found himself wrapped in his overcoat.

Chapter Seventeen

"Breva, why do you think Brooke didn't just wake me up last night?" Morgan asked the following morning during their morning coffee break. "It was obvious that I'd been waiting for her."

"Well—"

"I have to tell you, I think it was weird that she was wandering around my office while I was sleeping, too. What kind of woman does that?"

"Maybe the kind—"

He shook his head. "It's a bit of a letdown, if you want to know the truth. All this time I've been thinking about how Brooke and I could be perfect if we just had a chance to know each other better. But if this is her way of doing it, I'm not sure if she's worth—"

"Morgan, stop! You're about to dig yourself into a very ugly hole."

Morgan set his cup down before he dropped it. "Excuse me?"

"You really need to settle down. You're acting like a child. In fact, right now you are reminding me of Daniel when he was three."

Still feeling peeved by her tone, he asked, "Care to explain what you mean by that?"

"Sure." Breva took a sip of her coffee before indulging him.

"When Daniel was three, he wanted to do everything his older siblings did, but they didn't want him around."

"That sounds normal."

"Hush, Morgan. Let me tell this right," Breva chided. "The older kids didn't understand that Daniel would've been happy just to be with them, just to be in the same room, but he didn't know how to express himself."

She took a sip of coffee before continuing. "One day, when the older boys were trying to explain to him that he wasn't old enough to help them build a Lego tower, Daniel stood up and yelled, 'Cheerios!'"

Morgan felt a headache coming on. "And your point is?"

"That was the hardest word for Daniel to say. He only said it when he was really frustrated. Daniel needed help communicating. So do you, M.C."

"Brev—"

"Yep, your lack of skills in this area has really gotten you in a mess. Let's review."

"Let's not—"

She held up a finger, motioning for silence. "First, you wanted to be romantic with Sheri. When that didn't work out, you tried to be friends. And even though *that* wasn't really working out, you *still* asked her to the gala. Then, after she canceled on you and had the nerve to show up, sure you'd be sitting around mooning over her, you *still* managed to do things wrong. When you should've done nothing but give Sheri the cold shoulder, you *left* Brooke to go talk to her."

"Well—"

"Now, because you're so frustrated, instead of being happy that Brooke covered you up and wrote you back, you're finding fault where there isn't any." Breva glared at him. "Brooke is a good thing. Concentrate on making things work with her."

"Since you're not being shy about giving advice, anything else you think I should do?"

"Yes. Stop talking and help me organize these kits," she

added as she started to fill a basket with the latest product samples. She flipped open the cap on one of the bottles and sniffed the lotion. "I don't like this smell as much as our old one."

"The old one reminded too many people of their grandmothers. We have to use a new scent."

"I liked my grandmother," Breva said. Then she frowned and added, "Hey, I *am* a grandmother!"

Morgan hid a smile as he took another sip of coffee. This was why he loved working with Breva. Despite their age difference, they could banter about almost anything. And together, they were able to turn the worst task into a fun project. "You're a damn fine grandma. I'm sure other people like their grandmothers, too. They just don't want to smell like them."

Breva laughed. "You may have a point."

"So, back to my problem. What, exactly, do you think I should do about Brooke?"

"Write her back," she said after a moment's thought. "You two need to work some things out before you dive into a relationship. Learn about each other a little bit first." Breva dabbed another lotion on her hand, then looked up at Morgan with a dreamy expression on her face. "Actually, I think this whole note idea sounds rather romantic. You've told me before that you have a difficult time expressing your emotions. Maybe this is a good way to do it." She shooed him away. "Go try it. Write something about yourself that's meaningful."

He'd been hoping for easier advice. "Is this how Aaron courted you?" he asked.

"No, but Aaron's a *real* man. He didn't need notes to express his feelings," she said with a wink.

"Hey," Morgan objected, more than a little put out. "Just because I don't work outside on bridges and tall buildings doesn't mean I'm not a real man."

Breva's eyes sparkled in amusement. "Gotcha."

Morgan glared at her. She loved getting a rise out of him. His mind back on Brooke, he knew he hadn't meant any of the things he'd said to Breva earlier. He'd simply wanted to see her again, had been looking forward to it. To hide his disappointment, he'd lashed out at Brooke instead of admitting that he felt angry at himself for falling asleep.

Maybe this note idea had merit. He could try to explain to her why relationships were so hard for him. Shoot, expressing how he felt in writing had to be less difficult than doing it face to face.

But he still needed a little more help. "How long do you think this note should be?"

Only Breva would know he was being completely serious. "Ten sentences. Even you can do that."

"Thanks," he said dryly.

"It's worth a shot. After all, it's pretty obvious she doesn't want to talk to you until you make amends."

He pondered that for a while as he dutifully sniffed Breva's proffered wrist and shrugged at the smell. Seemed okay to him. Motioning to her to add the lotion to the baskets, he said, "So what is she going to do if I ever find her? Ignore me in person?"

"Maybe."

"She's going to bite my head off, isn't she?" he said, still feeling pretty guilty about his behavior at the party.

"It deserves to be bitten, or at least a little chewed on." Breva began sorting a pile of bath gels. "When I saw you together at the party, Brooke seemed really happy. She was glowing by your side."

The description gave him comfort. "You thought so?"

"I did. Her eyes sparkled and she had this dreamy look on her face—almost like my Diane on her wedding day." Breva glanced at him. "Have I ever described her wedding dress to you?"

Two stories in ten minutes was two stories too many. "Yes," he responded quickly.

Breva smiled to herself. "Well, I have a feeling you two

are meant to be together. You've just hit a little snag in your relationship."

"A snag," he repeated. Then her words registered. "Wait a minute. *Relationship?* Does one date and a couple of notes count as a relationship?"

Breva handed him a set of washcloths to fold. "Of course you have a relationship. My goodness, why are you even asking such a thing?"

"I don't know," he muttered. He hated it when she made him feel like he was back in tenth grade.

"Don't you like her? She's awfully cute."

"She is, but I don't think we have all that much in common," Morgan replied as he concentrated on making neat squares out of the washcloths.

"It looked as if you two had a lot to talk about that night," Breva countered. "You chatted the whole time Aaron and I were with you. What more do you want?"

"We have completely different backgrounds," he hedged. "At least, I think we do."

"But you don't really know, do you?"

Breva had no idea that Brooke was the company's janitor, but Brooke's job wasn't something that he, himself, had been able to ignore. To be honest, he didn't know what to make of it. He was raised to be proud of his family's social standing, of the privileges that came with it. Of his expensive education. "Even if we did find out that we're still attracted to each other, I doubt we'd have a future together. Everyone knows that common bonds are really important in a relationship."

"You sound like you're on a talk show."

Did he dare admit that he'd read more than one book about relationships? Not in this lifetime. "I'm a pretty astute guy."

But Breva kept talking as if he wasn't astute at all. "I thought her family sounded nice."

"I thought so, too."

"And I thought you told me the other day that you both like games and puzzles."

"She does. We do." Finally he decided to tell Breva everything he knew. "It's just that…she's a janitor, Brev." He bit his lip to keep from saying more. Why had he felt compelled to bring it up, anyway? Was he that shallow? Did her occupation bother him that much?

Breva's eyes widened. "Really? How'd you meet her?"

"She cleans our building. I met her here the evening Sheri canceled on me."

Breva gave a low whistle. "Really? After Sheri hung up on you, you turned to Brooke and asked her out?"

Morgan frowned. "Actually, I don't know if Sheri hung up on me. It was more like the conversation came to a mutual end."

"Morgan."

"All right. Yeah, I started talking to Brooke then. She was dusting in the conference room when I got off the phone with Sheri. We chatted for a while."

"And?"

"I was explaining to her about our dance classes, and how I doubted anybody else in Cincinnati knew how to ballroom dance, and then she told me that she could. Then…" Morgan's voice drifted off.

Breva clasped her hands together. "Then you asked her to the gala," she finished, her voice dreamy.

"I did. Well, it was sort of a business proposition. I think she said yes because I offered her money."

A slow smile crept across Breva's face. "Wow, who'd have thought?" she mumbled as she handed him a box of travel-size shampoo bottles to add to the baskets. "She doesn't look like any janitor I've ever seen."

"I know. She's as cute as can be. And bright and cheerful. And she's got a good heart. But don't you think she and I are kind of a strange combination?"

"Because you're a junior executive and she's a building custodian? Do you have a problem with people who work with their hands for a living?"

He glanced at her in shock, and Breva softened her tone. "Your differences shouldn't change how well you two get along with each other. What matters is what you both agree upon."

He felt his cheeks burn at her chiding tone. "Do I sound that full of myself?"

She brought her thumb and forefinger close together. "Only a little bit."

"I'm just trying to deal with realities here. I don't know if she'd fit in with my crowd. Or me with hers. I mean, what do you think she and Caroline would possibly find to talk about?"

"First of all, Caroline could have a conversation with an inchworm, and you know it." Breva shrugged. "And secondly, does it matter? I mean, you and your mother are cut from the same cloth, and you hate talking to her."

Breva had a point. "I'm getting a headache."

Breva looked as if she was about to hit him in the head. "Come on now, M.C. What do you think? That Brooke hangs out with other custodians all day, discussing mops and toilet cleaners? You two got along just fine at the Christmas party. And I think that says it all. If she can mix well with most of the people there, she can fit in anywhere. And you…you could use some diversity in your life."

"Thanks. I think."

Breva nodded smugly. "Anytime."

He had no excuse to delay the inevitable any longer. "I guess I'll go write that letter now. Ten sentences."

"That sounds like a fantastic idea."

"She won't think I'm being pushy?" he asked, stalling.

"No. Remember, she wrote you a note on your whiteboard. She's reaching out." Just then the phone rang. Breva hopped up from her position on the floor and raced to answer it in her Birkenstocks. "Go, M.C. You'll do just fine. I have faith in you."

I have faith in you. Her words echoed in his head as he pulled out another page of monogrammed stationery. Glancing at the whiteboard, he wondered what Brooke would be interested in knowing about him.

He tallied the things she already knew. His name. His job. His go-cart experiences.

She knew who his friends at work were. She knew about Sheri, the ex-girlfriend.

Puzzles. College. He paused. Tried to dig a little deeper, open his heart a bit more. Tried to rediscover what made him tick.

Finally, after chewing on the end of his pen for a while— something he hadn't done since fourth grade—he wrote:

Brooke,
    I like the stars, too. They make me think of the broad Texas skies and fireflies in the summer.
    I haven't done any decorating for the holidays yet. Growing up, my mother had to have the decorations just so…and my sister decorates enough for the whole city of Cincinnati. I always figured it wasn't worth it to try and hang my own. But maybe I will this year.
    When I was sixteen I used to drive down empty country highways too fast, listening to loud music and dreaming about being a man.
    I miss those days.
    I still have your shoes. Maybe one day soon we can actually meet.
Morgan

There. Ten sentences, some of them even more than four words long. Breva would be proud.

Carefully, he folded the paper into thirds, tucked it neatly into a crisp envelope, then took the letter to the front reception desk and asked the guard on duty to give it to Brooke…or Tomasina.

Surely there weren't any other Brooke Annes who worked the building. After walking back to his office, Morgan steeled himself for another four hours of work. And wondered what Brooke would say when she received the letter.

Chapter Eighteen

Brooke Anne sat at her makeshift desk at the Jovial Janitor headquarters and laughed at the banter among the three other women in the room. Yes, they were her employees, but they were her friends, too. They were also all slightly older than she was, had husbands and families and shared an outlook on life that was at once jaded and amusing. Currently they were discussing the things that were on many a woman's mind in the middle of December: Christmas gifts and holiday dinners.

"Sweet potatoes have to be mashed. With marshmallows on top," Vivian stated in a tone that dared anyone to disagree.

Karen wrinkled her nose. "No way will I ever have those slimy orange things at my dinner table."

"They're having a sale at Carson's," Monique, her newest employee, said. "Towels and home accessories are forty percent off."

Brooke Anne smiled to herself as she glanced around the room that housed her business. A large bulletin board outlined everyone's duties for the week. Closets neatly shelved a variety of cleaning supplies.

A few old chairs and an extremely worn coffee table served as their meeting place and rec spot, and the three other women in the room, along with Tomasina, comprised her employee roster. As they chatted away, she worked on the schedule which was an increasingly difficult task this time of year, du to all the holiday parties at both corporate and residential locations.

"Anyone want to go to the Kelsos' and clean tomorrow morning?" she called out.

"Who are they?" Karen asked, flipping through an old *Redbook* magazine. "Are they the ones with the two yappy dogs? I hate those dogs."

Brooke Anne had no idea, but she had a pretty good feeling that Karen wouldn't volunteer to put up with them if she didn't have to. She was all business when it came to cleaning houses. Dealing with annoying dogs wasn't something she did well. Scanning her file, Brooke Anne said, "Let's see here. They have five bedrooms. Oh, and a grand piano. Mrs. Kelso's message was really panicked. I guess her mother-in-law is coming to town and her house is a mess."

Vivian piped up. "I know them. They do have dogs," she said. "Poodles. And kids. A ton of them."

Brooke Anne glanced around. "Anyone?"

"Oh, heck, I'll do it," Karen replied. "I've got a mother-in-law, too. Vivian, want to come with me? We could knock it off in a few hours."

"Sure," Vivian replied, after quickly consulting the scheduling board.

Brooke Anne heaved a sigh of relief. "Great. I'll call her back and tell her it's a go." Eyeing the clock, she added, "Speaking of which, y'all better get a move on."

The women stood up and set about gathering their supplies, notes and cell phones from the supply closet. It was customary for Brooke to ask them to call her cell phone when they arrived and left each location.

Vivian spoke up. "Tomasina working tonight?"

"Yes. She decided to go straight from choir practice to the Royal Hotels building, though. Busy night."

After a few more instructions and goodbyes, Brooke Anne was finally alone, anxious to finish up her paperwork and go home for the night. She picked up the stack of mail from the corner of her desk and quickly began sorting it into piles, wincing at the number of bills the mail carrier had dropped off.

Then, one letter caught her eye. As soon as she saw it, addressed merely to Brooke Anne, her hands started to shake. A pink Post-it note from Tomasina was stuck on the envelope.

"I picked this up for you. And this is ABSOLUTELY the last time I deliver mail!"

Even though she was by herself, Brooke Anne glanced around warily. For some reason, she felt nervous that someone would see her handling the letter.

What could Morgan want?

There was only one way to find out. Opening the envelope, she pulled out a crisply folded piece of paper, and was amazed to see a handwritten note. Somehow she'd assumed all of Morgan's correspondence would be typed.

She read it quickly. Then read it again. *Stars. Fireflies. Decorations. Driving fast on empty country highways.*

Without knowing why she cared, she counted the sentences. Ten. The letter sounded especially chatty for Morgan. He hadn't seemed the type to convey so much about himself so readily. His printing was cute, too—a combination of upper- and lowercase letters were arranged in a way that would make a first-grade teacher groan. Or Brooke Anne sigh.

Just the thought of him going to so much effort left her mouth dry and her heart beating fast. She stared at the letter again. So he liked watching the stars, as well.

Closing her eyes, she imagined Morgan doing all the things he'd described. She thought about him decorating his house just so…and how she would teach him that things didn't always have to be perfect.

One day she'd love to be by his side, riding in a convertible down a wide-open road, going nowhere fast. She pictured what he would be wearing. Worn jeans and a soft button-down, the cuffs frayed from multiple washings. There would be excitement in his eyes, and he'd turn to her and smile, the wind ruffling his short hair.

"I'm so glad you're here with me, Brooke Anne," he'd say.

"I am, too. You need to relax more. Enjoy life."

"I enjoy life with you. I need you, Brooke Anne."

"I need you, too, Morgan. Pull over and kiss me."

And he would. He'd pull over to the side of the road on that lonesome highway and kiss her thoroughly, and she'd melt into his arms, the way she had at the ball. His lips would tease hers, then explore her mouth gently and the hard planes of his body would leave her breathless, as would the sure movements of his hands.

She'd curse the bucket seats in his sporty convertible, wishing they had more room to explore each other intimately. More room to get to know the corded muscles of his stomach, the feel of his lips on her breasts, the satisfaction of arching against him in complete ecstasy. She'd run her hands along his hips, down his thighs, memorizing every intimate detail through touch. She'd feel his hardness against her—and she'd be ready for him, not caring when a car whizzed past them on the road, only thinking of his body, his hands....

The fantasy was interrupted by the shrill ring of her cell phone.

Still in a dreamy state, she reached for the phone and winced as her hand slipped, sending it clattering to the ground. Finally, she grasped it securely and spoke. "Hello?"

"Brooke Anne? You okay? You sound kind of raspy," Tomasina said from her end.

Shoot. "Hold on one sec," she said, then pressed the phone to her chest and willed herself to get under control. She squeezed her eyes shut and counted to ten fast. Tried to think of cleaning toilets in sports arenas—anything to counter the pulsating of her body. After a few deep breaths, she placed the phone back to her ear. "Sorry about that. I'm okay. Just, uh, moving boxes around."

"Oh. Well, I'm over at the Hendersons'."

Brooke Anne sluggishly turned her attention to the board. "Great. That's your last job for tonight, right?"

"Bingo."

"How was choir practice?"

"Good. Can't wait for the concert."

"Me neither," Brooke said, now that her mind was firmly ensconced in the real world. "Have a good night. Tell Ronnie and Vanessa hi."

"Sure thing. You ought to go home, girl. You sound tired."

She was a lot of things. "I think I will, Tomi. And thanks for delivering Morgan's note."

Tomi grunted. "Did you read my Post-it?"

"I did."

"So, no more deliveries, right?"

"If I do write more letters, I promise you won't have to deliver them."

"Good. 'Night."

Hanging up, Brooke Anne folded Morgan's note and placed it carefully in her purse. She didn't know what to do next. Should she write back? Give him a call? Stop by Royal Hotels tomorrow?

And do what? Announce to the receptionist that she had a crush on a guy who owed her money?

The situation was enough to make her groan in exasperation.

Two DAYS HAD PASSED and Morgan hadn't heard a thing yet from Brooke. He wasn't happy about it. It made him uneasy. He hated feeling so out of control in their relationship—such as it was. He wanted to see her again, give her back her shoes, pay her the money.

See those gray eyes once more. Run his hands through her flyaway hair. Maybe catch her smile.

He wanted to make sure that he hadn't dreamed up such perfection. But at the moment, he had no idea how to go about that.

"So…I wrote her a note and haven't heard a thing, Breva. Now what?"

"It's only been a few days."

"Two. It's been *two* days. I need to move on to the next step."

"Give Jovial Janitors a call," Breva suggested.

"I did that. Actually, I've tried calling them three times. No one ever answers the damn phone. I finally left a message last night."

"Well, maybe no one wants to talk to you."

No, he didn't think that was it. At least, he hoped not. He wasn't ready to accept the possibility that Brooke might not want anything further to do with him.

Not when he couldn't stop thinking about her. Glancing at Breva, he wheedled again. "Come on. Give me some other ideas. What can I do?"

"I'm not really sure what to tell you, M.C."

"Oh, I bet you've been through something like this before. Or one of your kids has."

Breva folded her arms across her chest. "My kids didn't tell me as much as you might think."

"Please?" Morgan stuck out his bottom lip for good measure. Anything to stir up her maternal instincts.

She pursed her mouth. "All right. What do you have to go on? A note?"

"A note, a phone number that no one will answer and Brooke's buddy Tomasina. And a pair of shoes. And I'm *not* camping out at Jovial Janitors."

Breva smiled briefly, then stopped all semblance of work and stared at him. "Hold on. A pair of her shoes?"

Morgan shrugged. "She left them under the table."

"Boy, this is a new low for you, Morgan. Running off barefoot girls during Christmas balls. In the winter, no less."

"Are you going to help me or not?"

"Hand me the shoes. Maybe there's a clue on them somewhere."

Morgan doubted that, but he decided it couldn't hurt to let Breva see them. After retrieving the sandals from his file cabinet, he passed them over.

She grasped them and sighed with approval. "Now aren't these pretty!"

Morgan smiled at the way Breva was holding the sandals. What was it with women and shoes? It was as if they had some special connection. "They are kind of nice," he said. "They're gold."

"No, I mean these are no discount-rack shoes—these are designer sandals. You can only find these in exclusive boutiques and high-end stores," she clarified, tipping them one way and then the other. "Ooh, look at the rhinestone buckle."

"It's, uh, shiny."

Breva's blue eyes sparkled as she corrected him. "It's *gorgeous.*" She flipped the shoes over and examined the soles. "They've barely been worn. I bet she bought them just for the party."

"Okay. That's helpful."

Breva rolled her eyes. "What am I going to do with you? You need to think like a detective, Morgan. When did you ask Brooke to the party?"

"Two Thursdays ago."

"And when did she wear the shoes?"

"That Saturday."

Breva snapped two fingers. "All you need to do is find out where Brooke would've bought her expensive shoes that Friday or Saturday. Piece of cake."

"No, it's not! There are probably a thousand shoe stores in Cincinnati."

"Not *expensive* shoe stores. Not stores that sell shoes like these. That will narrow things down."

"I don't know. Seems like a long shot to me. What do you think? Are they a popular style? Would you wear these shoes?"

Breva looked at him as if he was crazy. "Of course I'd

wear them. Any woman would want to! Here, let me have one to try on."

Within seconds, Breva had shaken off her clog and was sliding her foot into the strappy sandal. But she quickly gave up and groaned.

"What's wrong? Did you break it?"

"No, I didn't break it. It's too small. This shoe was made for a tiny foot. What size is it, anyway?"

Morgan flipped over the sandal he was holding and found the size engraved on the bottom of the heel. "Size 5N."

"Five narrow! This girl has the tiniest feet I've ever heard of." Breva placed her foot firmly in her suede clog and handed the gold sandal back to him. "Well, now you won't have any problems."

"What are you talking about?"

"There can't be too many upscale shoe stores that sold a spiked gold sandal in size five narrow two Fridays ago."

Call him stupid, but he still didn't get it. "And I should care about this…why?"

"Because now you can go investigate, find out where Brooke bought the shoes. You can try and get some more information about her from the store." Breva sounded beyond excited.

He scratched his head. "I guess your idea has merit. I mean, that Tomasina girl wouldn't give me the time of day and no one will answer the Jovial Janitor phones."

His assistant patted him on the back. "It's a *great* idea. You're the one who likes puzzles—think of this as a missing piece."

She was right; he did like challenges. And he was sick of just sitting around and doing nothing. Even if he never actually got any information, at least he'd know he tried.

"All right," Morgan finally said. "I'm going to go out into the world and find the person who sold Brooke these shoes."

Breva raised her fist in the air. "Hurrah!"

He couldn't help grinning.

"So, you have a plan?" Breva asked him.

"I have a plan."

"Good." With a determined expression, she thrust a pile of shower caps into his arms. "Now help me finish these gift baskets."

Chapter Nineteen

Morgan only had one thing to say to Breva when he saw her next: Bad idea.

Trying to find the store where Brooke had bought her shoes was easier said than done. So far, out of the eleven shops he'd visited, four carried the shoes Brooke had worn. And at those four stores, no one was saying much. In fact, the salespeople looked at him as if he was crazy, asking them if they remembered who'd bought a pair of gold sandals in their store two weeks ago.

Of course, they all could have been lying.

Morgan sensed there was a whole confidentiality-clause thing going on with salespeople that he'd never been aware of. Retailers kept a closer guard on their clients' purchases than he would've ever imagined. One lady had actually gasped at the idea of divulging the names and whereabouts of her shoppers. He doubted that pharmacists were as vigilant about their prescriptions.

Three hours and two malls later, he decided to stop in at one last store, only two blocks from his office building. After that, he was quitting for the day. He'd given up most of his Saturday for this little investigation. He'd felt like a bag lady carrying the shoes around in a sack, daring people to ask why he didn't just put them away and forget about them—and he had nothing to show for his efforts except a pair of sore…uh…feet.

The last store, WJB Shoes, his last shot.

Peering through the window, he decided it looked exclusive and upscale. The storefront display depicted a mountain snow scene with shoes engaged in different winter activities. In spite of himself, Morgan was impressed. The window was eye-catching and humorous at the same time. Maybe it was an omen that the manager would be more forthcoming than his counterparts. And maybe, even if they didn't carry the shoes there, they'd know who would.

A discreet bell sounded as Morgan stepped across the threshold. Instantly, he became aware of the boutique's sedate atmosphere. He clutched his plastic bag a little tighter.

"Yes?" a rather elderly, butlerlike man inquired over a pair of half-moon glasses.

"Hi there."

"May I help you? New shoes, perhaps?"

Morgan glanced down at his feet. His shoes did look kind of scuffed and worn. He turned back to the gentleman. "Have anything in a size eleven, uh, Warren?" he asked, eyeing the man's discreet name badge.

"I do. Please sit down."

Morgan sat. It felt nice to finally relax in a shoe store, instead of stalking the help for information. He pulled off his wing tips and waited for Warren to return.

"Here we are, sir."

Warren opened the shoe box and presented Morgan with a brand-new pair of shoes, that while similar to the ones he'd been wearing, were, in fact, far more supple. Morgan was impressed. And after he tried one on, he knew for a fact that Warren was a genius. The shoe fit perfectly. It felt so good, he slipped the other one on, too.

It was time to get down to business, though. "I have a question for you, if you don't mind."

Warren took a seat. "Yes, sir?"

Feeling silly, but still determined, Morgan opened the bag and pulled out one of Brooke's gold sandals. "Does this look familiar to you?"

Warren glanced at the shoe, then at his feet. "Any particular reason why you enjoy carrying about gold sandals?"

Morgan scowled. "They're not mine. They were my date's."

Warren's gaze shifted from the shoes to Morgan with a new interest. "I see. Was there a problem with them?"

"No. Well, at least I don't think so. So, you do carry these shoes?"

Warren graced him with the slightest of nods. "We do."

Yes! Partial success!

"Any chance you could help me out? The gal that wore these didn't give me her phone number. I'm desperate to talk to her."

"Did you try the phone book?"

"She's not listed. I can't get any answer at her office, either. And…I can't get her out of my mind."

Warren crossed his knees and clasped hands on top of them. "And how did you come into ownership of the shoes, if I may ask?"

Morgan tried to ignore his sarcastic tone, as well as the uneasy feeling that had come over him. It was the same feeling when he'd been caught smoking in the boys' restroom in tenth grade. "My date…she left without them."

"Ah," Warren said.

Yep, there was that same exact sinking feeling he'd had in high school. He'd been busted and now Warren was going to make him squirm.

Desperation kicked in. "Look, it wasn't like that, so get any thoughts like that out of your head. It was a great date. Well, almost great," he amended. "She left the party early. We had a miscommunication. Now I'm trying to do the right thing by giving her back the shoes." And because he had nothing else to lose, he added, "And apologizing. I want to see her again."

Warren glanced at the gold sandal once more. "So you want to return the shoes…and maybe something more?"

"Maybe." Morgan wished he was a little closer to his father. Typically, a dad would be a far better person to talk to about relationships than Warren. "Did you sell these shoes?" he asked. "It would've been two weeks ago last Friday."

Warren took the sandal from his hand, inspected it closely, his eyes widening when he saw the size. "I did."

Relief coursed through Morgan. "Excellent. Do you think you have her address or phone number on file? That maybe you could pass either of those on to me?"

"I'm sorry, sir. It's not my policy to give the phone numbers or addresses of our clients out to people off the street," Warren said tersely.

"I'm not off the street—I'm the product purchasing manager for Royal Hotels."

Warren didn't look impressed. "And that means what, exactly?"

"I'm trying to make you see that I'm an upstanding guy who just needs a little help," Morgan said, and let out a sigh of frustration. "This girl, this woman…her name is Brooke. Does she come in often? Does she shop here a lot?"

Warren's eyebrows arched. "Does Brooke come here often? You obviously don't know her if you need to ask."

"We didn't talk about shoe-shopping habits when we were together," Morgan stated tersely.

"Perhaps if you did, you wouldn't be here," Warren replied in as succinct a fashion.

This wasn't working. Crossing a leg, Morgan tilted his head back and strove for patience. "Listen, I know if you were me, you would've handled things differently, but I need help, now. What do you think I should do?"

Warren rubbed at an invisible spot on his lapel. "It would all depend, sir, on why I wanted to see *Brooke* again."

"What do you mean?"

"I mean, if *I* was only wanting to return her shoes, I'd realize my efforts were futile, and I'd give the shoes to someone who'd appreciate them. But—" Warren sent him a pointed look

"—if there were other, more personal reasons why I wanted to see her again, I would ask someone else to give her a message."

"I've done that already," Morgan muttered.

"Have you?" Warren asked. "Because I happen to know that the woman we're speaking of has an open invitation to tea, right here in this shop. Perhaps I'd ask the manager, nicely, to relay a message…if it was the lady who mattered to me and *not* the shoes."

Morgan studied the older man. He sat so straight it was as though an invisible board was attached to his back. His expression was the epitome of good breeding, calm and interested. There was only one thing for Morgan to say.

What was in his heart.

He might not understand exactly what he was feeling, but Morgan knew without a doubt that it was more than misplaced guilt over a pair of shoes and a check that needed to be given.

He wanted to see Brooke again. He wanted to get to know her, take her out. She appealed to him and made him feel good.

He didn't think it mattered if she was the janitor or the CEO's daughter, but he wanted to find out…for both their sakes. It wasn't about pride or shoes or money owed anymore. It was about Brooke.

Finally, he spoke. "Warren, next time Brooke comes in for tea, would you please give her a message?"

Amusement and a tinge of compassion lit Warren's face. "I would."

"Would you please tell Brooke that I've been looking for her? That I've tried to call her, too? That I've missed her, and that I'd love to see her soon? That if she feels the same way, maybe she could give you her phone number so I could call her?"

Warren stood up, gave him a note card and a fancy fountain pen. "You better tell her all of that yourself. Write it down. If she comes in, I'll see she receives it."

Morgan did just that, thinking to himself that it had been decades since he'd written so many notes to be passed on.

Brooke,

I now know more about shoes than I ever thought possible. I have the Jovial Janitor number memorized. I practically ran over a lady yesterday because I thought she was you.

Give a guy a break, would you? Leave Warren your phone number...or call me. 555-1224.

I just want to see you again.

Morgan

"If you see her, and you give her this note, would you give me a call?" he asked.

Warren took the card and nodded. "I will. Would you like me to hold on to the shoes, and pass them to her, as well?" he asked, stretching out a hand.

Perversely, Morgan clutched the bag. "No. I'll just wait to give them to her myself." He'd had them this long; he was going to part with them for one person only.

"Now, as for your shoes, would you like to purchase them?"

Morgan's gaze dropped to his feet. The new shoes were so comfortable, he'd forgotten he had them on. "I would," he said. "But first I need to take them off. I'm going to get a Christmas tree, and there's no way I want to ruin them already."

"Excellent idea. It would be a shame to damage such fine Italian leather."

Fine Italian leather? "Warren, how much are those shoes, by the way?"

"Three hundred and twenty, sir."

Morgan leaned back in his chair as if he'd been pushed. *Three hundred and twenty dollars?* No wonder Brooke had wanted those shoes back.

If Warren noticed Morgan's slump, he didn't show it. "Cash or charge, sir?"

Morgan swallowed hard. "Charge," he mumbled. He only hoped Christmas trees were less expensive.

Chapter Twenty

Brooke Anne's mind raced with unfinished lists, but for once she didn't feel stressed. These lists had to do with fun things—Christmas presents, trees, icicle lights.

Not work. Not money troubles.

Tonight she was ready to become completely immersed in the Christmas season. She needed to get a tree and decorate her little apartment for the holiday. Maybe pick up some eggnog, too.

She realized that some people might think it frivolous that she was buying a Christmas tree, an ornament she'd been admiring, and new lights when she didn't have a lot of cash. But for her, having a merrily decorated home was as important to her well-being as eating a good breakfast—if doughnuts and coffee could be considered good.

So, armed with her wallet and in an exceptionally cheerful mood, Brooke Anne drove her Jovial Janitor van to the tree lot.

It was on an empty corner next to a convenience store and filled to the brim with trees. Each one had a six-inch cardboard price tag that fluttered in the light breeze. The unmistakable scent of fresh pine and the fainter smell of damp earth permeated the lot. A banner proclaiming Ed's Fresh Trees from Our Grand State, Ohio was tacked to the side of a small wooden building, about a third of the size of a mobile home. Twinkling lights and Christmas music completed the festive atmosphere.

Singing along with "Grandma Got Run Over by a Reindeer," Brooke Anne weaved her way through the miniforest, eyeing each tree critically and feeling exhilarated that she was finally doing something for herself. There were some people, she knew, who had a certain fondness for misshapen trees—the ones Charlie Brown would have loved. Not her.

She'd had too many beautiful trees during her childhood in Nebraska to settle for anything less. She wanted the fullest, most perfect one she could afford. Nothing but the best for her. The only thing stopping her was going to be a hefty price tag. Of which there were many.

"Ed," she said to the owner. "These prices are something else."

The man grinned broadly. "Yes, ma'am. Good crop this year. These trees come all the way from northern Ohio. The prices reflect that."

Ed sounded as if he came from the farm, too. Since they were right there in *southern* Ohio, she wasn't too impressed by the trees' origins. Or the exorbitant prices. "How's a girl supposed to get a nice tree when you're charging an arm and a leg?"

Ed didn't appear at all disturbed by her criticism. He took in her Jovial Janitor jacket and scratched his head. "Your problem is that you're looking at the high-end trees."

She glanced at the blue spruce next to her. "High-end?"

"I think, ma'am, you ought to go on down a few steps."

"Pardon?" Was he suggesting she wasn't good enough for the blue spruces?

"Try over there," he said, pointing to a few barren-looking, spindly trees, obviously in the low-rent section. Then he turned away, another customer having just pulled up.

Brooke Anne frowned. She wanted the beautiful, fresh, eight-foot blue spruce. But not for sixty-five dollars. For the first time in a while, she thought of Cassie and the glamorous women at the party. Of Ms. Hart and her mansion on the hill. And felt a tinge of jealousy. Wouldn't it be wonderful to be like them, to be able to buy exactly the thing she wanted? Not just what she could afford.

Overcome with indignation, she tromped over to the smaller trees, grumbling as she went. Well, Christmas wasn't about showy trees, was it?

Christmas was about love and faith and…

"Excuse me," a man said, as she narrowly missed running into him.

"Sorry, I was just imagining giving the world a piece of my mind…." Brooke Anne stated, before looking up at him. Then she gasped.

Morgan Carmichael. He seemed to recognize her at that precise minute, also. His face lit up with pleasure, and he actually chuckled. "Brooke! Unbelievable. I have been looking for you everywhere! I left a message on your business machine."

That had been a few days ago, when she'd been still reeling from her trip to Indian Hill, and her visit to his office when she'd covered him up.

He gripped her arm as if he was afraid she'd disappear. "I can't believe I decided to go buy a tree tonight and found you here. It's like it was fate."

It was amazing. That's what it was.

He looked so good, clad in a heavy coat and a burgundy-colored scarf. His cheeks looked ruddier than usual—he must've been in the cold for a while.

Brooke Anne stumbled around for something to say. "I didn't know you liked Christmas trees. You said in your note you didn't do much for the holidays."

"You've inspired me to do more." He looked amused by her comment. "And besides, even Grinches need trees."

He was right. Now she felt silly. "I…how's your girlfriend?"

"What?"

Brooke wished she could disappear from the lot. Vanish into thin air. Why had she done that? Only she would bring up another woman within the first two seconds of seeing the guy she liked. Did she secretly *want* to turn him away? Sheesh. Valiantly, she carried on. "Um, you know…Sheri?"

Morgan visibly winced. "Look, you don't know how I've been wanting to apologize to you. Sheri's not my girlfriend. She hasn't been for almost a year. We'd been trying to remain friends, but obviously that didn't work out, either," he said hurriedly. "That night at the dance, when she showed up…I'm so sorry. I was trying to get her to leave, but it wasn't working very well."

"But…Cassie said—"

"Cassie is a witch of a woman, and I'm sorry you ever had the misfortune of sitting next to her." His fingers edged down Brooke Anne's arm, then he reached for her mittened hand. Automatically, she clasped his outstretched palm, bringing back sweet memories of close contact with him. "I promise, our evening didn't go the way I would've liked at all…especially not the end," Morgan said.

It was hard to know what to believe. He seemed so warm and sincere now, just as he had when they'd been dancing. And as the cold air wafted around their bodies, he curved his hand around one of hers in a gentle, affectionate way. He looked as though he'd envelop her in a hug if she gave him even the slightest indication that she wanted one.

But she couldn't forget his first, cold, businesslike note or the way he'd completely ignored her at dinner. Her complete mortification when she'd realized she'd left her shoes under the table. Walking through the frigid parking garage barefoot. Sneaking back in, to discover that he wasn't around.

She couldn't forget how dashing and comfortable he'd appeared standing next to the attractive brunette at the soiree. Couldn't forget that she'd been asked to clean that house, not attend as a guest. Trying to play it cool, Brooke Anne said, "Well, I'm glad we got that settled once and for all. I guess I'd better go find my tree."

He looked confused. His hand tightened on hers, as if he didn't want her to go. "But, Brooke…I wanted to tell you that I was sorry I was asleep when you visited the office."

When she'd practically fondled him while he slept.

Mercilessly, heat rose to her cheeks.

Morgan was still talking. "So, you did get my notes, right?"

Just recalling the sweet words in his second note made her determination to remain aloof dissolve. "I did."

"And?"

The way he looked at her—his eyes wide and unsure—was the final straw. "They were very sweet. I liked them a lot. Especially the part about driving down the highway at night."

Morgan's lips curved for a brief instant, as if what she'd said pleased him, but he was embarrassed by it. "I, uh, thought I'd try and tell you some more about myself."

"I'm glad." What else could she say?

"I've been thinking of other things to tell you about. Do you have time for coffee or something? Are you hungry? Have you had dinner?"

His tentativeness was completely endearing. And almost believable. She couldn't get over the difference in him from the night he'd asked her out in his company's break room to this very moment. Brooke Anne wondered what had brought about the change. She seriously doubted it was her charm and good looks.

Which brought forth all her feelings of uncertainty. The memories she had of their dancing together and, later, kissing were wonderful. But, though a secret part of her knew she would love to be in his arms again, she couldn't forget the horrible feeling of loss she'd had that whole Sunday after the party. The humiliation of sitting beside his empty chair for almost fifteen minutes, of being asked to leave by someone who obviously belonged in those surroundings. The embarrassment of dodging him in that mansion. Did she really want to pretend for even a moment longer that they could possibly have a future?

Then there was the scarring experience of being jilted by Russell. She'd loved him, but it hadn't been enough. Without wanting to, Brooke Anne remembered Russell's announcement when he'd told her that he didn't want to marry her, after all. That it wasn't *her,* it was *him.* He wasn't ready to settle down. Not anytime soon.

But even then he'd already had Suzanne. And now he was married and had a baby with her.

Brooke Anne wasn't ready to trust her heart again.

"Thanks, but I have so much to do, I hardly know if I'm going to be able to get it all done." Brooke Anne forced a tight smile. Did she sound natural, carefree?

Morgan seemed desperate. "Tomorrow?" he asked, then grimaced. "Shoot, tomorrow I've got a dinner engagement. Thursday? Please?"

She felt herself begin to falter. He did care—to what extent, though, she couldn't know. "Well…"

"It's the least I can do," he said with a broad smile. "Besides, I've got to pay you—and give you your shoes."

Her hope dimmed again at the mention of the money. Was that what this was really about? "Oh, right…" That was what it boiled down to, after all. She needed every penny, while he had large bills to spare.

But Morgan didn't appear to notice her crestfallen expression; he was still planning. He had his PalmPilot out and was clicking down screens. "Hmm. I know that Tomasina girl said Royal Hotels was her account, but could you arrange to clean my office on Thursday? I could definitely stay late. I've got some work to do, anyway."

She was now completely deflated. She knew he was trying to be kind, but somehow that kindness only made all the differences between them even more pronounced. He thought she was just a cleaning lady. He owed her money. He had dinner engagements. Was working late, anyway.

She was looking for discount Christmas trees and romance.

He just seemed to be looking for a way to repay his debts.

If she ever needed a loud-and-clear sign that they weren't meant to be together, this was it.

"I'll take Tomi's place on Thursday. Why don't you just set my shoes and the check in a bag or something, and I'll pick it up when I'm there?"

"But…all right. What about dinner?"

She glanced around the tree lot. A family of four was currently circling a blue spruce, inspecting each branch. "I don't know. My schedule's back at the office. I have to check."

"Okay. You'll call me tomorrow?" He eyed her carefully. "Or maybe you'd rather have me call you?"

His persistence made her nervous. What were they to each other? Acquaintances? Friends?

She still felt on edge near him, as if she could never be sure what his next moves would be. "Yes."

His eyes twinkled. "Yes, you will? Or yes you want me to call you instead?"

Now completely flustered, she waved her hands helplessly. "Yes, I'll give you a call. In the morning."

"Promise?"

She closed her eyes. "I promise."

"Good," he said softly, little wisps of frosty air escaping as he talked. His eyes crinkled and he reached out his hand again. "I'll look forward to it."

The way he said the words made her think of so much more than holding hands and phone calls.

But was he *really* finished with Sheri? What about the gal on his arm the other day?

Would Brooke Anne ever fit into his world? And more important, would he ever fit into hers?

This was the perfect time to tell him about being at the Harts'. Then he would know she knew all about him. He would understand that she wore gold shoes only when she was pretending to be someone she wasn't.

As if sensing her churning thoughts, Morgan squeezed her hand, bringing her attention back to the present.

"Brooke, do you think we'll ever be able to just talk again?

"Of course," she said noncommittally.

"Really?"

"Sure." Though the only thing she was certain of was that she didn't know what to think. This was all too much.

She smiled weakly. "Oh my gosh, will you look at the time? I'd better get on home."

"But your tree...weren't you getting one?" Morgan paused. "How about I buy you one? One of those big blue spruces I saw over on the left? I could help you put it in your van."

The blue spruces. The ones she couldn't afford. "Uh...no. Don't buy me a tree."

He looked shamefaced. "I didn't mean that the way it sounded. It's just that Christmas is coming...." His voice drifted off.

"Christmas will come even if I don't have a big tree," she said with a shrug. "I'll get one another day. I...I should go."

"Okay," he agreed, relenting.

"I'll call you tomorrow. Good luck with your tree shopping. I hope you get a pretty one. You'll have to describe it to me. Bye. See you on Thursday."

BROOKE SCAMPERED OFF, leaving Morgan to watch her wind her way through the temporary forest. In the background, "The Christmas Song" began to play. Great. After days of trying to find her, he finally had.

And he'd managed to do everything completely wrong.

With a sigh, Morgan knew it was time to go home.

Chapter Twenty-One

Brooke was Morgan's first thought the next morning as he woke slowly to the sound of jazz playing on his clock radio. Brooke, with her mittened hands and jaunty red coat. She'd worn a fleece hat, as well, which covered her ears but left her cheeks and button nose to brave the elements by themselves. He'd wanted to hold her close and cover those exposed areas with warm kisses.

Shoot. He'd wanted to do a lot of things, he reflected, raising his arms and folding them beneath his head. The episode at the tree lot had both intrigued and puzzled him. She'd looked happy to see him, yet scared to death at the same time. And pensive. As if there were a few too many secrets she knew about him.

Like what? he wondered. What was she afraid of? Him? Her feelings? Something else?

Thinking back to their night together, he remembered how open she'd seemed. He'd been transfixed by her beauty and her lust for life. He'd loved how she'd laughed when she and Aaron had danced, as if she was happy just to be alive.

He'd felt their evening had been magical. She'd brought new energy to the party from the moment he'd seen her, looking like a fairy princess in that flowing gown.

Other people had noticed that about her, too, if the many interested glances in their direction were any indication. Brooke's vibrancy had attracted people to her like a magnet.

Even Breva had commented that her husband had spoken of her more than once.

It had to have been fate that had brought them to the tree lot at the same time. What else could it have been? He'd been all over town trying to find her…making friends with shoe salesmen…and had relearned the art of letter writing. He'd actually attempted to convey his feelings in ten sentences.

Brooke was like a gift to him, and he wanted to keep her. No way was he going to accept that she didn't suit him, or that she wasn't compatible for his lifestyle.

He wasn't going to lie to himself and say that he didn't enjoy the things that his money and drive had brought him, but he was now wise enough to know that those things were a small substitute for real conversations and genuine emotions. Sheri had taught him that if nothing else.

Soon Brooke would realize that he was perfect for her, too. He just needed to figure out how to make her see that. Her hesitancy to be with him had given him pause, but he had a feeling that he could win her over if he was patient. And she was going to call him that day—he could hardly wait to hear her voice on the phone.

Morgan had put on his robe and was pouring himself a cup of hot coffee when the phone rang, as if on cue. For a split second he wondered if he'd been on Brooke's mind, as well, this morning. If she hadn't been able to wait until he was at the office to speak with him.

"Hello?" he asked, half expecting it to be her on the other end.

"Morgan? It's your mother."

Every one of his nerve endings deadened at his mother's voice. Her calm, impersonal tone drove him to take a deep sip of coffee for fortification. It was rare for his mother to call him during the week. Rarer still to do it before 10:00 a.m.

Which brought up another thing. Was it only his family who announced themselves on the phone, as if he wouldn't recognize their voices? "Hi, Mom. What's new?"

"Well, I've been very busy, getting everything organized for the *holiday*." She emphasized the last word, as if Christmas was something on her appointment calendar to be expertly dealt with. No wonder he had such a hard time with other people! He took another gulp of coffee, glad he liked the dark brew very strong.

She continued. "Dear, I was just wondering when exactly you were coming home."

Great. In all of the excitement of meeting Brooke and then trying to find her, he'd completely forgotten about scheduling plans to go home for Christmas. Suddenly, it didn't sound appealing at all. "I'm not sure, Mom."

"Morgan. I need to know. I'm having a dinner party on the twenty-fourth and I'm trying to plan the table decorations. Did you want to attend?"

He winced. That would be "Christmas Eve" to normal people. His eyebrows furrowed in irritation. Only weeks before he would have thought nothing of her choice of words, of her worries over table decorations. He would have only thought that his mom was trying to make the holiday nice. To make it run as smoothly as possible.

But her concern over trivial preparations now seemed superficial and ridiculous. Her steadfast determination to turn the occasion into yet another social obligation annoyed him no end. Especially when he thought of Brooke and her efforts to find gifts for needy children.

That was what was important. The spirit of giving. The knowledge that there was a reason to celebrate Christmas—not merely get through it.

"Morgan? Are you still there?"

Barely, he realized with a start. Somewhere along his journey into adulthood, he'd made a conscious decision to become a better, more insightful person than his parents. He had left their world some time ago…and was in no hurry to go back. Just the thought of entering that environment made his stomach turn. "I may not visit this year, Mom," he said slowly, some small part of him waiting for her to try to convince him otherwise. "Probably won't."

"Morgan. What are you talking about? You always come to Dallas for the holidays."

"Not this year."

"But Caroline and Bob aren't coming, either. Caro's having some kind of midnight gala on the twenty-sixth."

"Boxing Day. Caroline is having a Boxing Day gala."

"Whoever heard of such a thing?"

His sister. His sweet, beautiful, too-rich sister who made everyone smile.

Who was the exact opposite of their mother.

"I just don't know what I'm going to tell everyone if neither of my children comes to visit."

His heart lurched, not at the words his mother said, but at all the things she didn't. At all the things he knew she never would say. She was a loving woman, but so hard in many ways. Obligations were paramount in her life, and she didn't forgive those who abandoned them easily. Rubbing his thumb along the rim of his cup, he said, "Mom, I've met a girl. I'm going to spend the holiday with her."

He took a sip of coffee as he waited out the long pause on her end. "Oh, Morgan. Really? When did you meet her?"

He had to smile at the change in her voice. It was now rife with hesitant expectation. He knew that she was already worrying about future holidays with in-laws, about a new daughter-in-law to talk to. "A few weeks ago. She's adorable. She's volunteering to be an elf at Children's Hospital. She's been shopping for dolls for the kids all month."

"What's her name?"

"Her name is Brooke, and she's as sweet as can be. She has flyaway blond hair and soft gray eyes. I can't wait for you to meet her."

"Where's she from?"

He frowned. His mother's voice was becoming noticeably chillier and chillier. "Um, Nebraska originally, I believe."

Another pause. "Well, I just don't know what to say to this, Morgan. I'm positively shocked you didn't let me know about this…Brooke earlier. I've made plans for you. For all of us. And Alexia Kilmore will be in town, also. She was looking forward to seeing you. You know Alexia. She and Caroline were good friends in college."

Morgan rolled his eyes. He knew how to read between his mother's lines so well. *If Caroline-who-married-well was friends with her…*

His mom kept chatting. "I told her mother you'd take her out. I thought we might have eggnog with her and her family on Christmas Day around two. After church, of course."

Of course. "You'll have to tell her hi for me."

"Alexia just graduated, dear. She's a little at loose ends…. You'd be so good for her."

But would she be good for *him?* Shaking his head, he replied, "I don't think so, Mom. I want to be with Brooke." As he said the words, he realized just how much he meant them. Somehow he instinctively knew that Brooke wouldn't care what her table looked like, or what he was wearing, or how well his stock portfolio was doing. He had a feeling she'd be more concerned with hokey decorations, red and green M&M's and steaming mugs of hot cider.

And a good-looking blue spruce.

His mother still hadn't said a word. He could already picture her deep in thought, planning her next offensive. He wondered what it would be. Perhaps she'd ask him to bring Brooke to Dallas with him. It would be uncomfortable, but with Brooke by his side, it might even be fun.

They'd be together Christmas morning. He could get her something expensive and pretty, like a porcelain figurine or a gold necklace.

And a puzzle. He could get her one of those crazy five thousand piece puzzles that he'd have to help her assemble.

"Oh. I see," his mother finally said, dispelling all warm, homey thoughts from his mind. "Well. Hmm. How is everything going at Royal?"

Disappointment surged through him, though he had to admit he wasn't completely surprised. Of course his mother wasn't going to beg him to come visit for the holidays. His family didn't do that. Of course she wasn't going to ask him to bring Brooke-from-Nebraska home with him. She was a stranger. A nobody.

Feeling slightly uncomfortable that he'd even put his mother in such a spot, he chose to simply answer her question. "Work's going well."

"Is it? I'm so glad. You always were a hard worker. I bet you'll be up for another promotion soon."

Biting back a caustic reply, he asked, "How's Dad?"

"He's fine. Playing golf. I'll let him know about your plans."

Yes, she would. They'd probably cross his name off their list of things to do, then move on to the next item.

There was nothing left to say now, really. "Thanks, Mom."

"You're welcome, dear. I'll send your present in the mail today, so you receive it in time."

"I'll do the same. And I'll call you on Christmas morning.'

"We'll look forward to it," she replied briskly.

"Bye, Mom."

"Goodbye, Morgan."

And that was it. That was his warm and fuzzy phone conversation with his mother. The one where he'd confided in her that he finally felt strongly enough about a girl that he'd skip out on a family Christmas in order to be with her.

No squeals of happiness. No fifty questions about Brooke.

Only a hint of irritation that he was messing up her seating arrangement and that she now needed to make an extra trip to the post office. Oh, and what was Alexia going to do?

No, that wasn't quite fair. His mother loved him, and he loved her.

His parents just didn't foster those touchy-feely emotions in their home. They were all about looks and outcomes and jobs well done.

Not gold sandals and slow waltzes, or silly childhood stories.

Or staying up to watch the stars at night.

Chapter Twenty-Two

"Nuh-uh. Nope. Not likely," Tomasina said firmly as she wiped down a bookcase in the interior design firm that Jovial Janitors cleaned on Wednesdays.

"Come on, Tomi. Just this once?"

"That's what you said last time. And knowing you, you'll say it again. Brooke Anne, you're worse than a heroin addict trying to get another fix."

"I hardly think my need for your friendship is on the same level as a drug addiction."

"You can't stop doing things that aren't good for you—or me. In my opinion, it's all the same."

Brooke Anne was scrubbing away so hard at a scuff mark on the tile floor that she was working up a sweat. "But I don't want to see him again. After the tree lot incident, I'm convinced he just thinks of me as an obligation to be taken care of," she told Tomi. Secretly, she was afraid he wanted so much more.

More than she was sure she could be for him.

"Doesn't matter if you don't want to see him again. You have to."

"But what am I going to say?"

Tomi straightened, set her hands on her hips and recited, as if she was back in grade school, "Thank you for my shoes and my money. I need to go pay my people so they can pay for expensive plastic log cabins they already charged on their Visa's."

Brooke Anne laughed at Tomi's theatrics. "Point taken. But you would do so much better than me. I know I won't be able to act tough when I'm around him. I'll just melt and get all gushy inside." She dipped her sponge in the water and tried scrubbing the scuff mark again, wishing she'd thought to bring a tube of toothpaste with her to remove the black marks. "You've met him. You know how cute he is."

"I have met him," Tomi replied as she shook her head at Brooke Anne's efforts.

"So…"

Tomasina crouched next to her and skillfully removed the mark with two swipes. "You need to grow some biceps, girl," she murmured, sitting back on her haunches. "Look. Just because you've found yourself some too-cute, brown-eyed hunk of a man who you don't know how to talk to doesn't mean I have to help you out."

"Khaki. They're khaki."

"What?"

"His eyes, Tomi. And you should feel how solid he is."

Tomasina's lips curved into a ghost of a smile, then she glowered at her for show. "I've got my own man to feel, thank you very much." Pulling out the vacuum, she continued, her voice a little more tender. "Listen. If you don't want to see him tomorrow night, then just get your stuff and give him a break. Even though he seems kind of needy in the romance department, he's obviously honest. Grab your check—which you earned, I might add—and get on with your life." She bent down in one economical motion, plugged in the vacuum and pressed the power button. "Don't you have more elf stuff to do?"

The reminder caused Brooke Anne's eyes to widen in alarm. "Yes. The big party is in two weeks."

"See…you can't be wasting your time."

Brooke Anne sighed. "That's my problem. I've got too much on my plate."

They worked another forty-five minutes, then made their way to the parking lot together. Brooke Anne was dropping Tomi off at choir practice after work, and her church was just a few blocks from Brooke Anne's apartment.

On the drive over, Brooke Anne felt bad that lately all their conversations had centered on her. She'd only been focused on her needs and not her friend's. "I'll still give y'all those bonuses I promised, Tomi. I will."

"That's good."

"So, how are things going with you? How's Ronnie doing?"

"Ron's good. Working hard at the UPS office. Good overtime, though."

"Do you know what he's getting you for Christmas?"

"Nope, but it better be small and fit in my stocking, if he wants a little ho, ho, ho."

Brooke Anne laughed. "I got the cutest toy for Vanessa."

Tomi grinned. "Did you?"

"Yep. It's a metal pot-and-pan set, complete with metal spoons to rap against them."

Tomasina gave her a look of mock horror. "All that racket! As if my house wasn't noisy enough already. You wouldn't do that to me, would you?"

Brooke Anne reached out and placed a hand on her best friend's arm. "You're right—I wouldn't. I got her these adorable Winnie the Pooh finger puppets."

"I love Winnie the Pooh. Is there a Tigger?"

"Of course."

"Gotta love Tigger."

"Yep." Brooke Anne smiled warmly at Tomi as they pulled up to the church, beautifully lit with white lights.

"See you tomorrow night."

Tomasina slid out of the passenger seat, looking like a different woman than when she'd gotten in. While they were driving, she'd slipped out of her Jovial Janitor jacket and pulled on her black-suede-and-faux-fur coat. Tennis shoes had been replaced with heels. The clips had been taken out of her hair and now it hung like a flag down her back. She looked glamorous and spunky…like Tomi. "See you later. You go see that man tomorrow. Let him fawn over you a little bit. Enjoy a night out."

"And if I only get my shoes and a check tomorrow?"

Tomi reached out and clasped Brooke Anne's hand tightly. "That's more than you've got at the moment, right?"

"Right."

Tomasina gave her hand another squeeze, then stood up, her leopard-print tote bag carrying her change of clothes. "I'd better go. I can't be late."

"I know."

"Brooke Anne, it's going to be okay. I have faith in you, girl. Tomorrow night will work out just fine. I can feel it."

The van door slammed shut and Tomi made her way up the lit sidewalk.

As Brooke Anne drove away, she wished she had a little of Tomasina's confidence.

Chapter Twenty-Three

Well, here she was again, outside Morgan's door, Brooke Anne thought to herself the following evening.

The good news was that he was obviously there, and even awake. She could hear papers shuffling and desk drawers opening and shutting. *What would they say to each other?*

Quickly, Brooke Anne rubbed her damp hands against her jeans. This time, she'd opted to wear her Jovial Janitor jacket instead of a sweatshirt. It was a little more flattering, if she could use such a word to describe the garment. Underneath, she had on a bright red turtleneck, and she was wearing high-heeled boots.

After all, she hadn't come to the office to clean this evening, she was there to meet Morgan. She'd offered to take over Tomi's shift for the night, but Tomi had refused to budge. She'd only worn the jacket to get past the security guard.

Taking a deep breath, she knocked briskly on the door frame and stepped in.

Morgan was already standing and circling his desk.

"I'm so glad you actually came," he said. "I was half expecting to see Tomasina in your place."

Brooke Anne was uncomfortably aware of just how close that had come to happening. "I told you when I called this morning that I'd be here."

"I'm glad you are."

That was his second "glad"! Happiness warred with suspicion in her heart. Was he really pleased to see her, or merely saying the right thing?

She glanced at a plain shopping bag on his desk. "So, are these my infamous shoes?"

"Yes, they are. There's an envelope with your money in there, as well."

"Thanks. That will come in handy."

When she was about to take the bag and run, Morgan stopped her with a hand on her arm. "Are you done cleaning for the day?"

"Actually, Tomasina will still clean the office tonight. I just stopped by to see you…and to, um, get my things," Brooke Anne added belatedly, feeling as if she'd already said too much.

"So you had to come all the way over here, just for this?"

"I told you I would."

"What about dinner? Would you like to get some?"

She knew what she should say to keep her heart intact. She should tell him she'd already eaten, then move on—shoes and money in hand. But she didn't. The thought of being in his company again was too tempting. *Give Morgan a chance, Brooke!* a little voice called out inside her. *Forget what happened with Russell, and take a chance again. You're worth it!*

"Sure. Dinner sounds fine," she finally replied. Besides, then she could tell him all about cleaning the soiree house and they could both be uncomfortable together.

"There's a diner around the corner."

The place he was talking about was Skip's. To say it was simply a diner was like saying a Cadillac was simply a car. Skip's had been a landmark as far back as anyone could recall. The food was good, and the restaurant was known for its soup, which would be perfect for a frigid evening like tonight. "Great," she said.

"Do you have a warm coat? For once it's not drizzling outside, just cold. We could walk."

"Yeah, my winter coat is in my van. If you'll give me a minute, I'll go exchange it for this jacket and then meet you there."

"No way. I'm not letting you out of my sight tonight," he said as he moved toward her, a new, almost possessive gleam in his eyes. "I'll walk with you."

Morgan held her bag for her and escorted her through the building to the parking lot. When they reached the Jovial Janitor van, he stood to the side as she unlocked the door, slipped the envelope into her purse and switched coats. Then they were walking down the sidewalk, braving a crisp wind that seemed determined to blow directly into their faces.

It felt natural when Morgan took her arm to keep her steady. It felt even better when she gave in to her desire and let her body fit against his. He wrapped his arm around her shoulders, enveloping her with his masculine scent. She felt warm and secure—as if she was on a real date.

The diner was crowded, filled with noisy customers who had come downtown to shop and celebrate the season. Loud music played, and the servers had donned Santa hats and reindeer-head buttons.

Morgan and Brooke Anne were led to a table immediately and given plastic-coated menus. "What a day," he said, once they were seated across from each other.

Brooke Anne eyed him. He did look a bit frazzled, but animated, too. The combination suited him. She couldn't decide whether she wanted to brush her fingertips along his brow or just sit back and listen to him talk. "Busy?" she asked, choosing the latter idea.

"Oh, yeah." He set his menu down and met her gaze. "Part of my job is to survey people about different items that are stocked in our hotel rooms. This past month Breva and I have had the dubious honor of restocking the toiletry articles for the guest rooms."

"I had no idea such a job existed." Brooke Anne leaned forward, intrigued.

"It sounds like it would be fun, right? Breva and I actually thought it was going to be a great project for December. Piece of cake. Last year it was table linens and silverware for the dining rooms."

"But choosing shampoos isn't fun?"

He scowled. "Everybody's a critic. First we had to test all the items and now we're in the process of weeding through hundreds of customer and employee responses."

"And it's driving you crazy?"

He nodded. "Breva and I thought we had everything under control…but the last batch of questionnaires came in today."

His joking tone was infectious. Brooke Anne couldn't help but get caught up in it. "Let me guess. Nobody likes your choices."

He grinned. "Not only that—*everyone* has something to say. Breva and I came to the conclusion around four o'clock that it's going to be impossible to please everyone."

"But you've known that all along, right?"

"I have…it's just coming as a surprise. I was kind of hoping that minibottles of shampoo and conditioner wouldn't mean much in the grand scale of things."

"You mean compared to…world peace?"

"Exactly. But I was completely wrong. We even had two people from the sales team come over to see how their choice was faring. I think they've got a betting pool going on over there."

"What are you going to do?" she asked lightly, completely taken in by his banter. She wondered if Morgan had any idea that his eyes looked green in candlelight. Or that his dimple appeared every time he frowned.

If he realized his shoulders looked especially broad in crisp button-downs.

"Breva and I are just going to stick with our original recommendations," he declared. "I'm sick of it all. And I'm finding out way too much about people's personal grooming preferences."

Brooke Anne wrinkled her nose. "I think I understand."

"I'm sorry," Morgan said. "You asked a simple question and I've completely bored you with my petty problems."

She wasn't the least bit bored. "I wouldn't have asked if I wasn't interested, Morgan."

He smiled at that.

After making their dinner selections and ordering hot coffee from Bernice, their server, they were alone again.

"So, tell me what you've been doing. Still shopping for Barbies?"

It was time. "Yes…and cleaning. Tomi and I actually cleaned a woman's house all the way over in Indian Hill two Friday's ago."

Morgan squirmed. No doubt the last thing he wanted to hear about was her cleaning toilets. "Is that right?"

This is good for you, Brooke Anne told herself. *Let him see that the two of you have no future. Now that you have your shoes and money back, you don't ever need to see him again.* "Yeah. It was a really pretty house. I think I might have seen you there."

He looked at her as if she was speaking Greek. "I doubt it. I don't go over to Indian Hill too often."

"I really think it was you I saw," she pressed, more than a little irritated now. Why in the world would someone pretend he wasn't rich? His attitude wasn't making any sense. "Do you know a Caroline Hart?"

Morgan's face went slack. "What?"

"I was…cleaning the carpet…when I saw you go in that house. With a very pretty brunette."

Instead of denying what she'd seen, Morgan sent her a piercing look. "Why didn't you say anything?"

"What would you have done? Invited Tomasina and me to the soiree?"

"Maybe." He rolled his eyes. "That silly soiree. That, Brooke, was my sister's house."

"What?"

"My sister's married name is Hart. Caroline married a rich trust-fund kid. And that brunette is my cousin Barbara."

Now Brooke Anne felt stupid. "Your cousin?" Once more, she tried to picture how he'd looked with that gal. Had Brooke Anne just imagined he'd been acting in a romantic way toward her?

"My cousin. Caroline is always coming up with weird party ideas. Last month we had to dress up and take part in some murder mystery. Barb and I always go together. I mean, who else would we subject Caroline to?"

Brooke Anne felt like sinking into a very large black hole. "I thought your sister was really nice," she said, more for herself than for him. Oh, why had she even brought this up?

"She is nice. She's a peach! But she's silly as all get-out." He shook his head. "I can't believe you were there at the same time. You don't know how hard I'd been trying to talk to you."

"I'm sorry. I guess I should've woken you up that night I stopped by."

"I wish you had, too, but it's sweet that you didn't." He treated her to a devastating grin. "It was nice to wake up with the knowledge that someone actually cared about me while I was sleeping."

Brooke Anne felt heat traipse up her neck as she recalled the nurturing instinct that had overcome her that night. How she'd tenderly traced the planes of his face. The slope of his shoulders. Fought the urge to caress more of him.

"You want to know a secret?" Morgan said. "I even tried to find you through the place you bought your shoes."

"What?"

"I put your shoes in a bag and visited as many nice shoe stores as I could, looking for the one you shopped at. I think I went to twelve."

She was intrigued and a little puzzled. It sounded as if he really had been as affected by their evening as she had. Perhaps she'd just imagined that he'd only been thinking about obligations and money owed. "Well…did you get any information?"

"Not even a little. Nobody wanted to give me any info."

"Nobody?"

"Well, I did get lucky and found Warren, the owner of that WJB shoe store down the road."

Brooke Anne smiled. "And what did he say?"

"He said that the shoes did indeed come from his store, but that he wasn't talking. That's pretty much what he told me, anyway. I ended up leaving a note for you there."

"Oh my gosh. I don't think anyone's ever tracked me down before."

"There's a first time for everyone, I guess."

They laughed, and once again Brooke Anne found herself being drawn in by Morgan's charming personality. He was interesting, somewhat self-deprecating…utterly darling. She wanted to know everything about him.

By the time their broccoli cheese soup and club sandwiches came, Brooke Anne was wondering why she'd ever had any doubts about their compatibility. Their conversation flowed easily, and the silences, when they were eating, didn't seem strained or tense. And she'd caught more than one brief glance from him that was anything but businesslike. Happiness filled her.

She was already looking forward to seeing him again. Maybe he'd want to accompany her to Tomasina's choir recital or to the hospital Christmas party. He seemed like the kind of guy who might appreciate grown women dressing in green-and-red elf suits.

Afterward, they could go down to Fountain Square…maybe even ice skate. Admire the trees and browse through the pretty designer shops.

Then they could go to one of the trendy restaurants nearby and have some dinner. They could laugh about the antics of the kids at neighboring tables and sympathize with the kids' parents. It would be fun.

"Brooke, there's something I've been meaning to ask you," Morgan said, interrupting her thoughts. "Two things, actually."

"Okay."

"Why were you taken off my business's account?"

"What?"

"Well, Tomasina seems to be the regular cleaning girl now," he explained, rubbing his teaspoon with his thumb. "Did something happen? Is that why you moved?"

Belatedly, Brooke Anne realized that she'd led him to believe that she wasn't the owner of Jovial Janitors, but one of the employees. "Morgan, I was just filling in for Tomasina that night. Jovial Janitors is my company." She handed him a business card from her purse as proof.

Surprise, then admiration, showed in his eyes as he read her card. "I had no idea."

"I'm sorry. I didn't mean for it to be a secret."

"How long have you been running your company?"

"About two years. Before that I was working for a cleaning service that was going out of business. It seemed natural that I take over the accounts. But…it's been hard."

"How so?"

Since he seemed genuinely interested, she elaborated. "Oh, there are just so many things that small business owners have to deal with. Hiring and firing workers, getting used to being the person on whom all the responsibility lies. Liability insurance, worker's comp, picky customers. Money."

"Money?"

She laughed. "Learning how to not have any! All my profits have been going into building the business. That's why I jumped at your offer. It's been two years since I've indulged in frivolous dresses or shoes. Everything I buy now has to serve multiple purposes."

"So you didn't say yes to get to know me, or because going to the party sounded like fun?" Morgan asked in a bemused tone.

What did he mean? "No. I said yes because my employees needed their Christmas bonus and I wanted those shoes." *Of course, within the first hour of their date, she'd wanted to know him better.*

Morgan looked deflated. Brooke Anne wondered if perhaps she'd been a little too honest with him. "It was fun, though, until…"

"Until I abandoned you? Glad to hear it."

They ate their food in awkward silence.

Brooke Anne wished she knew of a way to tell him that she'd found him attractive—that she still did—without embarrassing them both. Then she remembered that Morgan had said he'd had two questions for her. "What was your second question?"

"What? Oh, it's nothing. I was just wondering why you weren't in the phone book. I tried to call you."

Confused, she set her fork down. "Morgan, I am listed."

"No, there're only two 'Annes' in the phone book, and neither is you."

She laughed. "'Anne' isn't my last name, it's part of my first! My last name is Kressler. I'm Brooke Anne Kressler."

"I can't believe this," Morgan said. "I didn't even know your last name, *and* I thought you were just a cleaning lady."

"What do you mean, *just* a cleaning lady?"

He glanced at her, his expression unguarded. "Nothing. There's a big difference between working for a business and owning one, that's all."

"How? Like in the social scheme of things?"

The sharpness in her voice must have set him on edge. He suddenly seemed wary and spoke slowly, as if he was testing each word to see how it would fly. "I didn't mean to offend you. Obviously, once again, I'm having a tough time saying what's on my mind. I only meant that I can't believe I was going crazy looking for you when I didn't even know some basic information."

"I'm sorry," she said, contrite. "I shouldn't have snapped at you."

"It's okay. I know what I said came out completely different than I intended." He flashed her a sad smile. "Guess I should stick to notes, huh?"

His words defused her anger, but not her bruised feelings. Maybe if she hadn't already been so gun-shy because of Russell, she'd have no problem shaking it off. Maybe if her business and her shoestring budget weren't such a source of constant worry, then she'd be able to laugh at his misconceptions.

Maybe if she hadn't seen with her own eyes what he did in his spare time, she would have thought their differences were surmountable.

But they weren't, were they?

In her world, owning a janitorial service was an accomplishment.

In his…it was a consolation prize for not being able to do anything better.

Morgan reached for her hand. "Are you okay? Have you been listening to what I've been trying to say…very badly? I'm just sorry that I didn't know more about you before." Rubbing his thumb over the veins in her hand, he added, "It's good that we're together now though, right?"

She pulled her hand away with a sinking feeling. He was right about the two of them not knowing much about the other. Why had she thought she could trust Morgan with her heart, when Russell—a guy who'd known her forever—had broken it without a second thought? She needed to grow up and get her head out of the clouds. Some men were just not for her, and the sooner she realized that, the better off she'd be.

"I'm glad we found each other again, too," Brooke Anne said quietly. "And thanks for the dinner and my money and for bringing me my shoes. But—I think I'm going to go on home now."

He appeared completely stunned. "Wait a minute…"

"Merry Christmas, Morgan," she said, then pulled on her coat.

"Don't you think you're being kind of childish?"

"Childish?"

Morgan's fingers whitened as he tightened his grip on his mug. "I didn't mean that. Why don't you stay and we'll talk some more."

Talk some more? Throwing him one last glance, Brooke knew in her heart that it would be better for her—for both of them—if she ended things before they ever really began. They didn't belong together. "I'm sorry, but no," she said, then strode out of the diner.

As she walked back to the office building along the well-lit street, Brooke Anne tried to put things in perspective. She had her shoes back, and she could pay her employees without dipping into her savings.

Things were better, right?

At that moment, she knew they couldn't be more wrong.

Chapter Twenty-Four

"We're really going to miss you, sweetie," Brooke Anne's mother said over the phone. "Are you sure you won't change your mind?"

Oh, she wanted to. She wanted to feel more confident and happier with herself. It would feel really good to go home to Nebraska with her head held high. But Brooke Anne knew that making the trip now would be just one more thing to stress about. "I'm sorry, Mom. Not this year."

"So are you going to spend Christmas with that Morgan fellow?"

"Probably," Brooke Anne said, well aware she could be nominated for an Oscar, considering how perky she succeeded in making her voice sound.

"I'm glad you've found someone else. Oh…did you hear about Russell?"

"No." Did she want to?

"He and Suzanne were having trouble and are seeing a marriage counselor. I guess things aren't all peachy-keen between those two."

Only her mother could say "peachy-keen" with a straight face. As she was thinking that, Brooke Anne also realized that it didn't hurt as much anymore when she thought about Russell.

Maybe she really was getting over him— Finally. "That's too bad," she said.

"I still get fired up when I think of the way that snake treated you."

Brooke Anne smiled in spite of herself. "I used to, too. But now…I don't know. I guess what happened with us is history."

Her mom paused, then continued in a new vein. "You know what? You're exactly right. Russell is part of your past now. The past! Just like mud pies and green nail polish."

"Mom, do we have to bring up the nail polish again? That was in eighth grade."

"It's hard to forget when I see your hands in your junior high school graduation portrait hanging right in front of me."

One day she was going to pick up that portrait and carry it right out of her parents' home. "Mom—"

"Anyway, sweetie, I'm so glad we talked. You've always had such a good heart. It's a real gift, you know—the way you're able to forgive people, make them feel better about themselves. You're the most giving person I know. I'm so glad you're my daughter."

Her mother's words made her want to puff out her chest and go hide in a corner, all at the same time. She appreciated the compliment, but she was also well aware of what everyone back home would have thought about her relationship with Morgan.

They would tell her that she had no business dreaming about men like him.

That even if they did get along, she would be like a fish out of water in his crowd.

Remember who you are, Brooke! her mother would say. *You're a small-town girl who likes simple things.*

Brooke Anne's shoulders slumped. Was she really just like them? Was it possible to have a perfect match with someone so different? "I'd better go, Mom," she said hurriedly. She couldn't pretend to be happy a second longer. "I'll call you soon."

"All right, honey. Stay warm."

She always said that. "I will. You, too, Mom."

She hung up, and at that exact moment, the doorbell rang. Glancing at her watch, Brooke Anne wondered what in the world Tomi would be doing, coming over so early. "Tomi, I'm not even dressed yet," she called out as she quickly checked the peep hole, just in case....

She froze in place when she saw who was on the other side of her door.

"Hey, Brooke Anne Kressler," Morgan said. "I found you."

She opened the door a crack. "What are you doing here?"

He dared to grin. "Visiting?"

"It's early Saturday morning. Shouldn't you be...sleeping?"

"It's 10:00 a.m. Even I don't sleep in that late." He took in what she was wearing. "May I come in?"

"I'm in my robe and nightgown."

"I don't mind if you don't." He held up a hand. "I'll stay five minutes, tops."

What could she say? Grudgingly, she opened the door the rest of the way—and watched Morgan step into her tiny apartment as though he hung out in places like hers all the time.

It took everything she had not to apologize for the dishes in the sink and the state of her hair. Had she even brushed it?

"I like your puzzle," he said.

"Can I offer you some coffee?"

"I'd love some."

Morgan took a seat at the card table and started fussing with the puzzle pieces. "How long has this taken you?" he asked. "It looks like you're halfway done."

She poured his cup of coffee, and because she remembered, she added some milk and sugar, too. "A few weeks."

With a smile of thanks, Morgan took the cup and sipped gratefully.

She couldn't take it anymore. "Why, exactly, are you here?"

"I felt bad about the other night."

"Because..."

"Because I started talking without thinking," he replied, his voice earnest. "I didn't want you to spend the whole weekend thinking I'm a jerk. Besides, looking for you has kind of become my main hobby."

Don't melt, she chastised herself. *Don't forget that he's not the man for you.* "Well, you found me."

"I did." He moved two jigsaw pieces around some more and finally popped one in place. "So, would you like to go out again?"

The question caught her off guard. "With you?"

"With me."

"Why? Because you feel guilty?"

"Because I like you."

Brooke Anne swallowed hard. "Morgan, I don't know how to say this, but I don't think that's a good idea."

"Because…"

"Because you're rich and I'm…not." Her stomach churned. Leave it to her to point out the obvious.

"For some reason that seems to be a huge problem for you. And I'm not that rich, Brooke Anne. Not like my sister, Caroline." He toyed with another puzzle piece. "I did grow up with money, but I also grew up pretty lonely. Having money doesn't make a person happy."

"I know that."

"Well, then, why are you holding that against me?"

"You should know right now that I'm always going to be a Jovial Janitor."

Morgan burst out laughing. "Okay."

Mentally, Brooke Anne winced. "I didn't mean that the way it sounded."

"I hope not. Listen. I'm not saying let's go get married. I'm just saying, let's go out on a date. Now that we know the true colors."

Remembering her earlier conversation with her mom, when they'd talked about forgiveness, Brooke Anne knew it was time to follow her heart. "Tomasina has a choir concert next Saturday night. Would you like to go with me?"

"Sure. Pick you up at five-thirty? We could grab something to eat before the concert."

"I'll be here."

She stood up, feeling almost naked in her nightgown and robe. "Well, maybe you should go now."

"All right." He started to leave, then turned again to face her. Standing so close that his jacket brushed her robe, as his scent wafted toward her, he murmured, "So…will you ever forgive me for being a jerk?"

She already had. Not that she was going to tell him that right away. "Maybe."

He leaned closer, clasped her shoulders. "See you in a week," he whispered.

Before she even knew what was happening, Morgan kissed her on the lips—and then he was gone.

"Breva, has Aaron ever sent you roses?" Morgan asked as casually as possible on their way to a meeting Monday morning.

"A couple of times. Once when we were dating. Another time after we got in a fight," Breva answered. "Hmm. Then there was this time after a particularly lovely evening." She smiled to herself. "Why? Are you interested in sending me some roses, too? I like pink ones, just to let you know."

"I'll keep that in mind for Secretary's Day," he joked. Turning serious, he asked, "What about candy? Do you like chocolate?"

Breva slowed her pace and studied his worried expression. "What have you done? I thought things went well when you saw your Cinderella. Didn't you say she came by and got her check and shoes?"

"She did. We went to Skip's Diner, too."

"That's good. Everyone likes that place." She looked at him more closely. "And…"

"And after we visited for a while and things were going fine,

I decided it was time to gather some pertinent details about her life."

"Such as?" Breva asked, a small crease appearing between her brows.

"Such as her last name, her exact occupation—"

"'Anne' and custodian, right?"

"Wrong. It's 'Kressler' and she's the *owner* of Jovial Janitors."

Breva brightened. "Oh, well, that's even better…I mean for her, right?"

"Wrong," he replied, still feeling guilty. "I guess I sounded really happy that she owned her own company, instead of just being a cleaning lady. She took that as a sign that I cared about such things." He paused. "And then there was the whole Caroline thing."

"What?"

"It turns out she cleaned Caroline's house the night of her last party. Brooke Anne saw me there and came up with the idea that I live in Indian Hill, date my cousin and attend soirees on a regular basis."

"Guess you both made a couple of wrong assumptions."

That had a good ring to it. It reminded him that he wasn't the only one who'd made a mistake.

"So why are you sending her flowers?" Breva asked.

Morgan shrugged. "I went to her apartment on Saturday."

Breva stopped abruptly in the middle of the hall. "What? How did that happen?"

"I found her address and stopped by." He smiled at the memory. "It was great."

"Was it really? Hasn't your mother ever told you never to stop by a woman's house unannounced?"

"No, but I'm glad I did. We talked…and I'm going with her to a choir concert next weekend. I thought I might send her roses in the meantime, so she won't forget about me."

"I must say I didn't know you had it in you to be so romantic," Breva commented.

"I'm not. Do you think it's a good idea, though?"

"At this point, I think anything would help," she replied. "And flowers always do. Send them off, Morgan Carmichael." Breva glanced behind him and nodded to some people walking by. "Now, get ready to discuss next year's budget. We have to be alert or another department's going to try and take some of our money."

The anticipation of a good fight made him grin.

After lunch, Morgan called a local florist and had one dozen roses and a box of chocolates sent to Miss Brooke Anne Kressler. Along with a note that said,

Looking forward to Saturday night. Maybe this time we'll both be sitting at the end of the meal. I'm glad we talked.
Morgan

There. That was a good note—a whole three sentences. The ball was in her court now.

Chapter Twenty-Five

Brooke Anne read the note and smiled. Then she set the card down carefully and buried her face in the fragrant blooms. The pink and white roses, nestled in a bouquet of baby's breath and ferns, were lovely, and the designer chocolates that had accompanied them tasted delicious—at least the four she'd eaten.

And the card…it said it all. It was good they'd talked.

They needed to communicate more. There was an undeniable pull between them, a pull that had begun the moment they'd spied each other in the foyer of the hotel. They'd relied on attraction and chemistry instead of mutual interests and priorities to get them this far.

Not that that was necessarily a bad thing.

They'd certainly both been quick to jump to conclusions in the past. Morgan shouldn't have left to go talk to Sheri without telling her, but she'd let the gossip of one stranger guide her thinking.

Just as she was the one who'd automatically assumed, when she'd seen Morgan at Caroline's, that he must live next door and date the woman he'd come in with.

And with regard to their conversation at Skip's, Brooke Anne knew she'd let her temper get the best of her, when Morgan had just been trying to explain himself. She was so prickly about her business and her lack of funds that she'd overreacted to his comments.

It wasn't his fault that she was constantly worried about being a good boss and managing the company while operating on a shoestring budget.

It wasn't Morgan's fault that neither she nor Tomasina had told him that she was the owner of Jovial Janitors. And she was kidding herself if she thought being the owner didn't matter. She'd worked darn hard to achieve so much. Despite what she might have said to Morgan, she was extremely proud to be the owner of her company.

As she mulled over things she'd said, and others she wished she had, Brooke Anne knew it was time to face some hard truths. The other night she'd taken offense where none had been given, and had left the restaurant without even thanking Morgan for the meal. She felt guilty.

No one deserved that type of behavior. Her mother had taught her better. The least she could have done was thank him for dinner.

All morning she'd wondered what she should do. Tried to think of a way to start over with him. On an even footing.

But when she'd opened the door to the courier and received the bouquet and the chocolate…her heart had swelled up. *He was looking forward to Tomi's concert.*

Even though Tomi had been nothing but prickly toward him.

Earlier that morning she'd been thinking that maybe it was a little weird to expect a real relationship when all she and Morgan had done so far was dance to a few songs, exchange a couple of extremely extraordinary kisses…and then try to figure out what was going on between the two of them for the remainder of the time they'd known each other.

But the fact was she wanted to be around Morgan Carmichael. On a regular basis. She wanted to get to know him better. She was slowly falling…if not in love…then seriously in like with him. She thought about him while cleaning. She dreamed about his kisses at night.

She thought about things she hoped they'd do one day. Things that involved silky sheets and hours alone together.

There had to be a reason he was still in her thoughts after the ball. Surely he'd remained there because she had no desire for him to leave.

Morgan made her feel alive when she was with him, and she liked that feeling very much.

Floating on that emotion, she pulled out his business card, picked up the phone and dialed his number. She was going to thank him for the flowers. And then she was going to talk to him about their upcoming date.

And maybe even ask about going out another night, too?

After following the automated prompts to enter his extension, Brooke Anne took a deep breath as she heard the phone ringing.

A woman answered. "Good afternoon. Morgan Carmichael's office."

"Hello. May I speak with him, please?" Brooke Anne rubbed her free hand against her thigh. She was nervous. Did her voice give it away?

"I'm sorry, Mr. Carmichael is in a meeting. May I take a message?"

"Oh…all right. This is Brooke Anne Kressler. Would you please tell him I called?"

The secretary's voice instantly became friendlier and less businesslike. "Brooke Anne, this is Breva. We met at the ball, remember?"

"Yes," she replied hesitantly, wondering what Breva thought about everything that had been going on between Morgan and her. "Um, how are you?"

"I'm fine. Getting ready for the holidays. Dealing with Morgan."

Brooke Anne gripped the phone. "Is anything wrong?"

"I'm not sure, to tell you the truth. He might not even know himself," Breva said with a chuckle. "But I can tell you one thing—ever since he's met you, he's been a different person."

Something about Breva inspired Brooke Anne to speak frankly. "I feel different, too."

"Different good? Or different bad?"

Brooke Anne thought about that one. How did she feel? Her heart was beating faster, Morgan's ruddy good looks preyed on her mind like nobody's business…and things seemed brighter in her life, even though nothing in it was going smoothly. "Different good, I guess," she said finally. "Sometimes it's hard to tell, though."

"I know the feeling. Did you get your flowers?"

"Yes, I did." Brooke Anne felt vaguely uncomfortable that the woman knew about them. Obviously, Breva was conversant with what had been happening between her and Morgan. "How did you hear about them?"

"M.C. wanted to know my opinion about roses. I told him they were always in good taste. Well, what did you think? Did you like the colors?"

"They're beautiful—I like pink and white roses very much." Brooke Anne glanced at the bouquet again, caressed a soft petal. "It's been a long time since I've received flowers."

"That's terrific. He was worried about sending both the chocolate and the flowers, but I said why not? Come to think of it, I should get Morgan to give my husband a few hints."

Brooke Anne chuckled. "I was just phoning to thank him. Do you know when he'll be back?"

"Within an hour, I'm guessing. Oh, he's going to be sorry he missed you," Breva said, amusement lacing her voice. "I'll have him give you a call."

"Thanks," Brooke Anne replied, and hung up, feeling suspiciously like she did whenever she hung up the phone with her mother: as if she'd given away more information than she'd intended to.

WHEN MORGAN GOT OUT OF his meeting, Breva was sitting on the corner of her desk, smiling like a stuffed canary. Instantly he went on alert. "What happened?"

"Why would you think something happened?"

"You've got a look on your face that says you know something I don't." Mentally, he clicked through the projects they'd been working on. Shoot. The questionnaires.

"What happened?" he asked again, a feeling of doom settling in his stomach. "Brownlee said no to our recommendations and we have to do them all over again."

"Bite your tongue! There is no way on earth I'm going to go through those questionnaires one more time."

What else could it be? Warily, he scanned Breva's face. "You didn't get a promotion, did you?"

"No, I didn't, though that's a fine way to ask. Don't you want me to be promoted?"

Morgan didn't answer her. "You're pregnant and you just found out?"

"M.C., I'm almost sixty!" Shaking her head, she said, "This has nothing to do with work, or me."

That left…him.

Slowly realization dawned. There was only one thing at the moment that he'd been concerned about that didn't have anything to do with Royal Hotels. She was spunky, petite and liked to waltz. "Brooke Anne?"

Breva's eyes shone. "She called."

A lump formed in Morgan's throat. "What did she say?"

"Not much. She was looking for you. I told her you were in a meeting, so she left you her cell number. She says no one ever answers the Jovial Janitors main line."

He could vouch for that.

"So, how did she sound?"

Breva crossed her legs, one clog swinging lazily from her outstretched foot. "She sounded good."

"Really?"

"Really. She liked the flowers, by the way. I told you they were a good idea."

"You're indispensable, Breva. Thanks."

"No problem," she said as she hopped off her desk and practically pushed him into his office. "Now, go call her."

As soon as she closed the door behind him, he did exactly that. Brooke Anne answered on the second ring.

He'd know her sweet voice anywhere. "Hello, Brooke Anne. It's Morgan."

"Hi."

Did she sound hesitant? Pleased? "I heard you called earlier."

"I did. To thank you for the flowers. They're lovely."

"And my note?"

"I really liked your note."

Really sounded good. "I'm looking forward to Tomi's concert. That's in five days, right?"

"Right."

Was he imagining it, or did she sound a little disappointed that their date was so far away? "Any chance you might want to grab a bite to eat sometime sooner?"

"Tonight?"

Morgan had to smile at her suggestion. He scanned his calendar quickly and realized there wasn't a thing he had to do that he couldn't get out of. "Dinner?"

"Okay. You want to come to my place? We could order Chinese."

"I'll be there at seven," he said, before she could even think about saying no.

"Great."

Still smiling, Morgan analyzed the way she'd said that. She'd sounded breathless. Expectant. Good.

Kind of the way he was feeling himself.

"See you in a little while."

"All right," she said. "Bye."

Morgan hung up, already anticipating how their night might go. Maybe they'd kiss again.

He was looking forward to that. Thinking back to the

evening of the ball, he recalled how he'd been dying to kiss her lips from the minute they'd started dancing. They'd looked so soft and lush, and he'd been anxious to taste them. Taste her.

He hadn't been disappointed. She'd been so fresh. So honest in her responses to him. He couldn't wait to be with her.

Morgan leaned back in his chair and pictured her petite body. She was so small and feminine. Her breasts weren't overly large, just perfectly proportioned. She had a slim waist and a backside right out of his dreams. Firm. Compact.

It must be from all the cleaning she did, he mused. She looked toned and healthy, and he was ready to get reacquainted with every part of her.

If she'd give him the chance.

Chapter Twenty-Six

After slipping on a silvery-blue zip-up sweater and gray flannel slacks, Brooke Anne put a bottle of wine in the freezer to chill, placed her beautiful roses on her coffee table and sat down to work on her Christmas puzzle.

She was too excited about seeing Morgan to fuss with dusting and cleaning the bathroom, or to worry about her decorating style.

All that mattered to her at the moment was that they would be together—and without a heavy load of baggage between them this time. He would be seeing her exactly for who she was, with no wrong notions to muddy his perception.

If he was disappointed, then so be it. At least he'd be disappointed with *her,* not someone he thought she was.

She wondered if Morgan had any idea how often she thought about him—which it seemed she did constantly. She hoped it didn't show on her face. If it did, he'd realize that she was much more attracted to him than she'd ever let on.

When she heard his knock, Brooke Anne forced herself to wait three seconds before opening the door. There was no reason for him to know just how anxious she was to see him.

He stood in her doorway, looking debonair in khakis and an olive-green shirt. A tie printed with some kind of designer-looking fish hung loosely at his collar.

And he seemed very happy to see her.

"Hi."

"Hi," she said, then stood there dumbly. Her mind had gone completely blank. Even walking seemed like it was going to take some effort. "Um, come on in," she finally added, moving aside to allow him to enter. "I was about to get the phone book and place an order. Do you like anything in particular?"

His eyes crinkled at the corners, as if he was privy to some secret joke. "Anything is fine," he said. "If we're talking about Chinese food."

Her heart stilled. She tucked her hair behind her ears and pasted a bright smile on her face. "I have your flowers here."

His gaze cascaded down her form, and she thought she spied a look of approval. Then Morgan finally glanced toward her living room. "They're pretty, aren't they?" he asked in a pleased tone.

"Yes." Before she lost her nerve, Brooke Anne took a step toward him and started talking fast. "Listen, I'm glad you came over the other day. On Saturday."

"I am, too."

"I'm not really sure what's going on between us, but I think it's been all mixed up," she continued. "At the diner, I let my mouth get the best of me, when I should have been trying to see things from your side, as well as mine."

Morgan shrugged. "How could you? We've barely had any time together. Passing notes doesn't count for much."

"I don't know," she said wistfully. "I kind of liked those notes. I sort of felt like a kid again—I got the same rush of adrenaline I used to get when I'd find out the boy I liked liked me."

Morgan closed the distance between them, his eyes bright with interest. "Is that how you've been feeling?"

She'd been babbling so much, she honestly couldn't recall what she'd been talking about. "I…yes?"

He cupped her shoulders with his palms, his thumbs making lazy circles as he did so. "What? You mean you don't know?"

"I'm not entirely sure," she corrected, hardly able to keep track of their conversation because his hands had shifted to her back as he edged even closer. Tenderly, they massaged her tense body, and she slowly became enveloped in his arms.

Her fingers reached for his chest. Held herself steady.

He pressed her toward him. The next thing she knew, they were standing face-to-face, as close together as if they'd been dancing. Except she had a feeling that Morgan was far from thinking about fancy footwork.

What to do? Part of her wanted to pull from his embrace, yank him closer and feel his mouth against hers.

But she panicked. "Morgan?" she asked in a small voice. "About dinner—"

"Anything. I'll take anything," he replied. Then he kissed her.

His lips felt just as good as she remembered. He nibbled and teased, and chewed on her bottom lip when she gasped. Then he plunged his tongue deeper, making her forget all about gentleness and sweetness.

Suddenly, there was only the present. Nothing that had happened before mattered.

Neither did their future.

All that mattered was Morgan's lips against hers, the feel of his warm hands on the small of her back and the exquisite way his body molded to hers.

Visions of the two of them together, making love on her down comforter, filled her mind. She knew they would fit well together then, too. He would entice her with kisses, tease her with slow caresses, charm her with sweet words and tender requests.

There was a new level of intimacy to their kisses now—as if the last barrier between them had fallen. "Brooke, you're so sweet," Morgan murmured, punctuating each word with featherlight brushes of his lips along her neck…the base of her throat…her breast.

He lowered her zipper a few inches and slipped his hand inside her sweater. The contrast between his warm skin and the cool metal made her inhale sharply.

"I love this," she breathed.

Morgan must have felt the same way because her zipper was edging down, her sternum, past her waist. Finally, he unfastened it and smoothed apart the soft fabric.

"Look at you," he said quietly, appreciation evident in his voice.

Tilting her head back, she glanced at him questioningly.

But his attention had settled on her lavender bra, with the plastic-flower clasp in the front. With a flick of his fingers, he opened it, freeing her to his steady gaze.

He met her eyes. "You're lovely, Brooke Anne."

She could only speak the truth. "You make me feel that way."

Morgan palmed her gently, driving her crazy as he rubbed her nipple with a callused thumb. She shivered from the contact.

And moaned softly when he kissed her deeply again.

Brooke Anne gripped his hips and reveled in the sensations. She felt uninhibited. Special.

As if she was loved.

Love?

Was that what she was feeling?

Was she ready for that?

With a ragged sigh, she pulled away and was thankful when Morgan did nothing to stop her. Tugging the two halves of her sweater together, she stammered, "I think…I think…we ought to talk a little bit, now."

His eyes lit up. "Absolutely. I want you, Brooke."

Oh! "Not about that. About us. About our feelings." Trying to look tough even though her bra was unfastened and her sweater was unzipped, she said, "I still think we have some issues to resolve."

"What do you need settled?" Morgan murmured, running a hand through her hair.

"Our feelings."

Wariness entered his eyes. "What do you mean?"

"I mean what I said. I think we should have a clear understanding between us before we let ourselves go any further."

Stepping back, Morgan rubbed his forehead and cast her a regretful glance. Then he coughed. "I think I'd better go sit down."

Feeling bereft, Brooke Anne watched him cross the room. She turned her back, clasped her bra and zipped her sweater. Then, hesitantly, she sat next to him and tried not to think of all the things that they could be doing if she'd just kept her mouth shut.

"Brooke Anne? You…you're exactly right about the two of us needing to talk. I think we have a lot to discuss before we go any further."

Although this had been her idea, Brooke Anne was too afraid to start. Simply nodding, she waited for him to continue.

"I…I've kind of told you this, but not in so many words. My parents expected a lot from me. They wanted a kid they could be proud of." He looked at her from the corner of his eye. "Good grades. Good manners. Pleasant demeanor."

"And you had all those things?"

"I did. I did well in school. Went to a good college. Got my degree in the requisite four years. Got my MBA, too. Found a good job…got promotions."

She studied him. He had leaned forward and was resting his elbows on his knees. "I'm sure they were proud of you," she said.

"They were. Are." He exhaled. "I learned my work ethic from them—persistence, diligence, honesty—but not how to communicate." He waited for her reaction.

She fought hard to keep her expression neutral. Hurting for him, she rested her hand on his arm. "What do you mean?"

"I never felt especially close to them. We never really *said* much to each other. I never felt like if I had been sent to the principal's office, flunked out of school, or been fired, that they'd still feel the same way about me. I've never felt that un-conditional love."

Brooke Anne thought of her own family and of her last con-versation with her mother. She squeezed his arm. "I'm sure they do love you unconditionally, Morgan. You're their son."

"Maybe." He took a deep breath, as if summoning up a great deal of courage. "Brooke Anne, I know how to do a lot of things, but not how to convey my emotions very well. If I've seemed distant, it hasn't been because I'm that way inside."

Patting his arm gently, she said, "I like how you are, right now. I don't want to change you."

Now it was her turn. He deserved complete honesty after baring his soul. "Although you know how sensitive I've been about our differences in finances, I've been carrying around skeletons, too. Two years ago, before I moved here…I had a serious boyfriend. I thought…I thought we had a future to-gether, but it was obviously one-sided. He broke up with me in front of all our friends one night, after he'd had too much to drink."

"Oh, babe," Morgan said softly, pulling her into his arms.

Her lip trembled. "It gets worse. See, I guess he'd been see-ing someone else at the same time. Everyone had known about it but me. I was completely, publicly embarrassed."

"He sounds like a loser."

"Oh, he was…but knowing that didn't make what I was feel-ing any easier," she said, hoping Morgan realized just how hard it had been to share her story. "I've been afraid to trust anyone ever since."

Understanding dawned in his eyes. "Oh. Well. I see."

She shook her head. "No, you don't. What I've been trying to tell you is that I haven't been ready to start a new relation-ship, or to try to trust anyone until…you." She swallowed hard. "I really care about you."

His breath hitched, followed by a small chuckle. "Damn. You did it again."

Trepidation coursed through her body. Was he laughing at her? Right after she'd bared her soul to him? She moved away, only to be caught back up in his arms. "Brooke Anne, I meant you beat me to it again. I've been trying to summon up the nerve to tell you that you're special to me—really special—but you said it first."

She stared at him in surprise. "Really?"

"Really," he said, kissing her softly. "I care for you very much."

There. Finally. They'd each made their true, honest emotions known. Gone were the doubts and uncertainties that she'd harbored over the past two years since Russell broke up with her. That had plagued her during the past few weeks with Morgan.

Maybe their differences really didn't matter all that much.

At long last, she felt secure—as if she was on even ground. And because of that, she felt more desirable than she had in ages.

When she met his lips again, it was with pure pleasure and a new awareness of him. They had a real, solid relationship now. "Morgan, are you hungry?"

"God, yes," he said, brushing his hands down her body once more.

"I mean, for food? For Chinese?"

His gaze lingered on her for a moment, then he turned his head to the frosted windowpane, the card table littered with a thousand jigsaw pieces. "I am. Let's order Chinese food, do this puzzle and hang out, Brooke Anne."

"Just that?"

His expression whimsical, he nodded. "Just that. I'd like to spend a night just being with you. Getting to know you. We've got plenty of time ahead of us to do more, don't you think?"

"I do." Tears pricked her eyes as she realized the extent to which he cared for her. If he was willing to wait to make love until they knew each other better, it was a sure sign that he was completely serious about them building a relationship.

"Then go order some sweet-and-sour pork."

"I've got some wine, too."

"Terrific," he said with a smile. "I can't think of a better way to spend the evening."

She bit her lip to keep from saying anything.

"Almost," he amended with an answering grin. "I almost can't."

Chapter Twenty-Seven

Five days later, seated by Morgan's side at Tomi's concert, Brooke Anne found it impossible not to laugh. There they were again, dressed up and seated next to each other. And, just like at the ball, an unspoken tension seemed to accompany them. Both were torn between the happiness of being together and an increasing awareness that there were still issues between them that would one day have to be ironed out.

At least, that was Brooke Anne's take on the situation. But she'd be a liar if she pretended the only thing about Morgan Carmichael that interested her was his conversational skills.

There were quite a few other talents he possessed that were firmly rooted in her mind—the way he kissed for example. So slowly, so expertly, as if she consumed his thoughts when they were together.

And even when they were apart.

She couldn't wait to kiss him again…but that wasn't all she was looking forward to. She was anxious to reacquaint herself with the way he felt next to her, their bodies locked in a no-holds-barred embrace, and wondered how things would be if they progressed further than that.

Just the thought of the two of them being together, with no distractions, no words left unsaid, caused her pulse to quicken. She wanted to be alone with Morgan. Explore every inch of him. Feel his bare skin against her own. Savor the desire for him as long as she could.

Did he feel the same way? Was he as anxious as she was to venture into a new dimension of their relationship?

She hoped so. She'd dressed with care. Her rose-colored cashmere sweater was one that her mother had given her years ago. And the knit fabric of her long black skirt hugged her body in a way that made her appreciate all the exercise she got cleaning for a living.

She'd even bought a small bottle of new perfume. Thinking about where she'd applied it, Brooke Anne felt a little tremor go through her. Had she really been anticipating that he was going to be kissing all those places?

Well, to be honest… Yes.

Swallowing hard, she turned her attention back to the choir.

"You okay?" she whispered to Morgan, as the group sang a compelling version of "Hark, the Herald Angels Sing."

"I'm better than okay. The choir's terrific, and it's fun watching Tomasina."

Brooke Anne glanced over her shoulder to where three of her other friends sat. She smiled brightly at Vivian, Monique and Karen. All three of them had given her a thumbs-up when they'd seen Morgan. And he'd seemed happy to have the chance to meet them after the concert. That meant the world to her—that he wanted to meet her friends.

Morgan put his arm around her and she settled in closer to him, then turned her attention to Tomasina, who had just stepped up for a solo.

The special thing about her best friend was that she knew when she looked good, which was pretty much all the time. You could tell because there'd be a slight upward tilt to her chin, a little more attitude in her step and a gleam in her eye that dared any observer to think otherwise.

Brooke Anne was used to it. In fact, it was what made Tomi, *Tomi.* Brooke Anne had laughed when she'd heard Tomi's husband make a comment about it once. He'd teasingly stated that it was hard being married to a woman who woke up beautiful and only got better-looking throughout the day.

Tomasina had given him a nice kiss for that.

Tonight, dressed in a red satin robe with a snow-white collar, Tomi looked ethereal. As she sang "What Child Is This" more than one person dabbed at their eyes. Without a doubt, Tomi's voice was inspiring.

Brooke Anne looked over at Morgan to see his reaction. He appeared transfixed by Tomi's beautiful contralto voice. Brooke Anne was glad she'd brought him to the concert. In fact, she was glad about the general direction things were going with Morgan since that evening they'd spent at her apartment, eating Chinese food.

By now they'd put in enough phone time together to get a good sense of each other's likes and dislikes, Brooke Anne had the feeling that they'd be able to overcome their differences.

When the concert ended, after the crowd had given the choir a standing ovation, Brooke Anne took Morgan over to Vivian, Monique and Karen.

"Nice to meet you," he said, after all the introductions had been made. "I've been looking forward to it."

"The feeling's mutual," Monique replied.

Morgan laughed. Turning to Brooke Anne, he said, "What have you been telling your friends about me?"

The women shared secret smiles. "That's confidential," Vivian said sagely.

"Only that you're the best thing that's ever happened to her," Karen piped in.

Morgan pulled Brooke Anne toward him in a one-armed hug. "Whoa! Looks like I need to go hang out at your office."

As she thought about their endless jibes and girl talk, Brooke Anne shook her head quickly. "No way. You've got your own job. You stay there."

The three women laughed. "That's okay, Morgan. We'll expect to hear regular updates about you from now on," Karen said.

Embarrassed by the conversation, Brooke Anne eyed Morgan. She couldn't tell if the teasing bothered him or not. Then he gave her that smile—the one he saved just for her.

It suddenly felt as if her whole body was on alert, waiting for him to touch her again. Kiss her. Wrap her in his arms.

Take her to bed.

As Vivian and Monique smiled at her knowingly, Brooke Anne slipped out from under Morgan's arm. "Um, I think we'd better go find Tomasina and congratulate her," she said.

"Whatever you want," Morgan replied, much to the amusement of her girlfriends.

Quickly, they said their goodbyes, then went in search of Tomi.

"You were great, Tomi," Brooke Anne said once they found her, standing with Ron and Vanessa. "I think your voice just keeps getting better and better."

"It was a good night," she replied, her gaze panning from Brooke Anne to Morgan. "Where are you off to now?"

Brooke Anne was confused. "Aren't you having a party, like usual?"

"Yes, but it's just a *family* party this year," Tomi said with a smile for Vanessa. "I'm afraid you two will have to find something else to do."

Her friend's words were a complete surprise. "Tomi, what are you talking about? I thought you said—"

Tomi glanced at the clock on the wall and gasped. "My goodness, will you look at the time!" she said. "I've got to go. The mall closes at nine and I promised Vanessa we'd get her picture taken with Santa before heading home. Y'all have a fun time tonight."

Tomasina turned her back on Brooke Anne and Morgan and within seconds was lost in the crowd.

"I can't believe that!" Brooke Anne exclaimed, as she and

Morgan walked out to the parking lot. "I've always gone to her house after the Christmas concert."

"I think it was her not-so-subtle way of saying that we ought to do something a little more romantic instead." Morgan opened her car door for her. "Just the two of us."

"You think so?"

"I do."

"Any ideas?"

He gave her a speculative glance. "A couple."

Memories of being wrapped in his arms on her couch came tumbling forward. "How about a late dinner?"

"Sounds good by me."

They drove along the narrow downtown streets, the hilly terrain making Brooke Anne's stomach jump—or maybe it was Morgan who'd put the butterflies there. By contrast, he looked so calm, so self-assured. Focused.

Brooke Anne was more aware of him than ever. His scent, his laugh…that wayward curl that fell across his forehead. Oh, she wanted to be near him. She hoped dinner would be quick.

An hour later, Morgan rubbed his thumb over the fine bones of Brooke Anne's hand and wondered if it was possible for their server to be any slower. He was in a hurry to get out of the restaurant, find somewhere secluded and pull Brooke into his arms. And if her heated glances were any indication, she was in a hurry, too.

It had been too long. Too many days had passed without any body contact, without her kisses. He'd spent hours daydreaming about how it would feel to hold her close again.

When had he gone from being attracted to her to…in love?

He poked at his chicken, then set his fork down again. He had no interest in food.

"Aren't you hungry?" Brooke Anne asked him.

"What? No, not really. How about you? You haven't touched much of your meal, either."

She looked at her plate. "Gosh, I haven't. I guess my mind has been on other things."

"Such as?"

A slow wash of red spread across her face. "Nothing important…really."

He recognized that catch in her tone, that look of longing she was trying to hide, because he felt the exact same way. "What do you want to do?" he asked, the huskiness of his voice betraying his innocent question.

She licked her lips. "I want…I want to be alone with you, Morgan, to tell you the truth."

He stared at her mouth, at the spot where her tongue had darted out, and swallowed hard. Signaling their waiter, he said, "Check, please."

Brooke Anne smiled at Morgan. "You know what this means now, don't you?"

He couldn't wait for her to tell him. "What?"

"We're leaving yet another meal unfinished."

"Let's just stop eating. Food doesn't seem to work for us."

She met his gaze. "I couldn't agree more."

Chapter Twenty-Eight

Morgan took her to his town house. He hadn't meant to. He'd planned on going for a walk after dinner, enjoying some scintillating conversation, then charming her into kissing him again.

But the weather had turned rainy, he had no conversation and she already wanted to kiss him.

The least he could do was make sure they had privacy—and they were both too old to go parking.

If Brooke Anne felt uncomfortable being at his house, she didn't say a word. She just smiled at him as soon as he closed the front door, and stepped into his arms.

Just like that.

Her body felt every bit as petite and feminine as he remembered. Taking care not to crush her, Morgan curved her close to him and, unable to stop himself, slipped a hand underneath her sweater.

She had smooth skin. Like velvet. He flattened his palm against her back, savoring every inch of her, little by little. Somehow they made it to his couch.

"Brooke Anne, I've missed you," he said softly, as he bent to kiss her. "I've missed being this close to you…." His voice drifted off at her inviting smile.

"Then come here," she said, and pulled him toward her.

The offer was impossible to resist. Morgan touched her lips with his, sensed her passion. Her welcome. He traced the line of her mouth with his tongue…tempted her to let him in. And grunted with pleasure when she did just that.

Within minutes, they were lying on the couch, and he was helping her off with her sweater. She seemed so sweet to him. His fingers trembled as he brushed them across each of her ribs, and finally reached the edge of her bra.

She didn't even hesitate. Looking him in the eye Brooke Anne unhooked the clasp nestled between her breasts. Creamy flesh spilled forth. The lacy garment fell to the floor. And Morgan's blood heated up another hundred degrees. "Brooke Anne," he said quietly. "I've wanted you so badly."

She inhaled shakily. "Me, too."

She met his lips and he caught her up in his embrace. She was giving herself to him. In trust.

The knowledge made him heady.

Because they had all night, he held her close and then leaned back, prepared to take his time. He gazed at her torso, noticed the spattering of freckles along her collarbone. Drank in the sight of her firm pale flesh, each breast tinged in pink…and he cupped her tenderly.

She responded by moaning, raising her arms and kissing him greedily.

It was only natural for him to trail his lips lower. To her jaw. To the line of freckles. To the places his fingers had already been.

Brooke Anne buried her hands in his hair, as if she didn't want him to stop.

He flicked his tongue against her nipple. Watched with pleasure as it hardened into a tight bud. Glanced up to see Brooke Anne's reaction.

Her eyes were closed, her back arched.

Morgan smiled.

This was exactly how he knew making love to her would be. Slow. Exquisite. Thoroughly enjoyable. He ran his fingers over the jut of her hip. Skimmed the small indention at the top of her thigh. Felt the satin of her underwear…and explored some more. Brooke Anne gasped and turned her head to one side.

This was good. Very good.

The sheer feel of her—and the knowledge that she was offering herself to him—did more for his body than any amount of sexual expertise ever could. Her hands stroked his back, coaxing him on.

He couldn't wait to enter her…to luxuriate in her warmth. He had the distinct thought that Brooke Anne was transforming him, making him a better person, a more complete man….

"We ought to move to my bed," Morgan said, pressing quick kisses to her lips.

She sat up slowly. Stared at him in confusion, breathing heavily, as if she'd just run a race. "Oh. All right."

He stood, bringing her with him. Circling his hands around her waist, he kissed her temple. She nuzzled his neck and looked up at him uncertainly. "I, uh, haven't had much experience with this."

He didn't care. "It's okay." Tenderly, he picked her up and laid her on his bed. Her white pale skin contrasted sharply with the dark plaid of his comforter. "You're beautiful, Brooke Anne," he said reverently. Slowly, he pulled off his slacks, then his boxers, until he stood naked in front of her.

He met her gaze and hoping his obvious enthusiasm didn't scare her, forced himself to stand still while she quietly took in the sight of him.

All she did was hold her arms out to him. "Morgan," she whispered, as he bent over her.

Hooking his thumbs under the elastic band of her panties, he edged them down over her thighs. Then he pressed her to him, gasping when their bodies made contact.

It felt so right. So *real*. Morgan slid his hands around her, smiling when he felt how ready she was for him.

She moved her hips against his. Eyes wide, Brooke Anne moaned.

Deftly, Morgan retrieved a condom from his bedside table, opened the packet and sheathed himself. She covered his shoulder and his neck with little butterfly kisses as he did so.

"Brooke Anne," he said, positioning himself over her. "You've got to believe…there's no one else…."

"But you," she finished, when their bodies finally joined. "There's no one else for me but you."

There was nothing more to say.

BROOKE ANNE WOKE UP several hours later, her body curiously sore, yet completely relaxed. Then she remembered what she'd been doing before she went to sleep.

She blushed at the memory. It was as if a dam had been broken in their relationship. Suddenly, all they wanted was to be alone with each other. Naked. Exploring.

Stretching against Morgan's sleeping form, she recalled the patience and care he'd shown the first time they'd made love—and the passion he'd displayed when they'd done so again, the fierce expression in his eyes in the second before he'd climaxed.

Right at the moment when she had.

It was the stuff fantasies were made of.

"Brooke Anne? You awake?" Morgan asked groggily, flopping his calf over her thigh.

"Yes."

He propped his head up on his hand and caressed her with a sleepy, shimmering gaze. "You okay?"

"Oh, yes."

That brought a smile from him—an incredibly masculine one. "Me, too." Yawning, he asked, "What time is it?"

"Almost midnight, I think."

"You want to stay here with me?"

Did she? Part of her never wanted the night to end…but another part was ready to go home and let the past few hours sweep over her in private. "Maybe I should get on home."

Morgan studied her face, then cast his eyes downward, skimming her body with a heated look.

"Why don't you stay just a little longer?" he asked, as he bent to nuzzle her neck.

"Umm," she muttered, distracted by the feel of his stubbly cheeks rubbing against her tender flesh. "I...probably should..."

He raised his head, leaving her body practically screaming in dismay. "You should what?" he rasped, devilment in his eyes.

What could she say? Her body was in charge now. "Stay," she murmured.

As he brought his lips back down to her neck, Morgan whispered into her ear, "Good choice."

WHEN BROOKE ANNE WOKE again, she peered at the digital clock next to the bed, then at Morgan. Those khaki eyes were wide open and staring at her intently. "Hey," she said.

"Hey."

"It's 10:00 a.m.," she mumbled, waiting for him to slide an arm around her and pull her closer. "I can't believe it's so late."

Instead, he sat up. Glanced away. "I can't, either. I've got to get going."

"Where?" she asked, a warning bell sounding in her head.

"Work."

"Work? It's Sunday."

"I...I've got a project that's due on Monday morning. I wasn't able to spend enough time on it this week." For a moment it looked as if he was going to say more, but then he shook his head. "Sorry. I'd better hit the shower," he said before climbing out of bed and disappearing from the room. A few seconds later, the bathroom door clicked shut.

Well, so much for inviting her to shower with him, Brooke

Anne mused. Still wrapped in a warm haze from their wonderful night, she looked around his taupe-colored bedroom. She noted the expensive custom curtains and bedspread, the mahogany wood floor and the intricately woven Persian carpet over it. The antique figurine that looked as if it had cost a year's salary. Slowly but surely, a sense of foreboding coursed through her.

What was she doing here? Had what they'd just shared been a mistake? Old feelings of being betrayed by Russell assailed her. The memory of cleaning Caroline's house while Morgan breezed in for a party tumbled forth.

Panic set in.

The sound of the shower coming to life spurred Brooke Anne to action. She suddenly felt embarrassed and all too naked. Exposed. Vulnerable.

She eased herself out of bed and slipped on her clothes, then found her shoes where she'd kicked them off last night.

She made the bed because the sight of Morgan's expensive sheets and designer coat lying in a mess at the foot of his plasma TV made her feel at loose ends.

The water pipes groaned as Morgan shut the shower off, causing Brooke Anne's heart to beat a little faster.

Not wanting him to find her sitting on his bed when he came out, she ventured into the kitchen. Gleaming stainless-steel appliances lined the walls. The countertops were made of mottled brown granite and felt cool and sleek under her hands. The cool surface helped calm Brooke Anne's nerves. Maybe she was just overreacting. Maybe she was being ridiculous— Morgan really did have to go in to work. He hadn't meant to be so abrupt.

When Morgan appeared in the kitchen doorway, smelling of soap and aftershave, she smiled, ready to forget the awkwardness of the last few minutes.

"You're still here," he said.

Yes, she was. Her bottom lip trembled. She bit it hard. Struggling to keep her voice calm, she said, "I couldn't leave. I don't have a car, remember?"

For a second, he looked guilty. "Sorry, I didn't mean that the way it sounded. I just thought when I saw the bed made and you gone that…" His voice drifted off.

"You thought what, Morgan? That I'd cleaned your house and then left?"

Something in his gaze flickered dangerously. "That's not what I said."

"Well, I have all my things together, if you're ready to take me home."

He glanced at his shiny designer coffeemaker. "Do you want coffee or something?"

Or something? Like a little warmth, perhaps? "No, thank you."

"Okay, I'll drive you home, then."

The car ride home was painfully awkward. Brooke Anne did everything she could to keep her mouth shut and her expression vacant. What good would it do to tell him that she'd expected some sweet words and a loving hug this morning?

The two of them were obviously completely different. Oh, they enjoyed each other on a certain level, that went without saying. But as far as a basis for a long-term commitment went, they didn't have much.

She wasn't sure anymore.

After what seemed like hours, Morgan pulled into her building's parking lot. "I'll call you soon, Brooke."

"Don't worry about it."

He raised an eyebrow. "What are you talking about? After last night…"

"I'm not sure if last night was a good idea. This morning is telling me that maybe it wasn't."

"I don't know why you're saying that."

"You don't know why? Morgan, you practically bolted from your bed after you saw me in it."

"That was only because I was late for work."

She felt so used and uncomfortable, she couldn't resist snapping at him. "On a Sunday?"

He looked away. "I've told you that I'm not great at expressing myself."

"And I've told you that I don't deal very well with rejection."

The words hung between them. Morgan stared at her warily. Brooke Anne fought hard to stare back and not let herself become overwhelmed by emotion.

"I'm sorry about this morning. Really." He ran his fingers through his damp hair and sighed. "Look, how about I stop by later tonight? Tomorrow?"

"I'm going to be busy with the hospital. The Christmas party for the kids is on Thursday."

"Do you need some help?"

"With what? Are you going to help me wrap Barbies?"

"I thought maybe I could give a donation."

It took every ounce of her strength not to fling something at his head and tell him that giving someone a couple of hundred dollars was *not* going to make everything okay.

But then…her mind stilled. Who was she kidding? She'd taken money from him in a heartbeat. And, Lord knew, the Christmas fund at the hospital could use all the help it could get.

"Do what you want, Morgan," she whispered.

His earnest expression collapsed. "Brooke—"

With that, she got out of the car, and walked up the three flights of stairs to her apartment.

So different than Morgan's town house that it was almost laughable.

Chapter Twenty-Nine

"Did you get the packages I sent last week?"

Brooke repositioned the phone under her ear and strove for patience. "I did, Mom, thank you. I'll have mine out to you soon."

"Don't worry about presents this year, sweetie. It'll be enough just to know that you're happy."

There was something in her mom's voice that made her wary. "What are you talking about?"

"Brooke Anne, can we be frank with each other? I know you're having a difficult time financially right now—"

Her shoulders slumped. "I am."

"—And I know you're not quite ready to see Russell yet."

"No, I'm not." Brooke settled more comfortably on the couch and felt the weight slowly lift off her shoulders. It felt so good to finally be honest with her mother. Why hadn't she told her the truth in the first place?

"*Is* there a Morgan?"

"Yes…but things with him are confusing."

"Why?"

"He…he's completely different than me. He's emotionally closed-off, and rich."

"I see…."

"I think I love him," Brooke Anne continued in a rush, "but I never know how's he's going to act from minute to minute."

"Sounds like he needs you, my dear."

She couldn't help smiling. Her mother thought so highly of her. "I don't know. Everything about him—his job, his house, his clothes, his friends—screams money. And just when it seemed like we were finally past all that, he started acting weird and distant."

"Gosh, Brooke Anne. He sounds awful."

"No. No, he's not."

"What's he like, then?" her mom inquired.

"He's fun, and he tries hard. Morgan didn't have a lot of love growing up…. His mom's not like you. He has a hard time expressing his feelings." She shrugged her shoulders to loosen them. "But he did write me some notes. And he sent me roses once."

"Ah."

Ah? "What does that mean?"

"Just that it sounds to me like you two might be a pretty good match, after all. *You* need *him* to remember what love is like…and *he* needs *you* to show him what love is really all about."

"Do you think so? You don't think we're too different? That a relationship between us is doomed?"

"No. No, I don't, Brooke Anne."

"But, Mom—"

"Honey, everything about you and Russell seemed so right…but it wasn't at all, was it? You can just never predict what's going to happen in the future, so you have to take your chances."

No, SHE COULDN'T PREDICT anything, Brooke Anne decided, as she sat at her desk the following morning and visited with her employees. On the spur of the moment, they'd decided to have an impromptu Christmas party, and for some reason, they'd made her the guest of honor.

"I don't know if I should tell you this," she said, glancing at each of the four other women, "but the boss is supposed to treat the employees to a Christmas lunch. Not the other way around."

Tomi picked up another one of Vivian's sand tarts before replying. "Who says?"

"It's just how it's done."

"If we waited for you to organize our party, we'd probably still be waiting on Groundhog Day," Karen said between bites of a pecan tart.

Brooke Anne couldn't deny that. She really had been overwhelmed.

"We know you've been working hard," Monique said gently. "You shouldn't feel bad about us doing this."

"Yeah. You can repay us by telling us what's been going on with you and Morgan."

Vivian nodded. "We heard all about the incident at the soiree house."

Brooke Anne laughed but deftly changed the subject. "If Tomi and I had had any idea that place would be so big, we would've stopped by every one of your houses and made you come with us."

"I'm glad you didn't. Cleaning expensive stuff makes me nervous," Karen said.

While the others argued the benefits of cleaning houses versus office buildings, Brooke Anne stared at the treats spread out in front of them and tried to think of another way to deflect the conversation from her love life. "Thanks again for throwing that feast," she said, when the conversation had died down. "At least, I do have a little something for all of you, as well—your Christmas bonuses."

The women smiled as she produced the envelopes, but none of them held out their hands. In fact, the way they were sharing glances made Brooke Anne feel totally confused. "What's going on?"

Tomi shifted restlessly. "We got to talking and, well…we don't know if we really need bonuses this year."

"What?"

Tomi looked at her co-workers, who nodded. She bit her lip. "We were thinking that this party is enough. We'll plan on bonuses next year."

Brooke Anne was stunned. "But, Tomi—what about that Visa bill and everything?"

"Ronnie got a good bonus of his own."

"We know money's tight for you, too, Brooke Anne," Karen said. "And with everything you've been through with Morgan… It just doesn't seem right to take money you made by going on that date. We don't need the checks that bad."

Brooke Anne opened her mouth, then shut it just as quickly. Her employees' refusal of their hard-won bonuses had completely thrown her for a loop.

Tomi popped open a bottle of fake champagne. "Who wants some of this fancy cider?"

"I'll have some," Monique said, holding up a plastic cup. "Gosh, look at us, acting all high-class. Having our own little office party."

Brooke Anne fought hard to regain control. "Listen. You're all going to take these checks, and you'd better go buy something nice with them, too. I'm proud that I'm able to give them to you."

Karen's eyes shone with respect, but she kept her hands tucked firmly in her jeans. "You spend it, Brooke Anne."

"Oh, no. I *want* to do this. Really! I've worked hard to be able to do this. If you don't take them, I'll feel horrible."

"It's practically blood money."

No. No, it wasn't. It was money rightfully earned, and her employees deserved every cent. "Everything that's been going on with Morgan, that's my business. It has nothing to do with the fact that you *deserve* your bonuses. And the problems Morgan and I have been having are mostly because of some stupid hang-ups about love."

"So…you like him?" Vivian asked.

"I do," Brooke Anne whispered. "I like him a lot."

"And does he know that?"

She thought about the night they'd made love. About the way they'd parted in the morning. The things they'd said to each other…and hadn't. "Yes. He does. At least I think he does."

"Humph," Tomi sniffed.

"So, please take the checks and let me tell you Merry Christmas."

The other women looked at each other, then one by one stepped forward and accepted an envelope. But instead of receiving a smile and thank-you, Brooke Anne found herself being hugged by each one of her employees. The contact reinforced what she'd long suspected—no matter what, going to the dance for the bonus money had been worth it. She loved her friends, and loved that she was able to show her appreciation in a way that would make their holidays brighter. Blinking furiously, she said, "Merry Christmas."

"Merry Christmas right back at ya," Vivian replied with a laugh. "Now, who's ready for another pecan tart?"

"WARREN, DO YOU HAVE A minute?" Brooke Anne asked as she poked her head into WJB Shoes the following afternoon.

Warren glanced up from the catalog he was reviewing with a tall, model-thin woman, and instantly motioned Brooke Anne inside. "Now, you are a person who's been on my mind lately," he said, smiling.

"Why is that?"

"Well, a certain someone came in here looking for you."

"He told me," she said. "I still can't believe Morgan did that. I think he went to every shoe store in Cincinnati looking for me."

"Ah, but he found his answers here."

She chuckled, then got to the reason for her visit. "I was wondering if you might have a half hour or so to have some tea today? I think there's a nice tea shop around the corner."

He shook his head. "Oh, no."

Taken aback, Brooke Anne turned toward the door. "Oh. I'm sorry. I'll just—"

"No, my dear. You didn't let me finish. I have everything we need for tea here."

She looked around the shop. "Here?"

Warren pointed to his back room. "There. Why don't you take a moment and look around? I'll go make the tea. Elise will assist you if you'd like to try anything on."

As Warren glided away, Brooke Anne felt Elise's jet-black eyes boring into her.

"I'm just going to look around," she said.

Elise nodded. "No problem."

"Does he really make tea back there?" Brooke Anne couldn't resist asking.

Elise's perfect features broke into a genuine smile. "Like nothing I've ever tasted. It almost puts the Excelsior Royal Hotel's tea to shame."

"Really," Brooke Anne murmured, wondering if Warren had been talking with Elise about her situation.

"Yeah. Well, again, let me know if you'd like to try anything on."

Brooke Anne wandered around the salon, thinking about how, just a few weeks ago, she'd been too afraid to even set foot inside this shoe store. Now here she was, about to have tea with the owner.

And feeling pretty good about it.

Warren appeared in the back doorway. "It's ready, love."

Warren's office was impressive—every bit as elegant as the showroom, yet more inviting. A sitting area with heavy wood furniture graced one corner, and a small kitchen, consisting of a compact refrigerator and stove, flanked the far wall. On the antique cherry coffee table stood a beautiful tea service, complete with a silver sugar bowl and china cups and saucers.

"This is amazing," Brooke Anne said, as she seated herself. "Maybe I should stop by here more often."

"I hope you will." After they'd both sipped the exquisite tea, Warren gazed at her directly. "How *is* Morgan?"

"He's fine. We're trying to come to grips with some things."

"He seemed quite smitten when he was here searching for you."

"We're pretty different, you know."

"Different can be nice."

"I suppose. Morgan has some trouble expressing himself. And I...I guess sometimes my insecurities still get the best of me."

He smiled. "Everything didn't magically get better when you put on your gold slippers and a new dress?"

"No. The pretty things gave me some confidence, but they didn't solve my problems."

"So, do you know what you need to do?"

Brooke Anne took a deep breath. "Stop blaming myself for what happened with Russell. Be willing to trust someone so different from me."

"And have you done those things?"

She thought about that. "I'm able to do them some of the time. Eighty percent, maybe."

Warren sipped his tea. "Some would say eighty percent is impressive."

"Would you?"

He looked surprised. "Of course. We all have problems, my dear. Even me. The key to living is to work through them until you find happiness." Warren walked over to the kitchen and picked up a tray of beautifully decorated cookies. "Have a cookie, Brooke Anne. I just purchased them from the bakery down the street."

She took one without hesitation—and bit into bliss.

Chapter Thirty

Morgan was taking a stab at cleaning off his desk when his sister showed up at the office.

"Hey!" Caroline said, plopping into the chair across from him. "I haven't seen you since the soiree, so I thought I'd pay you a little visit."

"Must be my lucky day."

If she was caught off guard by his sarcastic comment, she didn't show it. "What's new?"

He shifted in his seat. "Nothing much."

Her eyes glowed. "That's not what I heard."

"What have you heard?"

"I heard you've been escorting a certain attractive blonde around town lately."

"Who told you that?"

Her lips twitched. "I have my resources…and I bumped into Breva at the diner two days ago."

Wasn't there supposed to be some kind of boss-secretary confidentiality privilege? One that prevented secretaries from divulging private information? "Is that why you're here?"

"You guessed it. Who is she?"

"You don't know her. Not really…"

"Now I'm even more intrigued. Come on. Tell me about her. What's her name?"

"Brooke Anne Kressler."

Caroline scrunched up her forehead. "For some reason that name sounds familiar."

"Maybe. She cleaned your house the other day. Brooke Anne owns Jovial Janitors. She cleans on occasion."

Surprise, then speculation, entered Caroline's brown eyes. "Well, my goodness."

Morgan immediately rushed to Brooke Anne's defense. "What is that supposed to mean?"

"It means that it's about time you finally fell in love."

An odd sense of bewilderment came over him. "I thought you'd be disappointed. Weren't you and Mom trying to set me up with Alexia? Mom made it sound that way."

Caroline made a face. "Mom always liked Alexia more than I did. Besides, Alexia's had a lot of work done recently," she added in a stage whisper. "I mean, she's hardly the same girl I used to know."

He wasn't sure whether to be intrigued or appalled. "You…don't think it's strange that of all the women in the world, I've fallen for a tiny janitor?"

"If you want to know the truth, I'm amazed you've managed to find anyone who'll go out with you. I love you. And I'm glad you're my brother. But you've got serious emotional attachment issues."

"I'm working on those," Morgan said. "And I've gotten pretty good at letter writing."

"That's a start. So, what's next for the two of you? Want to bring her over for holiday tea?" She snapped her fingers. "I know! Why don't the two of you come to my Boxing Day gala!"

"I'll have to see. Brooke Anne's awfully busy right now. She volunteers as an elf for the Children's Hospital Christmas party."

"That's a great cause. I bet she'll be adorable. Bob and I donated some money to Children's Hospital to help out with gifts. Did you?"

"No." His shoulders slumped. "I offered, but it didn't come out right."

It's not too late, you know," Caroline said softly. "Actually a little bird told me they're in desperate need of a Santa for their Christmas party."

He stared at her in surprise.

"Don't worry, Morgan. One day I'm sure you're going to be a great communicator." And with that, his sister blew out of the room.

As her words hung in the air, he halfheartedly attempted to place the stacks of papers on his desk in some kind of order. There, in the middle of it all, were two sheets of his mono-grammed stationery—the kind he'd pulled out weeks ago when he'd given that first note to Tomasina.

A lot had happened since he'd first desperately attempted to communicate with Brooke Anne. Repeatedly, he'd pushed himself to become better at it. He still had a ways to go, but he'd definitely improved.

And he was determined to keep trying.

BROOKE ANNE AND TOMI were cleaning the interior design firm again. It was an opportunity for them to catch up with each other—although, admittedly, Brooke Anne did most of the talking. Tomi just nodded a lot and uttered the occasional word of understanding. So far they'd already covered Brooke Anne's visit with Warren and the impromptu Jovial Janitors party, and had now moved on to the topic of Brooke Anne's mother.

"Isn't it something how my mom was able to read my mind from hundreds of miles away?" she asked her friend.

"It's amazing, all right."

"She seems to think I should keep being patient with Morgan."

Tomi glanced up from the chair she was dusting. "Did he call you today?"

"He did. I think he feels bad about how he acted the morn-ing after…you know."

"He should."

"I know he likes me, Tomi, but I'm worried about what this relationship will be like a few months from now."

"Months from now?" Tomasina scoffed and arched a perfectly plucked ebony eyebrow. "Girl, you worry too much about stuff you can't control. What are you talking about?"

"I'm talking about whether we'll still have enough to talk about. If we'll still like each other."

"I don't know why you're so worried. Everything will work out fine," Tomi said, as they moved on to a particularly messy conference room. "You'd think these people never heard of a garbage can," she muttered.

Brooke Anne eyed the empty pizza boxes, paper plates and plastic cups, and wrinkled her nose. "It is a mess in here. You'd think designers would party more neatly." Scooping the used materials into her trash bag, she said, "I think you're being awfully flip about this. I'm really worried, Tomi."

Tomasina reached for a bottle of cleaning spray. "You, worried? The girl who started her own company two years ago? Who agreed to go on a date with some stranger so she could pay her talented, efficient workers their Christmas bonuses?"

"That was different—that was business."

Tomi sighed. "Don't you get it, Brooke Anne? None of us knows what's going to happen in the future, if that special someone in our life is still going to be the right person for us twenty years from now. You hope so. You pray so…but things happen." She pulled out a rag from the cleaning cart and started wiping down the table, cake crumbs falling to the carpet as she did so. "Take Vanessa, for instance."

"What do you mean? That baby is just as cute as she can be."

Tomi gave her a knowing look. "Of course she is, but she was also quite the little surprise. Ronnie and I weren't planning to have kids for a while." She shook her rag out in the garbage. "And what about in the future? What if Vanessa turns into a teenager?"

"Tomi, of course she'll turn into a teenager."

"Well, shouldn't I be worrying about that?"

"But this is different. You expect kids to change."

"You need to expect change in relationships, too, Brooke Anne. And not all changes have to be bad ones. Sometimes changes bring you closer."

"So…"

Tomasina rolled her eyes in mock irritation. "So, if Morgan makes you happy, be happy. If you love him—which you do, I might add—then love him. Appreciate what you have." She waved her arms dramatically, like a circus ringmaster. Raised her voice. "Bask in his attention. Put some effort into this relationship. Know that he's doing the same."

Tomasina was getting worked up. "All right…." Brooke Anne said.

But Tomi didn't hear her. "And, girl, stop analyzing each and every conversation and worrying about how things might be twenty years from now." She waved a finger at her. "Damn, you're making me crazy."

"Thanks, Tomi."

Her friend smiled. "Anytime."

They split up to finish the job—Tomasina vacuumed and Brooke Anne tackled the bathrooms. After about an hour, they met up again at the front door. Tomi removed her ankle weights and stretched her legs. "So…you off to your elf party tomorrow?"

"I am," she answered. "Want to change your mind about coming?"

"Nope."

"That's what I thought."

Tomasina grinned. "There are some things in life you can count on, Brooke Anne Kressler. You will always love Morgan Carmichael…and I will never dress up as an elf."

Brooke Anne nudged her playfully with the cleaning cart. "I'll be sure to remember that."

Chapter Thirty-One

Being an elf was not as easy as it looked. Kids cried and whined and parents grew frustrated, many of them choosing to stand back and watch, while Brooke Anne and the other volunteers made fools of themselves.

But then Santa Claus showed up and worked his magic. He ho, ho, hoed and chuckled merrily, patiently taking dozens of children on his lap and listening to their Christmas wishes. Brooke Anne watched as the kids once again became the sweet children she'd visited in the arts and crafts room over the past few months. They laughed and told jokes and munched their candy canes happily. Whoever played Santa this year deserved a special prize, she thought to herself.

After Santa left, things went much more smoothly. The elves handed out cookies and punch and presented the kids with their gifts, which was Brooke Anne's favorite part of the evening. Finally, the children left the hall, happy and worn-out.

Brooke Anne was jubilant and proud and more tired than she could ever remember being. She, along with the other twenty committee members, had made Christmas special for some very sick kids, and had given their parents a brief respite from the worry and exhaustion that permeated their lives.

It felt good; now, she just had to finish cleaning up.

Luckily, most of the mess had already been picked up by

the volunteers before they'd gone home. All that was really left to do was to mop the floor and wipe down the doors and walls.

Brooke Anne, the good Jovial Janitor that she was, had volunteered her company to do the cleanup. And since it just happened to be December 22, and her four employees were busy with their families, she was taking on the task by herself.

Retrieving a mop and bucket from their nesting place in the back of the kitchenette, she got to work. She filled the pail with soapy water, pulled on some gloves and began the cleanup in earnest.

She was about a fourth of the way through when she caught her reflection in a small circular mirror on the wall. There she was, in an elf costume, mopping the floor. The quintessential jovial janitor, in fact. No wonder Tomasina had passed up the experience. Tomi had probably envisioned what she'd look like doing this job, and knew better than to embarrass herself in such a way.

Brooke Anne worked steadily. Wiped a chocolate streak off the wall. Removed a scuff mark from the gray-and-blue linoleum. Rinsed and squeezed her mop, then scrubbed some more.

Faced with the wide expanse of floor, she was reminded of a much different experience she'd had about a month ago.

When she'd been wearing the opposite of a green-and-red elf suit—a beautiful ivory dress....

And she'd been dancing in Morgan's arms, twirling gracefully, matching her steps to his. She'd laughed, asked him about his childhood and told him about hers.

Knowing no one was around, Brooke Anne bowed to her mop. "Certainly, yes, you may have this dance." One tennis-shoe-clad foot slid to the left.

Slide…step, step. Slide…step, step. Step, step, spin.

She rose onto her tiptoes, pretending she was wearing beautiful shoes. "I dance beautifully? Why thank you. I've had years of lessons, you know…."

In her mind, Tchaikovsky's "Waltz of the Flowers" was playing. She closed her eyes and recalled the night when strong hands had held her tightly. Morgan had pressed her close. She remembered his look of appreciation. Her breathless excitement. "I like to waltz best, too," she said softly to the empty room. "And I especially like waltzing with you, Morgan."

Slide, step, step. Step, step, spin.

"I'm so glad you asked me here…. You want to go dancing again, soon? Well, let me see… Why don't I call you when I get home, after I check my calendar."

The music played on…its tempo soaring toward a crescendo. Her feet moved faster. She felt like Ginger Rogers—elegant, beautiful, garbed in feathers….

Or at least something prettier than an elf costume. Maybe a red gown? Blue?

Something in organza?

"Brooke? Brooke Anne?"

The music stopped.

Brooke Anne opened her eyes and found herself staring at Morgan. He stood in the doorway, his overcoat unbuttoned, wearing a dark pin-striped suit and a bemused expression.

"Morgan," she said. "You're here."

He pointed down the hall. "I've been here for a while. The woman at the reception desk told me you were still here, too."

He'd been there for a while? She swallowed. Glanced around. She was dressed like an elf and hugging a mop. Footprints marked the section of freshly washed floor. "I was just…cleaning up."

He stepped into the room. Right onto the wet floor. "So I see."

"I'll be done in a few minutes," she said, watching him approach. "Um, what did you mean when you said you've been here for a while?"

His eyes twinkled. "Ho, ho, ho."

She about dropped the mop. "You were Santa?"

"My sister said something…. I realized I wanted to do something from the heart."

"I didn't mean you were supposed to…"

"Shh. I wanted to. Besides, I did a pretty good job, don't you think?"

She was still trying to come to grips with the fact that Morgan Carmichael had donned a fake beard and a red velvet suit to play Santa. "Yes. I…I thought you were great." Because she didn't know what else to do, she started pushing the mop around. "Did you need something?"

He shrugged. "I need a lot of things. I need to remember that time and relationships count for more than presents and money…. I need to learn to say good-morning with kisses instead of concerns." He eyed her outfit.

"And since you're dressed for making wishes come true, I might as well tell you that what I need most of all…is you."

She stopped mopping. "What did you say?"

"Brooke Anne, you and I both know I'm terrible with speeches, but what I need more than anything in the world is you. I need you in my life, every day."

Brooke Anne could only stand there dumbly, trying to absorb his words.

He seemed to think she was rejecting him. He took a step forward, his sole squeaking on the linoleum. "Please don't give up on us."

"I…" She shook her head. Words were clearly impossible. Morgan was saying things she'd only previously imagined.

And she gripped her mop a little bit tighter so she wouldn't fall over.

Morgan stepped closer, removing the mop from her hands and pulling her into an embrace. "So, may I have this dance?" he whispered.

"There's no music," she said, although she had a sneaking suspicion he'd seen her dancing earlier without it.

"That doesn't bother me." He gazed at her questioningly. "Does it bother you?"

"No…not at all."

Morgan clutched her right hand and slowly began to lead her in a waltz. They danced for minutes in silence, and then he spoke. "I've been meaning to tell you, I'm so glad I met you that day at the office."

"Me, too."

"And I'm glad we're dancing right now."

"I wish I wasn't wearing this elf costume," Brooke Anne admitted.

The corners of his eyes crinkled. "You look cute."

They danced to the back of the room—no, *glided*. She was amazed that they could keep in step without any music.

"You've made me happier than I ever thought possible," Morgan continued. "You make me laugh and *feel* more than I ever thought I could. And you've helped me open up…be more honest with my emotions. Those weeks when I couldn't find you, I thought I'd go crazy."

It was her turn. "I was afraid to take a chance after Russell. And…I thought we were too different."

Their feet stilled. Brooke Anne raised her hands to circle his neck. Morgan closed his eyes briefly, as if he was savoring her touch.

"We both know that isn't so," he said quietly. "Brooke Anne, you make my life magical. Special. Happy."

No one had ever said anything that sweet to her before. Tears pricked at her eyes.

"I love you, Brooke. I love you so much."

Her eyes widened. His words, his tone—they were so romantic, so honest, so heartfelt. For once, their roles were reversed and she was the one who didn't know what to say.

"I'm doing the best that I can, Brooke Anne," he murmured. "I mean, I've barely learned to write a decent note."

A tear slid down her cheek and she smiled. "You're doing an excellent job."

He clasped her hands with his own. His grip was gentle, his expression sincere. "Brooke Anne, would you marry me?"

That was when she realized dreams really could come true. Cinderellas really could get their men, and princes really did live in her world.

"I love you, too," she said. "And yes, I will. I will marry you."

Morgan spun her in a circle, gazing at her as if there was no one else in the entire world.

Brooke Anne laughed.

Her laughter echoed through the room. Out the door and through the hospital corridors. More than one person smiled at the sound. A few people chuckled, too.

After all, some things were just meant to be shared.

Epilogue

Brooke Anne,
 Merry Christmas! Come over at ten this morning. I have a gift for you.
 I love and adore you,
Morgan (I know it's only three sentences, but I'm trying!)

Dear Mom,
 Thanks for the new flannel nightgown and slippers! I'll put them to good use this winter. Morgan and I had a wonderful Christmas together. As I told you on the phone, I'm having a hard time taking my eyes off of my beautiful diamond engagement ring. I still can't believe it was threaded over the strap of a new pair of shoes! I'll call you soon.
Love,
Brooke Anne

Dear Brooke Anne,
 Don't forget that I'm taking Friday off. Ronnie and I hired a babysitter and are going out. We've got romance on our minds. Hope you have a good Valentine's Day, too.
Tomi

Dear Morgan,

I cannot believe you're going to miss my Easter soiree because of a trip to Nebraska! Hope Brooke Anne's family is nice. Please tell them I look forward to meeting them at your rehearsal dinner next month.
Caroline

Oh, sweetie,

The whole town is still talking about your glow. You and Morgan make such a nice couple. I love the way he couldn't seem to stop looking at you. And his obvious discomfort around your relatives didn't bother me at all. Don't worry, dear. We'll get him used to hugging in no time. And your father is sure Morgan will enjoy camping once he gets the hang of pitching a tent.
Love,
Mom

Dear Brooke Anne,

I can't believe it's finally our wedding day. The moment I met you, you changed my life. I can't wait to see you walk down the aisle…wearing this pearl bracelet.

By the way, have I ever told you that I've become a fan of letter writing? We'll need to keep a chalkboard in our house, just to continue our habit. See you in four hours.
All my love,
Morgan

Brooke.

This is THE LAST TIME I'm delivering your mail. Enough already! Walk down that aisle and don't look back. The best is yet to come.
Tomi

* * * * *

It's time for some BLOND JUSTICE! This is Kara Lennox's third book in her trilogy about three women who were duped by the same con man. Sonya Patterson's mother has been busy preparing her daughter's wedding—and has no idea the groom-to-be ran off with Sonya's money. Will the blondes finally get their sweet revenge on the evil Marvin? And how long can Sonya pretend that she's going through with the wedding—when she'd rather be married to her long-time bodyguard, John-Michael McPhee? We know you're going to love this funny, fast-paced story!

Airplane seats were way too small, and too crowded together. Sonya Patterson had never thought much about this before, since she'd always flown first class in the past. But this was a last-minute ticket on a no-first-class kind of plane.

She'd also never flown on a commercial airline with her bodyguard, which might explain her current claustrophobia. John-Michael McPhee was a broad-shouldered, well-muscled man, and Sonya was squashed between him and a hyperactive seven-year-old whose mother was fast asleep in the row behind them.

She could smell the leather of McPhee's bomber jacket. He'd had that jacket for years, and every time Sonya saw him in it, her stupid heart gave a little leap. She hated herself for letting him affect her that way. Didn't most women get over their teenage crushes by the time they were pushing thirty?

"I didn't know you were a nervous flier," McPhee said, brushing his index finger over her left hand. Sonya realized she was clutching her armrests as if the plane were about to crash.

What would he think, she wondered, if she blurted out that it wasn't flying that made her nervous, it was being so close to him? Her mother would not approve of Sonya's messy feelings where McPhee was concerned.

Her mother. Sonya's heart ached at the thought of her vibrant mother lying in a hospital bed hooked up to machines.

Muffy Lockridge Patterson was one of those women who never stopped, running all day, every day at full throttle with a to-do list a mile long. Over the years, Sonya had often encouraged her mother to slow down, relax and cut back on the rich foods. But Muffy seldom took advice from anyone.

Sonya consciously loosened her grip on the armrests when McPhee nudged her again.

"She'll be okay," he said softly. "She was in stable condition when I left."

A comfortable silence passed before McPhee asked, "Are you going to tell me what you were doing in New Orleans with your 'sorority sister'?"

So, he hadn't bought her cover story. But she'd had to come up with something quickly when McPhee had tracked her down hundreds of miles away from where she was supposed to be. She'd already been caught in a bald-faced lie—for weeks she'd been telling her mother she was at a spa in Dallas, working out her pre-wedding jitters.

"I was just having a little fun," she tried again.

"A little fun that got you in trouble with the FBI?"

This is the first book in an exciting new miniseries from Jacqueline Diamond, DOWNHOME DOCTORS. The town of Downhome, Tennessee, has trouble keeping doctors at its small clinic. Advertising an available position at the town's clinic brings more than one candidate for the job, but the townspeople get more than they bargained for when Dr. Jenni Vine is hired, despite Police Chief Ethan Forrest's reservations about her—at least in the beginning!

"Nobody knows better than I do how badly this town needs a doctor," Police Chief Ethan Forrest told the crowd crammed into the Downhome, Tennessee, city council chambers. "But please, not Jenni Vine."

He hadn't meant to couch his objection so bluntly, he mused as he registered the startled reaction of his audience. Six months ago, he'd been so alarmed by the abrupt departure of the town's two resident doctors, a married couple, that he'd probably have said yes to anyone with an M.D. after his or her name.

Worried about his five-year-old son, Nick, who was diabetic, Ethan had suggested that the town advertise for physicians to fill the vacated positions. They'd also recommended that they hire a long-needed obstetrician.

Applications hadn't exactly poured in. Only two had arrived from qualified family doctors, both of whom had toured Downhome recently by invitation. One was clearly superior, and as a member of the three-person search committee, Ethan felt it his duty to say so.

"Dr. Gregory is more experienced and, in my opinion, more stable. He's married with three kids, and I believe he's motivated to stick around for the long term." Although less than ideal in one respect, the Louisville physician took his duties seriously and, Ethan had no doubt, would fit into the community.

"Of course he's motivated!" declared Olivia Rockwell, who stood beside Ethan just below the city council's dais. The tall African-American woman, who was the school principal, chaired the committee. "You told us yourself he's a recovering alcoholic."

"He volunteered the information, along with the fact that he's been sober for a couple of years," Ethan replied. "His references are excellent and he expressed interest in expanding our public health efforts. I think he'd be perfect to oversee the outreach program I've been advocating."

"So would Jenni—I mean Dr. Vine," said the third committee member, Karen Lowell, director of the Tulip Tree Nursing Home. "She's energetic and enthusiastic. Everybody likes her."

"She certainly has an outgoing personality," he responded. On her visit, the California blonde had dazzled people with her expensive clothes and her good humor after being drenched in a thunderstorm, which she seemed to regard as a freak of nature. It probably didn't rain on her parade very often out there in the land of perpetual sunshine, Ethan supposed. "But once the novelty wears off, she'll head for greener pastures and we'll need another doctor."

"So you aren't convinced she'll stay? Is that the extent of your objections?" Olivia asked. "This isn't typical of you, Chief. I'll bet you've got something else up that tailored sleeve of yours."

Ethan was about to pass off her comment as a joke, when he noticed some of the townsfolk leaning forward in their seats with anticipation. Despite being a quiet place best known for dairy farmers and a factory that made imitation antiques, Downhome had an appetite for gossip.

Although Ethan had hoped to avoid going into detail, the audience awaited his explanation. Was he being unfair? True, he'd taken a mild dislike to Dr. Vine's surfer-girl demeanor, but he could get over that. What troubled him was the reason she'd wanted to leave L.A. in the first place.

"You all know I conducted background checks on the candidates," he began. "Credit records, convictions, that sort of thing."

"And found no criminal activities, right?" Karen tucked a curly strand of reddish-brown hair behind one ear.

"That's correct. But I also double-checked with the medical directors at their hospitals." He had a bomb to drop now, so he'd better get it over with.

This is the final book of Dianne Castell's FORTY & FABULOUS trilogy about three women living in Whistlers Bend, Montana, who are dealing (or not dealing!) with turning forty. Dixie Carmichael has just had her fortieth birthday, and gotten the best birthday present of all—a second chance at life—after the ultimate medical scare. One thing she's sure of—now's the time to start living life the way she's always wanted it to be!

Dixie Carmichael twisted her fingers into the white sheet as she lay perfectly still on the OR table and tried to remember to breathe. Fear settled in her belly like sour milk. *She was scared!* Bone-numbing, jelly-legged, full-blown-migraine petrified. It wasn't every day her left breast got turned into a giant pincushion.

She closed her eyes, not wanting to look at the ultrasound machine or think about the biopsy needle or anything else in the overly bright sterile room that would determine if the lump was really bad news.

She clenched her teeth so they wouldn't chatter, then prayed for herself and all women who ever went, or would go, through this. The horror of waiting to find out the diagnosis was more terrifying than her divorce or wrapping her Camaro around a tree rolled into one.

God, let me out of this and I'll change. I swear it. No more pity parties over getting dumped by Danny for that Victoria's Secret model, no more comfort junk food, no more telling everyone how to live their lives and not really living her own, and if that meant leaving Whistlers Bend, she'd suck it up and do it and quit making excuses.

"We're taking out the fluid now," the surgeon said. "It's clear."

Dixie's eyes shot wide open. She swallowed, then finally managed to ask, "Meaning?"

The surgeon stayed focused on what she was doing, but the news was good. Dixie could tell—she'd picked up being able to read people from waiting tables at the Purple Sage restaurant for three years and dealing with happy, way-less-than-happy and everything-in-between customers. *Oh, how she wished she were at the Purple Sage now.*

The surgeon continued. "Meaning the lump in your breast is a cyst. I'll send the fluid we drew off to the pathologist to be certain, but there's no indication the lump was anything more than a nuisance."

Nuisance! A nuisance was a telemarketer, a traffic ticket, gaining five pounds! But the important thing was, she'd escaped. She said another prayer for the women who wouldn't escape. Then she got dressed and left the hospital, resisting the urge to turn handsprings all the way to her car. Or maybe she did them, she wasn't sure.

She could go home. In one hour she'd be back in Whistlers Bend. Her life still belonged to her, and not doctors and hospitals and pills and procedures. She fired up her Camaro and sat for a moment, appreciating the familiar idle of her favorite car while staring out at the flat landscape of Billings, Montana. This was one of the definitive moments when life smacked her upside the head and said, *Dixie, old girl, get your ass in gear.*

You've wanted action, adventure, hair-raising experiences as long as you can remember. Now's the time to make them happen!

Welcome back to Laramie, Texas, and a whole new crop of McCabes! In this story, prankster Riley McCabe is presented with three abandoned children one week before Christmas. Thinking it's a joke played on him by Amanda Witherspoon, he comes to realize the kids really do need his help. Watch out for Cathy Gillen Thacker's next book, *A Texas Wedding Vow*, in April 2006.

Amanda Witherspoon had heard Riley McCabe was returning to Laramie, Texas to join the Laramie Community Hospital staff, but she hadn't actually *seen* the handsome family physician until Friday afternoon when he stormed into the staff lounge in the pediatrics wing.

Nearly fourteen years had passed, but his impact on her was the same. Just one look into his amber eyes made her pulse race, and her emotions skyrocket. He had been six foot when he left for college, now he was even taller. Back then he had worn his sun-streaked light brown hair any which way. Now the thick wavy strands were cut in a sophisticated fashion, parted neatly on the left and brushed casually to the side. He looked solid and fit, mouth-wateringly sexy, and every inch the kind of grown man who knew exactly who he was and what he wanted out of life. The kind not to be messed with. Amanda thought the sound of holiday music playing on the hospital sound system and the Christmas tree in the corner only added to the fantasy-come-true quality of the situation.

Had she not known better, Amanda would have figured Riley McCabe's return to her life would have been the Christmas present to beat all Christmas presents, meant to liven up her increasingly dull and dissatisfying life. But wildly exciting things like that never happened to Amanda.

"Notice I'm not laughing," Riley McCabe growled as he passed close enough for her to inhale the fragrance of soap and brisk, wintry cologne clinging to his skin.

"Notice," Amanda returned dryly, wondering what the famously mischievous prankster was up to now, "neither am I."

Riley marched toward her, jaw thrust out pugnaciously, thick straight brows raised in mute admonition. "I would have figured we were beyond all this."

Amanda had hoped that would be the case, too. After all, she was a registered nurse, he a doctor. But given the fact that the Riley McCabe she recalled had been as full of mischief as the Texas sky was big, that had been a dangerous supposition to make. "Beyond all what?" she repeated around the sudden dryness of her throat. As he neared her, all the air left her lungs in one big whoosh.

"The practical jokes! But you just couldn't resist, could you?"

Amanda put down the sandwich she had yet to take a bite of and took a long sip of her diet soda. "I have no idea what you're talking about," she said coolly. Unless this was the beginning of yet another ploy to get her attention?

"Don't you?" he challenged, causing another shimmer of awareness to sift through her.

Deciding that sitting while he stood over her gave him too much of a physical advantage, she pushed back her chair and rose slowly to her feet. She was keenly aware that he now had a good six inches on her, every one of them as bold and masculine as the set of his lips. "I didn't think you were due to start working here until January," she remarked, a great deal more casually than she felt.

He stood in front of her, arms crossed against his chest, legs braced apart, every inch of him taut and ready for action. "I'm not."

"So?" She ignored the intensity in the long-lashed amber eyes that threatened to throw her off balance. "How could I possibly play a prank on you if I didn't think you were going to be here?"

"Because," he enunciated, "you knew I was going to start setting up my office in the annex today."

Amanda sucked in a breath. "I most certainly did not!" she insisted. Although she might have had she realized he intended to pick up right where they had left off, all those years ago. Matching wits and wills. The one thing she had never wanted to cede to the reckless instigator was victory of any kind.

Riley leaned closer, not stopping until they were practically close enough to kiss. "Listen to me, Amanda, and listen good. Playing innocent is not going to work with me. And neither," he warned, even more forcefully, "is your latest gag."

Amanda regarded him in a devil-may-care way designed to get under his skin as surely as he was already getting under hers. "I repeat," she spoke as if to the village idiot, "I have no idea what you are talking about, Dr. McCabe. Now, do you mind? I only have a forty-five-minute break and I'd like to eat my lunch."

He flashed her an incendiary smile that left her feeling more aware of him than ever. "I'll gladly leave you alone just as soon as you collect them."

Amanda blinked, more confused than ever. "Collect who?" she asked incredulously.

Riley walked back to the door. Swung it open wide. On the other side was the surprise of Amanda's life.

Home For The Holidays!

While there are many variations of this recipe, here is Tina Leonard's favorite!

GOURMET REINDEER POOP

Mix 1/2 cup butter, 2 cups granulated sugar, 1/2 cup milk and 2 tsp cocoa together in a large saucepan.

Bring to a boil, stirring constantly; boil for 1 minute.

Remove from heat and stir in 1/2 cup peanut butter, 3 cups oatmeal (not instant) and 1/2 cup chopped nuts (optional).

Drop by teaspoon full (larger or smaller as desired) onto wax paper and let harden.

They will set in about 30-60 minutes.

These will keep for several days without refrigerating, up to 2 weeks refrigerated and 2-3 months frozen.

Pack into resealable sandwich bags and attach the following note to each bag.

I woke up with such a scare when I heard Santa call…
"Now dash away, dash away, dash away all!"
I ran to the lawn and in the snowy white drifts,
those nasty reindeer had left "little gifts."
I got an old shovel and started to scoop,
neat little piles of "Reindeer Poop!"
But to throw them away seemed such a waste,
so I saved them, thinking you might like a taste!
As I finished my task, which took quite a while,
Old Santa passed by and he sheepishly smiled.
And I heard him exclaim as he was in the sky…
"Well, they're not potty trained, but at least they can fly!"

HARRECIPETINA

If you enjoyed what you just read,
then we've got an offer you can't resist!

Take 2 bestselling love stories FREE!
Plus get a FREE surprise gift!

Clip this page and mail it to Harlequin Reader Service®

IN U.S.A.	IN CANADA
3010 Walden Ave.	P.O. Box 609
P.O. Box 1867	Fort Erie, Ontario
Buffalo, N.Y. 14240-1867	L2A 5X3

YES! Please send me 2 free Harlequin American Romance® novels and my free surprise gift. After receiving them, if I don't wish to receive anymore, I can return the shipping statement marked cancel. If I don't cancel, I will receive 4 brand-new novels every month, before they're available in stores! In the U.S.A., bill me at the bargain price of $4.24 plus 25¢ shipping & handling per book and applicable sales tax, if any*. In Canada, bill me at the bargain price of $4.99 plus 25¢ shipping & handling per book and applicable taxes**. That's the complete price and a savings of at least 10% off the cover prices—what a great deal! I understand that accepting the 2 free books and gift places me under no obligation ever to buy any books. I can always return a shipment and cancel at any time. Even if I never buy another book from Harlequin, the 2 free books and gift are mine to keep forever.

154 HDN DZ7S
354 HDN DZ7T

Name _____ (PLEASE PRINT)

Address _____ Apt.# _____

City _____ State/Prov. _____ Zip/Postal Code _____

Not valid to current Harlequin American Romance® subscribers.

Want to try two free books from another series?
Call 1-800-873-8635 or visit www.morefreebooks.com.

* Terms and prices subject to change without notice. Sales tax applicable in N.Y.
** Canadian residents will be charged applicable provincial taxes and GST.
   All orders subject to approval. Offer limited to one per household.
   ® are registered trademarks owned and used by the trademark owner and or its licensee.

AMER04R   ©2004 Harlequin Enterprises Limited

Home For The Holidays!

Receive a FREE Christmas Collection containing 4 books by bestselling authors

STELLA CAMERON

VICKI LEWIS THOMPSON

ANNETTE BROADRICK

RACHEL LEE

Harlequin American Romance and Silhouette Special Edition invite you to celebrate Home For The Holidays by offering you this exclusive offer valid only in Harlequin American Romance and Silhouette Special Edition books this November.

To receive your FREE Christmas Collection, send us 3 (three) proofs of purchase of Harlequin American Romance or Silhouette Special Edition books to the addresses below.

In the U.S.:	In Canada:
Home For The Holidays	Home For The Holidays
P.O. Box 9057	P.O. Box 622
Buffalo, NY	Fort Erie, ON
14269-9057	L2A 5X3

-- ✂

098 KKI DXJM

Name (PLEASE PRINT)

Address   Apt. #

City   State/Prov.   Zip/Postal Code

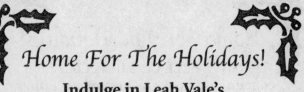

Home For The Holidays!

Indulge in Leah Vale's great holiday recipe

Family Fattigmann
Traditional Norwegian Christmas Cookies

Have at least one beloved family member or friend within shouting distance. The more the merrier.

6 egg yolks	1 tbsp whiskey
3 egg whites	2 1/2 cups flour
6 tbsp sugar	Vegetable oil for frying
6 tbsp canned milk	Powdered sugar

(and no nipping from the bottle—there's hot oil to follow!)

Beat egg yolks until creamy. Add sugar, milk and whiskey. In a separate bowl, beat egg whites until stiff, then add to egg mixture. Add flour to make soft dough. Chill in refrigerator. No, it's not time for that hot whiskey toddy, yet! When dough is almost ready, heat the vegetable oil in a deep saucepan. It should sizzle, but not smoke. Once dough is stiff, roll out until very thin—about 1/16 inch thick—on a lightly floured surface. Use a floured knife to cut dough into diamond shapes approximately 2 by 1 inch. Cut a slit lengthwise in the center of each diamond and pull one end through the slot to make a sort of knot. In batches, deep-fry the cookies until they are golden brown, then drain on paper towels and cool. Place cookies in a clean paper bag with some powdered sugar, roll the top closed and then dance around the kitchen shaking the bag. Store cookies in airtight containers.